ECHO

HUNT BROTHERS SEARCH & RESCUE

JESSICA ASHLEY

B.A.D. PUBLISHING CO

BLURB

A soldier tormented by the past. A woman with no memory. A love neither of them saw coming.

Elliot "Echo" Hunt carries the weight of his past, haunted by the one person he couldn't save. When he finds an injured woman on his ranch, he rescues her without hesitation—only to realize she looks eerily like the one he couldn't protect.

"Jane Doe" wakes with no memory, no identity—just an overwhelming sense of connection to the man who saved her. The attraction between them is undeniable, yet Elliot, scarred by his past, keeps her at arm's length, terrified of what a second chance at love could cost.

As the danger surrounding Jane intensifies, so does their bond. With every passing day, their hearts grow closer, but secrets from her past threaten to tear them apart.

As Elliot faces his greatest fears, he must decide if he's

willing to trust in God's plan for a love that might heal them both—or risk losing it forever.

Dive into a gripping tale of love, redemption, and unshakable faith. Get your copy of Echo and experience a heart-pounding Christian romantic suspense story that will leave you breathless!

To those who are searching for direction.
Psalm 23.

ECHO

Hunt Brothers Search & Rescue

By Jessica Ashley

Copyright © 2025. All rights reserved.

Edited by HEA Author Services
Proofread by Love Kissed Books, LLC
Cover Design by Covers by Christian
Photographer: Wander
Model: Blaze

NOTE FROM THE AUTHOR

Mistakes.

We've all made them.

Over and over again. Some of them were minor—setting a hot plate on a brand-new table (woohoo, white spots!), or a bit more serious—accidentally scraping the side of your car against a yellow pole (been there, done that).

Then there's the more serious ones. The times in our lives that cling to us like shadows. I've definitely made more than a few of those, and some days it feels like they'll never leave me alone.

That I'll be haunted forever.

That I'm forever tainted by a past I'd much rather forget.

In those moments, it seems impossible to remember that God's grace extends beyond ALL of our comprehension. He loves us so much that He sent His son to die for our sins.

So that we would be washed clean by His blood.

His sacrifice is our salvation.

Ephesians 2 says:

> *"**Once you were dead because of your disobedience and your many sins.** You used to live in sin, just like the rest of the world, obeying the devil—the commander of the powers in the unseen world. He is the spirit at work in the hearts of those who refuse to obey God. All of us used to live that way, following the passionate desires and inclinations of our sinful nature. By our very nature we were subject to God's anger, just like everyone else.*
>
> ***But God is so rich in mercy, and He loved us so much, that even though we were dead because of our sins, He gave us life when He raised Christ from the dead.** (It is only by God's grace that you have been saved!) For He raised us from the dead along with Christ and seated us with Him in the heavenly realms because we are united with Christ Jesus. So God can point to us in all future ages as examples of the incredible wealth of His grace and kindness toward us, as shown in all He has done for us who are united with Christ Jesus.*

We are washed clean when we repent for our sins and turn away from the darkness that we once allowed consume us. It's a hard journey, and temptation litters the very air we breathe, but as long as we remain steadfast in Him, we are saved.

So even in those moments when your past sneaks back into our minds, reminding us of the mistakes we've made— of the sins we've committed. We only need remind ourselves that we are bathed in the blood of Christ, and He has made us clean.

-Jessica

If you are in need of prayers or just someone to talk to, reach out to me at jessicaashley@authorjessicaashley.com. I will add you to my prayer list and send more prayer warriors your way!

CHAPTER 1
JANE DOE

He's going to kill me.

There's not a single doubt in my mind that I won't live to see another sunrise. Unless, of course, I'm granted a miracle. *Dear God, please grant me a miracle.*

I pump my arms, urging my body to move faster as my breathing comes out in ragged puffs of air, thanks to the cool spring night. I'm thankful for the cold, though, because it's helping to dull the full extent of the pain from my impact with the car a few hours ago. After managing to pop the trunk open and jumping out at that stop sign, I thought I'd finally gotten my chance at an escape.

Unfortunately, he showed no qualms about literally running me down. My hip aches, my side right along with it, but thank God, nothing feels broken.

Not yet, anyway. Adrenaline pulsing through my

system, I try to decide which route I should take. I could take my chances and maybe climb a tree—though then I'll be trapped. The only thing I do know is that I can't keep running. And when he catches up to me, I won't be walking away. Not this time. My bare feet burn, but the cuts covering them are the least of my problems.

A gunshot rings out, and I stumble, slamming my knee into a rock. I choke on a scream. I can't let him know where I am. It's dark now, and the shield of trees is keeping me relatively hidden. Out of sight, out of the crosshairs.

I just have to live until morning. By then, this park will be busy with hikers, and murdering me will be too risky. Even for him.

Another shot. Wood splinters off the tree beside me, and I fall once more, shredding the hem of the men's dress shirt I'd managed to grab on my way out the door. It helps to shield my body from the cold, covering skin the black dress I'm wearing beneath it doesn't.

Fabric tears as I push up from the ground.

The Lord is my Shepherd; I have all that I need. I start repeating Psalm 23. My mother told me to write it on my heart for moments just like this.

Tears sting my eyes.

He lets me rest in green meadows; he leads me beside peaceful streams.

Every move is agony, but I keep going. Keep moving.

He guides me along right paths, bringing honor to His name.

I have to keep fighting until there's no more breath in my chest. I won't go down without a fight. Too much has been lost already, and if something happens to me, the truth will also be buried six feet beneath the cold, hard ground.

Ahead, I can see the bright illumination of headlights on the highway. Hope fills me with renewed strength. If I can get up to the roadside, I can get into a car before he reaches me. Then I'll be able to survive. Then I can get help.

I push harder. Faster. *I've got this.*

Until—I slide to a stop at the edge of a river.

Water roars, blocking me from the highway. Thanks to the heavy rains we've had over the past couple of days, there's no hope of me getting across without being swept away. Still, maybe—

"I told you I'd find you. I will *always* find you."

Even when I walk through the darkest valley, I will not be afraid, for You are close beside me.

Dread coils in my belly as I turn to face my attacker. His smile is sinister, his eyes dark. How I ever trusted him, I'll never know. Unfortunately, it's a mistake that will likely cost me my life. "What, you don't think you can take me on without that?" I ask, eyeing his weapon, trying to keep my tone level.

Your rod and Your staff protect and comfort me.

He raises the gun and levels it on me. "I have nothing to prove to you, darling. I gave you a chance. You failed. Now I have no choice. You gave me no choice. Why couldn't you just take the deal? Why couldn't you play ball?"

"You know me well enough to know I never would have gone along with it. You sold your soul, and that's something I'll never do."

You prepare a feast for me in the presence of my enemies. You honor me by anointing my head with oil.

"Always dramatic. Things could've worked out. I'm sorry, but you've truly not given me any choice."

My cup overflows with blessings. Surely Your goodness and unfailing love will pursue me all the days of my life...

A single tear slips down my cheek. If this is the end, at least, I stayed true to myself. At least, I didn't—a gunshot echoes through the trees, and the bullet tears through the flesh of my abdomen.

Pain.

So much blinding pain.

And I will live in the house of the Lord forever.

CHAPTER 2
ELLIOT

"That ought to do it." I finish turning the wrench one final time then slide out from beneath the old truck. As soon as I'm standing, I tap on the olive-green hood so my brother, Riley, can turn the motor over.

It purrs to life, sounding better than it has in over a decade.

Riley grins at me. "Good work, brother."

"All in a day," I reply then head into the shop to retrieve a bottle of sweet tea from the refrigerator. It's not nearly as good as the stuff Mom makes, but it'll do in a pinch. "Want one?"

"I'll take one, thanks."

I hand Riley a bottle of tea, and we both take seats on the old couch kept in the auto shop. It's worse for the wear, with grease stains and the smell of motor oil clinging to it, but it's comfortable and reliable. And after a day of working underneath a truck nearly as old as my own father, it feels darn good to sit on.

My service dog, Echo, lies on an old blanket in the corner alongside Riley's dog, Romeo. Both German shepherds are enjoying a relaxing afternoon. You wouldn't know by looking at them that they can be lethal—or that they spend a good portion of their lives chasing bad guys and bringing people home to their families.

Hunt Brothers Search & Rescue is a job that leads us down some dark roads but one I wouldn't trade for anything. We bring lost people home, and that's a calling that I'll answer until the very last breath is drawn from my lungs.

Even if there are days it's haunted by failure.

Grief burns my throat, but I wash it away with sweet tea because there's nothing I can do to fix the past. Not when it's dead and buried.

"It's so hot already. How is this April?" Riley asks, rubbing an old handkerchief over his forehead.

"That's Texas for ya," I joke. "One day it's freezing, and the next, it's summertime. Who knows, maybe tomorrow it'll be winter again."

He laughs. "Isn't that the truth?" Riley downs the rest of his tea then gets up. "You coming in yet? I'm guessing Mom will have supper ready to go here in the next hour or so."

"I'll be in soon," I tell him. "I want to check a few more things before calling it a night."

"Sounds good." He turns and offers me a wave over his shoulder. "*Heel*, Romeo."

His dog hops up and joins him, and the two of them head out of the shop together.

Even though we each have our own houses on the ranch, Mom still insists on cooking dinner at least once a week. More if she can get us there. She loves it, and frankly, so do we.

I'm helpless in the kitchen, despite her best efforts to teach me when I was growing up. So, during the winter, when grilling is unpleasant, it's frozen dinners or takeout for me. Except on the nights she cooks. Given that I'm thirty-five now, I probably should have figured out how to cook at least a basic meal without a grill, yet here I sit, still hopeless. But when Mom's meatloaf is on the menu, that's something I can live with.

After taking a deep breath, I toss my bottle into the recycling bin then head out into the early evening. It's not quite six yet, so it's still bright enough that I can get one final ride in before the end of the day.

Since I spend most of my time repairing vehicles, tractors—anything with a motor—I like to end my day on horseback. It's so freeing, so comfortable. Therapy when I can't sleep well. Which I haven't been doing for quite some time now.

I head out of the auto barn and start toward the barn where we keep our horses. *"Heel,"* I order Echo. He falls into step beside me, the dog never straying far from my side. He's my best friend and the greatest partner I could ask for. Truth be told, he's saved my life in more ways than one.

When I got back from my final deployment, I was a mess. The things I saw—

I shake my head, not even wanting to relive them for a moment. I'd struggled with the transition into civilian life. Even starting our search and rescue team hadn't culled that pain. Not until we all nearly lost our lives during a rescue after an enemy flanked us. When we got home, Bradyn had the idea to get service dogs so they could alert us to any movement we might miss.

And here we are.

Getting and training Echo was the best decision I ever made.

Each of my four brothers has his own service dog. Bradyn has Bravo, Riley has Romeo, Dylan has Delta, and his twin brother, Tucker has Tango. All brothers themselves. German Shepherds we trust with our lives. They're our lifelines.

Or at least, that's what I consider them. Attachments that have tethered us in the real world when we'd felt so lost. They continue to tether us still when things go wrong. Which, unfortunately, they sometimes do.

The barn is empty right now with our three ranch hands likely finishing the new section of fencing dividing a pasture into two. Most of the horses are gone, including Bradyn's horse, Rev, and his fiancée's horse Midnight.

"Hey there, boy." I reach over and run my hand over the forelock of Bobby, my quarter horse. His intelligent brown eyes close as he rubs his face against my palm. "You ready to go out?" I saddle-broke and trained Bobby when I was home on leave after my first deployment, and now he's like an extension of me.

I retrieve his halter, slip it over his head, then open the gate and guide him over to the tethering post. After brushing him out, getting a saddle onto him, and slipping the bridle over his large head, I guide him out of the barn.

"Hey, just heading out?" Bradyn's fiancée, Kennedy, asks as she dismounts from Midnight. Her blonde hair is braided down her back, and when she smiles, there's no longer darkness hidden behind her bright blue eyes.

Bradyn has been good for her. Just as she's been good for him.

I'd be lying if I didn't admit I'd been a bit jealous. Not of Bradyn and Kennedy, of course, but of what they have. Attachment is something that I used to long for.

Back before I realized that this life takes too much from us. And falling in love again could be deadly for an already broken man like me.

"Yeah, I want to take a quick ride over the ridge. Spent

all day working on that old Chevy, so I'm ready to stretch Bobby's legs a bit."

"Totally get it." She beams at me. "The new fencing looks great. Bradyn's finishing up out there then heading in himself. You should check it out if you get the chance."

"Awesome. Will do. Thanks. So is it date night tonight?" I ask, knowing that they're in the final preparations for their wedding and likely spending the evening going over the last-minute details before their walk down the aisle in a month.

"Yes." She grins. "We're so close to having everything ready. I can't wait."

She currently lives in one of the ranch hand cabins on the property, though she spends quite a bit of time with her parents in town. They just bought a house a few weeks ago, and she's been helping them get everything unpacked and in its rightful place.

"It's going to be great to have you in the family." I smile then climb onto Bobby's back.

"Hey, I thought I already was a part of the family?"

I laugh. "You know what I mean."

"That I do. See you later!" she calls out.

"See ya!" I urge Bobby into a trot while Echo runs silently beside us. The ridge is a nickname my brothers and I gave the tallest hill on the ranch. It leads into some thick oak trees we used as cover when we'd play army as kids.

A game that turned into a desire to serve our country for

the better part of a decade. Until we all felt pulled back home.

I reach the bottom of the ridge then ride up, stopping only once we've made it to the top. From here, I can see the entire ranch. Two hundred acres of beautiful bliss, with our houses scattered throughout, just far enough apart that we get privacy but close enough that family is never too far away.

It's home.

Clicking my tongue, I urge Bobby to head down the other side. With it being spring, we've had a lot of rain recently, more so than usual even at this time of year. Not that I'm complaining. The creeks are all full, the pastures green, which will make for happy, healthy cattle.

Ahead, the largest creek on our property is overflowing with glistening water. It's fed by the Red River that runs along the border of Oklahoma then splinters through our property and even on into the next ranch.

My brothers and I spent many summers swimming in this creek as it's a good fifteen feet across and typically has at least a foot of water in it at all times. Though, thanks to the storm last night, it's nearly spilling over.

When we were young and the creek was at its lowest point in the summer, my brothers and I would come up here with our youngest sister, Lani, and spend the day eating fruit and playing in the water. A wonderful summer afternoon in the sun.

At this level, though, it's dangerous. The current is far stronger than I care to combat even as an adult. All it takes is one wrong step, and you'll be carried away, lucky if you even get the chance to resurface.

I keep riding, continuing up the creek a bit, enjoying the solitude. Birds chirp overhead, and somewhere a bullfrog calls out. Man, I love spring. It's my favorite time of the year. How everything just comes back to life. If only it worked on people, too. Heaviness settles over my heart, an anchor dragging me into the depths of the past.

It's been three years, but I still see her everywhere.

Echo lets out a warning bark. Instinctively, I reach behind me, hand closing over the grip of my pistol. It's more than likely a coyote or other wild predator, but just in case, I withdraw my firearm and climb down off Bobby.

He's not the least bit spooked, which isn't typical if there's an animal nearby. The hair on Echo's back is standing up, his ears forward.

"What is it, boy?" I ask, walking to Echo's side.

He lets out another warning bark then heads toward the creek. I follow on foot, leading Bobby behind me.

We make it five steps, and I see exactly what caught his eye. Dread coils in my belly, and fear ices through my veins. *Oh no.*

No longer worried about the strong current, I drop the reins and rush forward, holstering my weapon as I jump into the creek. The water is cold against my legs and hits up to my waist, but I push forward through the strong current, adrenaline surging through my veins as I fight the water on my way to the other side of the creek. A slender body is draped over a fallen limb, partially hidden, thanks to the canopy of trees over this side of the creek.

Shoving the branches aside, I get my first full view. Bright red hair falls in a curtain over her face, her arms dangling over one side of the branch. The blood drains from my face. *No. It can't be.* Water sloshes around my waist as I move closer, shoving the impossibilities aside and focusing on the now.

Renee is dead. But this woman might be alive.

A cascade of soaking wet red hair is matted and tangled in the bark of the fallen tree, but I manage to brush it aside. Her eyes are closed, her lips tinted blue. "Come on, please be alive." I slip my fingers along her cool skin toward the side of her throat so I can check for a pulse.

It's there. A weak *thud, thud.* But it's still something. "I'm going to get you out of here, okay?" I tell her.

Her hair is so tangled I can't get it free, so I reach into my pocket and withdraw my knife. Working quickly, I cut her free, leaving a good bit of hair on the log. After sticking my knife back into my waistband, I gently roll her body back and into my arms. She falls limply, eyes still closed.

I note blood on the front of a white men's shirt. Saturated enough that even the creek didn't wash it away. There's so much. *How is she still breathing?* Her face is covered in scratches and bruises, her legs the same. Even her feet have been torn up, though the injuries there have been washed clean by the creek.

"Hang in there," I mutter to her as I carefully make my way across the creek. I nearly fall twice, thanks to the strong current, but somehow, I manage to make it to the other side. As soon as we're on the embankment, I lay her down and strip out of my jacket.

Echo rushes over and starts licking her face, whining as he moves around her body, trying to wake her up. He lays directly beside her, likely realizing just how cold she is. I brush the hair from her face, noting a silver cross dangling from her neck. It's the only jewelry she's wearing.

Quickly, I cover her with my jacket then carefully raise it and the shirt to check her injury to make sure there's nothing immediate that needs tending to. The black dress beneath the shirt has a hole in the abdomen. Blood streaks from it, adding fresh stains to the clothes she's wearing.

A gunshot wound. *Oh no.* Working quickly, I strip my T-shirt off then grip the bottom and tear it into one long strip of fabric. Taking as much care as I can, I lift her body and slide it beneath her then tie it around her waist, pulling it just tight enough to hold sufficient pressure on the wound so she hopefully won't bleed out before I get her to the hospital.

She begins to tremble, her lips parting slightly. Eyelids

fluttering, she's trying to come out of it. Echo whines at my side, whimpering as he nudges her with his long snout.

"I've got you, okay? You're safe." I have no idea if she can hear me.

Bleeding momentarily tended to, I reach for my cell phone. But when I pull it from my pocket, I'm greeted with wet metal and a dead screen. I shove it back into my pocket and lift the woman into my arms. Draping her carefully over my shoulder, I climb onto Bobby then reposition her so she's leaning back against my chest.

"*Heel,* Echo!" I push Bobby into a run, and we race over the ranch.

I just hope we get there in time.

CHAPTER 3
JANE DOE

I'm moving.

My body is cold, unbelievably cold, and I begin to shiver as I come awake. I'm leaning back against something hard. I open my eyes, eyelids fluttering as the light assaults me. When my vision finally clears, I tilt my face up and see a man's strong, stubbled jaw, his hard eyes focused straight ahead.

The man is wearing a baseball cap backward, and I'm leaning back against his bare chest as we race down a dirt path. One of his strong arms is banded around my waist, the other holding leather reins.

A horse? I'm on a horse?

The animal jumps, and I hiss as pain shoots through my body. The first real thing I've felt in the moments since I first opened my eyes.

The stranger looks down at me, and our gazes hold.

Beautiful hazel eyes that somehow seem so kind and harsh all at the same time. "Hang in there, okay?" he says to me, his voice deep. "You're going to be all right."

"Okay." I'm not sure what else to say. Hang in there for what? My body aches, my stomach heavy as though it's full of stones. I manage to tilt my head forward enough to see that I'm covered in his jacket.

Pain. So much pain.

Panic thrums through my veins. "What happened to me?" I try to sit forward, but the stranger holds me tighter.

His arms feel strong. Good. But the panic mutes whatever comfort he's trying to offer.

"What happened?" I ask again. Fear shoves the rest of the cloudiness out of my mind, and I'm suddenly very aware of the danger I'm in.

"Stay still," he orders. "You're safe now, but we don't know how extensive the damage is yet. I'm getting you help, okay?"

Help.

Safe.

I close my eyes and nod, obeying him because leaning against him and remaining still is easier than moving.

"Bradyn!" he roars. "Help!"

A dog barks urgently.

We come to an abrupt stop, which jolts me again, and I cry out as agonizing pain shoots through my entire body.

"What is it?" a second man calls back, his tone

panicked. He comes into view, tall, muscled—his hazel eyes full of concern. "Who is that?"

"I have no idea. I found her in the creek. She's been shot."

"I'll call an ambulance."

Creek? Shot?

I've been shot?

"Here, let me help." Another man steps into view, nearly as tall as the first man, though his hair is darker. He reaches up and pulls me down. Then, as soon as the man who rescued me is off the horse, he takes me back into his arms.

"Ambulance is on the way," the first man says.

"What happened?" a woman asks. I turn my face to look at her, but my vision is blurry from tears of pain.

"She was shot," my rescuer replies.

"Let's get her inside," the woman says.

"Is Lani nearby?"

"I called her," the second man says. "She was on her way for dinner already and should be here any minute."

The man doesn't reply as he carries me gently, cradling me against his chest. We head up onto a sprawling porch. Warmth envelops me as we step into a house.

"I'm going to lay you down gently, okay?"

"O-okay," I stammer through chattering teeth. I'm so cold. So unbelievably cold.

"It's still likely to hurt, so just hang in there, okay?"

I nod, and the man sets me down on a couch, moving slowly so he doesn't jolt me again. Pain shoots up through my abdomen, and I hiss through clenched teeth, but as I lie still, it begins to subside.

Strangers flow around me in a blur of movement, but my hazel-eyed rescuer is all I can see. All I can focus on. Like a beam of light in the midst of my darkness. He kneels beside me, brushing some of my wet hair from my face. "Who did this to you?" he growls. "Who hurt you?"

"I don't—I don't know," I stammer. I try to remember, but everything is blank. Everything except for this man's beautiful face when I woke.

"We need to get her dry." An older woman kneels at my side then removes the large jacket from my body. She quickly undoes a band of white fabric from around my waist then presses a pale-blue towel to my abdomen.

I cry out, pain shooting through me. My body arches off the couch, and I grind my teeth together to keep from screaming as my rescuer's strong hands grip my shoulders. "Easy," he says, his voice a low rumble.

My teeth chatter so hard I'm sure they'll break right out of my mouth. The man grabs a blanket from the back of the couch and pulls it over my chest while someone else drags one down over my legs.

"I'm sorry, sweetie, I need to keep pressure on it. I'm Ruth Hunt," she says. "What is your name?"

"I—" I trail off. What is my name? Panic pushes

through the pain. Why can't I remember? Why don't I know? "I-I d-d-don't know my n-n-name." My heart pounds and I close my eyes to try and block out some of the light. "Why can't I r-r-remember? Who am I?"

"Easy," the handsome stranger says again, reaching up to rest his hand on my forehead. The moment he does, a calm washes over me. As though everything will be okay now.

I'm safe.

I open my eyes to stare up at him. How can he calm the storm so easily? Who is he?

"Hey! I'm here!" Another woman pushes through the crowd, and the man pulls away, leaving me lying alone on the couch. I want to call him back. My heart begins to hammer again, and I try to steady my breathing, but the panic is too much.

It's all too much.

What is happening to me?

The newcomer kneels at my side, her nearly black hair braided back.

The woman's face is serious as she raises the towel then lifts my shirt and checks the wound on my abdomen. "Is there an exit wound?" she asks.

"I didn't check," the man who'd brought me here says from somewhere out of view. "Bradyn called an ambulance."

"Good." The woman reaches into her pocket and withdraws a light then holds open my eyelids and shines it in. The brightness leaves me seeing spots. "What's your name?"

"She said she doesn't know it," Ruth answers.

The other woman nods. "She's likely in shock. My name is Lani. We called an ambulance, but I'm a doctor, okay?"

"O-okay." I want to ask where the beautiful man went. I want him back here, at my side.

"Do you have any idea what happened to you?" Lani questions.

"No." I suck in a breath as a fresh wave of pain shoots through me. "He said I was shot?"

"I found her in the creek. She was draped over a fallen branch. Still in the water."

There he is. Come back. Please. He steps into view, and my heart slows just a bit. Do I know him? Is that why I feel so calm in his presence? But I immediately brush that thought aside. If I knew him, he would know me. Which means he'd know my name.

Unless—did he do this to me?

But that's another thought I disregard the moment our gazes hold. *"Who did this to you?"* Would he really ask that if it were him? Would he have tried to save me if he'd been the one to put me in that creek?

My vision blurs, and I close my eyes. I'm so tired.

"I need you to stay with me, okay?" Lani says, gently rubbing my arm. "Stay awake."

"I'm so tired."

"I know you are, hon, but I need you awake."

I try to open my eyes, but they're heavy. Everything hurts. I just want it to stop hurting.

"Keep her awake," Lani says.

"I'm so tired," I say again.

"Stay with me." The deep voice says as hands gently cup my face. *I want to stay with you.* But as I try to open my eyes so I can see him, I can't. And with every passing moment, the voices begin to fade, and a numbness settles over me.

Maybe if I can just linger here long enough, I'll be okay. Just a few minutes, and everything will come back to me. If only I can remain in this place of peace.

I COME AWAKE SLOWLY. My brain is foggy, my vision a bit blurry. I rapidly blink to clear it and find myself lying in a hospital room full of beeping machines.

How did I get here?

I try to sit up, and pain shoots through my abdomen. I suck in a sharp breath and lie back. The moment I do, the pain subsides. Cold air shoots up my nostrils, thanks to a tube running beneath my nose.

"Easy, you need rest, honey." A familiar woman comes into view and gently presses me back onto the bed.

"Ruth?" I choke out. That was her name, right?

She smiles softly. "Yes, honey. That's right. Do you happen to remember your name too?"

I shake my head and lie back down. Whatever drugs they have me on have eased the pain now that I'm lying still. I glance down at my belly. I'm covered by a blanket, so I slowly push it down and gently touch the outside of the gown. Through it, I can feel a thick bandage. "I was shot."

"Yes. Doctors had to go in and get the bullet out. You were just moved here from recovery about half an hour ago."

"Who shot me?"

Her mouth flattens in a tight line. "We don't know, honey, but we'll get it figured out, okay? You don't worry about such things right now. You worry about getting rest."

"Where is the man?"

"What man, honey?" she asks, her eyes full of concern.

"The man with the baseball cap. The one who saved me."

The concern fades, replaced with understanding. "Oh, Elliot. He and his brothers are combing the ranch, looking for any evidence that could point to what happened to you."

Elliot. "His name is Elliot?"

She nods, a soft smile replacing the worry. "He's my son."

The door opens, so I turn my head as the dark-haired woman I'd seen before—Lani? Was that her name?—walks in, carrying a clipboard and wearing a white coat over light-blue scrubs.

She looks up and smiles. "I see you're awake."

"Am I going to live?"

"Yes, you'll be fine," Lani assures me. "We were able to get the bullet out and stop the internal bleeding. Do you remember being hit by a car?"

"I was hit by a car?"

"You have a few bruised ribs, as well as a contusion on your right hip. I don't think the car was going fast, but you were definitely hit. That or you fell off a roof and landed on that one side."

"Hit by a car," I repeat again.

"Before you were shot is my guess. We're not sure how long you were in that water. I'm guessing somewhere around five hours, based on the condition of your skin, but I do know that the only reason you survived is because of it. The cold slowed the bleeding. Otherwise, you probably would've bled out before Elliot found you. Honestly, I'm not even sure how you avoided hypothermia. It's a miracle, that's for sure."

Hit by a car and then shot? Who would do that to me?

"I would have died?"

She nods. "You don't remember anything that happened to you?"

I try to think back. To come up with anything that answers her questions, but I come up completely blank. "No. I have no idea."

She nods in understanding then turns to Ruth. "Mom, can you give us a minute?"

"Of course. I'll be right outside." She gently squeezes my foot then leaves. As soon as the door's closed behind her, Lani sets the clipboard aside.

"What is it?" I ask, her silence only making my anxiety grow.

Lani takes a deep breath. "I want your permission to check you for signs of assault."

My stomach plummets. "Assault? What?"

"You were found in a party dress with a man's shirt wrapped around you. The tox screen came back clean, but since you can't remember anything, I want to make sure."

"I wasn't drugged?"

She shakes her head.

"You didn't do it while I was in surgery?"

"No. It's invasive, and I won't perform it without explicit permission. If you don't want me to look, I won't. But the longer we wait, the less likely I'll be able to tell if you were sexually assaulted. If something happened, then we might be able to pull some DNA. That's if the water didn't wash it all away."

Tears blur my vision. Surely this nightmare won't get worse, will it? "I don't feel different." My stomach rolls at the mere idea. Would I feel different? Surely I would, right?

"It's totally up to you," she says softly. "No pressure from me at all. I cannot even begin to imagine how confused you are, and the last thing I want to do is be pushy. It's completely your call."

I swallow hard then nod.

She reaches down and squeezes my hand gently. "I'll come back in and do it in just a few. Right now, there's a deputy from the sheriff's department here, and he wants to speak with you."

"Okay."

"We'll get you taken care of, okay?"

Unable to stomach saying the word 'okay' even one more time when I feel anything, I simply nod.

"Come on in, Gibson," she calls out.

The door opens, and a man wearing a brown and black sheriff's uniform strolls in, notepad in hand. His brown eyes are friendly as he offers me a hesitant smile. "Ma'am," he says. "I just wanted to ask you a few questions."

"I don't know how helpful I'll be. I don't even remember my own name."

"We can get all of that figured out." He reaches into his pocket and withdraws a device that looks like an oversized cell phone. "With your permission, I'll scan your finger-prints; then we'll run them through our database, see what pops."

"Yes, please." Eager to find out who I am, I offer him my right hand. He quickly scans my fingerprints by pressing them onto the glass screen then shoves the device back into his pocket.

"I'll let you know if we find anything." He makes a note on his pad. "Now, can you tell me the last thing you remember?"

"I remember waking up and seeing Elliot. Right after he found me."

"Not anything prior to that?"

I shake my head.

"That's okay," Lani insists. "Sometimes a traumatic event can cause memory loss."

"Will it come back?" I ask Lani.

Her expression is one of hope. "I'm hopeful it will. But only time will tell."

The officer makes a few notes on his notepad then puts it back into his pocket. "Until then, ma'am, we'll do everything we can to find out who you are and what happened to you."

CHAPTER 4
ELLIOT

Angry and exhausted, I step through the front door of my house. My brothers, our dogs, and our three ranch hands, Kennedy included, scoured the creek bed all the way to the edge of our property, looking for anything that might clue us in to what happened to the mystery woman.

Unfortunately, aside from some trash that washed down the creek from the ranch over, we've got nothing. No sign of a struggle, no evidence that she was ever even there. Even the branch she'd been draped over had washed down the creek by the time we got back to it.

I know it should make me happy, given that she clearly wasn't attacked right under our noses, but if there's no evidence, and she can't remember what happened, how do we make sure it doesn't happen again?

Even as we've only been looking for a day, I can't help

but feel the failure settling on my shoulders like a heavy reminder of what was lost before.

Echo pads over to his bed and lies down, clearly exhausted. Desperate to feel clean again, I head into my bedroom so I can get ready to wash the day away.

I strip out of my dirty shirt, tossing it into the hamper then remove my wallet, keys, and phone from the pocket of my jeans. As I'm setting them on my dresser, my phone rings. Lani's name flashes on the screen.

I answer without hesitation. "How is she?"

"She'll survive," she tells me. "We had to go in and get the bullet out then remove part of her liver, but she'll live."

"What kind of round was it?"

"A 9mm. FMJ."

"Not a hollow point?"

"No. Which is one of the only reasons she's still breathing. It got lodged in part of her liver."

"Any idea how long ago?"

She sighs. "We can't quite figure that part out. She doesn't remember, but if I had to take a guess—" She trails off, and I know it's because Lani hates making assumptions even though she's got great instincts.

"What do you think?"

"I'd say she was in that creek at least five hours. Her skin was wrinkled and pale, and she was incredibly dehydrated."

"How did she not bleed out?"

"God," Lani replies. "And really cold water. It slowed her heart rate, which then slowed the bleeding."

"A walking miracle."

"Exactly. If you hadn't found her, though—" She pauses. "Elliot, it would've been a dead body that washed up."

The stranger's face swims into view. Wide green eyes so full of fear. Her red hair a blast of color against alabaster skin dusted with freckles. She's beautiful, there's no doubt about that.

Was it a crime of passion that sent her into that creek?

Or something else?

"She wasn't assaulted." As though she can read my mind, Lani continues, "I looked her over myself. She's also covered in scrapes and small cuts, conducive to running through brush."

"So she ran from whoever was after her."

"That would be my guess. One look at her feet will tell you that. They're torn up. She was hit by a car, and I'm wondering if it wasn't a hit-and-run gone wrong. Someone trying to finish the job."

I piece together what we know, trying to paint a picture. "A woman dressed in a cocktail dress and man's overshirt gets hit by a car then shot and dumped in a creek."

"That's what it looks like. Were there any signs she was attacked on our property?"

"No. We didn't even find tire tracks. We're headed to

the Jackson ranch tomorrow to ask them if we can take a look around."

"You think she was dumped there?"

"I'm not sure." The Jacksons are a bit different than anyone else around here. They don't partake in town activities, keep to themselves, and are among some of the rudest people I've had the displeasure of dealing with in the past. But I never would've thought them murderers. "Doesn't hurt to look around though."

"If they let you." Lani scoffs.

"Even if they don't, I'll still take a look around. I just figured I should ask first. Give them a chance to do the right thing."

"Good idea. My money is on a big fat no, though."

"Probably." We fall into silence for a moment. "So, how is she? Mentally I mean."

"Shaken up. Still doesn't know her name. Gibson ran her through the system, so we're hoping something will show up. We'll know more tomorrow."

"Keep me posted."

"Will do. You know, she probably would like to see you."

"Me? Why?"

"You saved her. Right now, you're the friendliest face she knows."

"You're friendly."

Lani laughs. "I am delightful, but I'm not the guy who

pulled her out of a creek. I'm just saying, maybe swing by and check in."

"I don't see how I would help."

"Because, my dear brother, you have a comforting nature about you. When you're not being a total pain in the rear."

I snort. "I'll think about it." Truth is I'd love to see her again. If only to assure myself that she's going to survive. Seeing her draped over that branch, unsure if she were alive or dead…it threw me right back into everything I've been trying to forget.

"Fine. Be difficult," she says. "I didn't want to pull this out, but you should know—she asked about you."

"She did? Why not lead with that?"

"Because I didn't want you to feel obligated. I thought you'd want to come by to check on her yourself."

"I do."

"Then what's the hang-up?"

She looks like the ghost haunting me. "Nothing. I'll swing by tomorrow." My tone is clipped now with frustration at myself for not checking on her sooner and irritation that my sister is pushing me to do it. If she notices, though, Lani couldn't care less.

"Great. Well, I'm pulling up in front of my apartment. I'll talk to you tomorrow. Night, Elliot! Love ya!"

"Love you too, Lani."

The call ends, and I toss my phone onto the bed then

head into the bathroom. I stop in front of the sink and grip both sides of it, staring at my reflection. So many times, I've tried to bury what happened that night three years ago. A mission that went awry from the first moment we took it. I lost more than anyone knows that night.

The same red hair swims into my memory, though Renee's eyes were hazel, not green. And the sight of them frozen open will forever be branded into my mind.

No matter how badly I wish otherwise.

***

The coffee might as well be mocking me with how little it's doing to curb my exhaustion. I tossed and turned all night then spent three hours working myself into a sweat and hoping exercise would exhaust me enough that I'd pass out.

Unfortunately, it didn't.

"You look out of it. You okay?" Riley questions, taking a bite of his pancakes. Since Dylan and Tucker left for a quick search and rescue in Florida and Bradyn is handling ranch business, Riley and I met for breakfast at the Pine Creek Café downtown.

"Fine, why?"

He eyes me. "You know why."

"I don't think I do."

"Jane Doe shares some similarities with Renee."

Hearing him say her name is like a dagger to my heart. "She's not Renee."

"I know that," he replies. "I just want to make sure you do, too."

It shouldn't surprise me that he knows where my head's at. We're all like that with each other—all four of my brothers and I can read each other like an open book. Lani too. Side effect of growing up so close. While it comes in handy occasionally, right now, I wish I could hide the pain that's been resurfacing ever since I pulled Jane Doe out of that creek.

"I do know," I snap then take a drink of my coffee.

"Good." He's not at all bothered by the irritation in my tone. "Now that that's covered. What do we know about our mystery woman?"

"Nothing. But the local police will handle it, so there's not much we need to know."

He arches a dark brow. "I thought we were spending our afternoon at the Jackson's place to look into this."

"Sure, but that's only because, if they think local police are sniffing around, they won't play ball. If we go and find something, we can alert the authorities. If we don't, then we can let them know that too."

He arches a dark brow. "You're not taking this case?"

"Why would I?"

He continues staring at me. "Why wouldn't you? The woman has no idea who she is or who shot her. Given that we find people, both sides of this case are what we do."

"Except for one thing. She didn't ask for our help."

"Neither did Kennedy."

I eye him in frustration. "That's different."

"Two women in danger. Sure, the circumstances are different, but as far as I'm concerned, they're two sides of the same coin."

Arguing with Riley is futile. He always has a response to everything. It would come as no surprise to anyone that debate was something he excelled at when we were home-schooled. So much so that my mom had him join a debate team that competed all over the country. But I *cannot* take this case. Beyond dealing with the Jacksons, nothing good can come of my involvement. She looks too similar to Renee. And I'm still too broken. Untrusting of myself.

I'll do what I said and swing by the hospital to check in, but that has to be it. Last night proves that. "Fine. Then you take it."

"I'm busy already."

"With what?"

"Leg work for a new case that came in last night." He finishes off his coffee. "You, however, have nothing on your plate."

"Doesn't mean this will fit on it."

"Sure it does."

"She never even asked for our help." That familiar

suffocating panic sets in, something I've been dealing with since I lost Renee. I try to shove it down, but it rears its ugly head over and over again, determined to drown me in my past mistakes.

"Probably because she doesn't know you can offer it."

I see his logic, but the idea of getting any closer to her is terrifying. She's too familiar and a complete stranger all at the same time. "The cops will find something."

"The cops are burdened by red tape," he says with a knowing grin. "A condition we are not afflicted with."

I glare at him, that vise squeezing so hard it might as well be suffocating me. "Why are you so insistent on me taking this case?"

"Other than because I truly believe we're her best hope at getting answers?" He arches a brow. "I think it'll be good for you."

"Good for me. Why? Because you think I'm holding on to the past?"

He leans back and studies me. "I *know* you're holding on to the past. You haven't worked a solo missing persons case since Renee."

"I needed time."

"What happened to her wasn't your fault, brother, and if you keep blaming yourself for it, you're going to spend your life in suffering."

"It was my fault. I missed the connection."

"We all did, Elliot. None of us saw it until it was too late."

My throat constricts, but I fight the grief back down. "It's been three years. I'm fine."

"Then where were you on March second?"

I swallow hard, hating that my brothers know me so well. "It was her birthday. I always visit on her birthday. That doesn't mean I'm holding on to the past; that just means I want to offer support."

"Gotcha. Then did you actually go in this time?"

His words are a punch to the gut. "They don't want to see me."

Riley takes a drink of his coffee. "I guess it's a good thing you're not holding on to the past, then."

CHAPTER 5
JANE DOE

This hospital room is going to drive me insane. It's only been a day, and I'm already stir-crazy. It's not even like I have memories to keep me occupied. I can't even remember my own name, let alone things that have happened in the past. No matter how many times I try to make myself remember, I get nothing but a haze. Seriously, how does someone forget something they literally spent their entire life memorizing?

Who knows how many years I've walked this earth? I made a joke to the nurse earlier about cutting me back open and counting the rings so we could figure it out. She did not find it funny.

The TV is on, some show about a mother and daughter who talk fast and are burdened by forced family dinners on Friday nights. I have no idea if I've ever watched it before, and I checked out about an hour ago because I'm unable to focus on anything but my desperate need for freedom.

I'm frustrated. Hungry. And beyond tired of being cooped up.

The door opens, and Lani breezes in, a big smile on her face. "Good morning," she greets then steps in front of the monitor to check the readout. "How do you feel?"

"A little sore," I admit. "But I also really want to get out of this room."

Lani taps a couple of things on the tablet in her hand then crosses her arms and folds it against her chest as she faces me. "We can see about getting you an escort to take you out for a walk. How does that sound?"

"That depends. Do I get to go outside?"

"Yes, of course. The hospital has some great gardens you can stroll through. We just have to wait until we can spare someone. I would love to take you, but the hospital is massively understaffed right now. Hence why I'm here and not seeing my patients in my clinic."

"I would love a walk. Please. I'm willing to beg."

She chuckles. "No begging necessary. As soon as we have someone who can help, we'll get you on your feet. It would be good for you to move around a bit."

I open my mouth to plead with her to take me now when there's a soft knock on the partially opened door.

"Hey, come on in," Lani calls out.

The door opens all the way, and the man who saved me

steps in. He's wearing the same baseball cap he had on before as well as dark jeans, a black T-shirt, and a brown jacket that's hanging open in the front.

As I drink in the sight of him, the air is sucked out of my lungs, and my heart begins to pound. I may have been mostly dead a day ago, but I can still appreciate the sheer masculine beauty that is the man who pulled me from that creek. "Elliot," I whisper.

Both he and Lani shift their attention to me.

His gaze darkens, and he shoves both hands into the pockets of his jeans.

"Your mom told me your name," I reply quickly.

"I figured." He clears his throat. "I, uh, just wanted to check in on you and see how you were feeling."

"Much better. Thank you." Nerves twist in my stomach, and I begin fidgeting with the top of the blankets. He's a presence—a gorgeous yet haunted presence.

"Good."

Lani looks from me to him. "Actually, we were just hoping to find someone to escort Jane here out for a walk."

Jane. I hate when they call me that. It feels so impersonal. And it just reminds me that I still have no idea who I am. Not even a blip of memory. I'd even take the first letter of my name at this point. Do I prefer coffee or tea? How do I like my eggs? *Anything.*

"Oh, I can get out of your hair," he says and starts to back toward the door.

Please don't leave.

"Nonsense." Lani crosses over to him and grips his arm then tugs him back into the room. "You're a big, strong guy. You don't mind getting her out of the room, do you? She's desperate for some fresh air."

His hazel gaze narrows, and his jaw clenches. "Oh, I don't know, I need to get back to—"

"You can spare fifteen minutes. Come on, big brother, I'm swamped, and she needs fresh air."

"It really is okay," I say, feeling the disappointment settle in. Why doesn't he want to be around me? I don't have to know who I am to see that this man would rather be anywhere but here. He's practically trying to bolt out of the door.

"Nonsense. You don't mind, do you?" Lani asks.

He shifts his gaze from Lani to me, and the earlier annoyance dissipates. "Of course not. I'm happy to take you out, Jane."

Jane. When he says it, it doesn't sound so bad. "It really is okay," I repeat again. "I'm tired anyway."

"Stop saying something you don't mean just to spare Elliot. He doesn't mind."

"I really don't," he assures me. "I was just caught off guard. I've got time if you want to go outside."

A moment of silence settles around us, and while I still get the sense that he would rather be anywhere but here, my desire to escape these four pale yellow walls is apparently stronger than my pride. "If you don't mind escorting me for a walk, I would truly appreciate it."

"Not a problem." He smiles tightly. "I'll be in the hall when you're ready." Without another word, he leaves the room and closes the door gently behind him.

Lani sets the tablet down on the table at the end of the bed then folds the blankets back.

"I feel bad that you just backed him into that corner."

Lani waves a hand in dismissal then helps me sit up and swing my legs over the edge of the bed. The move brings a wave of pain through my abdomen, but I bite back a groan, unwilling to let her know how uncomfortable it is. *I can do this.*

"Elliot really doesn't mind. His hesitation has nothing to do with you."

"Then what does it have to do with?"

She smiles sadly. "My brother has been through hell and back. Really, they all have. But Elliot most recently. It's not my story to tell though, so that's all I'll say."

Even as curious as I am, I know poking at a painful memory is not the best way to handle a conversation. I might not know my name or the day I was born, but at least manners weren't lost along with everything else. "Understood."

After five minutes, a pair of sweats, and an oversized sweater, I'm on my feet. Since my IV was disconnected earlier this morning, I only have the catheter in my arm.

Which thankfully means I don't have to drag that large pole on wheels around.

I'm shaky on my feet though and doing everything I can to hide the bone-deep ache radiating through my body out of fear she'll make me get back into bed.

Lani pulls the door open, and Elliot pushes off the wall he was leaning against. His gaze is guarded, his expression neutral. What does a man like that think about? Is he running over a to-do list? Thinking about future plans? Plotting an escape? All of the above?

"She's ready." Lani transfers my arm from hers to his, and I have to keep my gaze trained down to keep from staring at him. Aside from the brief hazy moment of being awake on that horse, this is the closest I've come to Elliot Hunt.

He smells amazing.

Like leather and sunshine. If the latter could be a smell, anyway.

"Keep your arm on her at all times. And no more than thirty minutes, okay?"

"Yes, doc," he replies.

"Good." She turns to me. "You doing okay?"

I force a smile even though the pain in my abdomen is far worse than I thought it would be. "Doing great."

Her expression reflects the fact that she clearly doesn't believe me. "Uh-huh." A phone clipped to her waist rings, so she offers us a wave as she steps away to answer it.

Elliot and I begin walking, and thankfully, with every step, my body seems to loosen up just a bit. By the time we've reached the door, the stabbing pain has subsided to more of an intense ache.

The glass doors slide open, and I'm hit with a cool blast of air that erases all of the stress I'd felt at being kept inside.

I smile. It feels great to be outside.

"She was always bossy."

"Huh?"

"Lani," Elliot replies as we cross the pavement of the drop-off area and reach the garden on the other side. "Even when she was little. She'd carry around a spatula and tell us that she was queen and we were her loyal subjects."

I smile, trying to picture the competent doctor playing royals as a child. "And I'm betting you listened?"

"To every word," he replies with a smile. "She was the queen, after all."

"True."

We pass by a glittering fountain surrounded by tiles that appear to have been hand-decorated by people of various ages. I lean closer, noting the titles of Bible verses written on some of them while others have paintings of a cross or crown of thorns. "This is beautiful."

"Our church donated this prayer garden, and the kids in the Sunday school classes painted all of the tiles."

"It's beautiful."

"Jogging any memories?"

"Unfortunately not. I know they're from the Bible, but I couldn't tell you what any of them mean." Disappointment resonates deep within me. One more thing I don't remember. Reaching up, I touch the cross around my neck.

It's honestly the only thing that stirs emotion within me. Even if I can't remember when I got it, I know it's important. This silver cross and my faith tell me that everything will be okay. That I will survive this because I'm not doing it alone.

Elliot uses his free hand to point to one that reads Proverbs 17:22. "A cheerful heart is good medicine, but a broken spirit saps a person's strength."

I study him. "You have that one memorized."

"I have a lot of them memorized." He smiles, and even as it doesn't quite reach his haunted gaze, it feels like a piece of me slips back into place. I still can't remember anything, but it feels closer somehow.

"I wonder if I knew any."

"I'd say it's likely." We start walking again. "You were wearing that cross when I found you. Do you know where you got it from?"

I twirl it in my fingers and glance down at the silver. "No. I know what it is; I know who He is, but that's where it ends. I guess if I'm going to remember anything, faith is a good place to start."

"It's all we need," he says, though there's a tone to his

voice that is a bit hollow. Almost as though he's not quite sure. We continue walking, and I shift my attention to the garden around me.

Even as cold as it is outside, flowers have begun to bloom in the garden, making for a beautiful and colorful backdrop. I like flowers. And being outside. Two things I didn't know about myself before. I mentally file them away, hoping that these building blocks will be the foundation I need to build on in order to remember.

"Thank you, by the way."

"You already said that," he replies.

"No, not for this." My cheeks heat. "For saving me. You're the only reason I'm alive."

"I did what anyone would have done."

"Maybe. But it was you who saved me," I repeat. "And I will always be grateful for that."

He doesn't respond, just continues walking and staring straight ahead.

After a few moments, he clears his throat. "Sorry about the haircut I had to give you. I think I cut off quite a few inches in the back to get you free of the log."

I reach back behind my head. "I couldn't tell."

He smiles, the joke landing just as I'd hoped. "Fair enough."

Minutes tick by in silence, and before I know it, we're coming back around the prayer garden with the hospital straight ahead.

Anxiety begins raging within me, those walls already closing in despite me still being outside. "Can we just sit for a minute?"

"Lani said thirty minutes," he replies, checking his watch. "We're coming up on that."

"Please?" I ask. "Just a few more minutes."

He starts to shake his head but then stops, likely noting the panic that must be present on my face. "I don't see what a few minutes will hurt."

"Thank you."

Elliot guides me over toward an "In memory of" bench, and we take a seat side by side. He releases my arm. "Has anything about your life come back?"

I lean back and close my eyes, basking in the warm rays of the sun even as the air around me is cool. "No. It's so weird, it's all a blank slate. I mean, I remember waking up on the horse with you. But before that—" I trail off, trying to come up with something that describes this feeling accurately. "I feel like there's something there, but my brain has blocked me from accessing it. Like there's a wall that I can't get through. Does that make sense?" I turn my head to look at him.

Light hits his gorgeous hazel eyes, showcasing golden flecks within the greens and browns. Stunning. This man is stunning. "It does make sense." He breaks the eye contact by shifting his gaze straight ahead. "Lani said it might be temporary."

"Maybe."

"You don't sound so sure?"

I laugh. "It's not that, it's just—do I *really* want to remember?"

"Why do you say that?"

"Someone clearly tried to kill me. While I do want to know who, for the obvious reason of not having someone attempt to remove me from this world again, what if the things I forgot make me a bad person?" I vocalize the biggest fear I've had since I woke up in that hospital bed. I'm not even entirely sure why it worries me. It's not like there's any actual proof that I've ever done anything wrong.

But what if?

"You think you're a bad person?"

"I don't feel like a bad person. If that makes sense. But I worry I might have been. How many good people do you know have gotten shot? To be wrapped up in something that would end like that, I must not have been around the best people."

"I've been shot. As have each of my brothers—Tucker excluded. Though he's been stabbed a few times."

My jaw drops open. "What?"

Elliot chuckles. "We were soldiers. Special Forces in the Army."

I let out the breath I was holding and press a hand over my heart. "Okay, sir, that is not the same. I doubt I was a soldier."

He shrugs. "There are different types of soldiers. Different battles to fight." The way he says it settles around me, lifting the fear from my shoulders. "Either way, good people get hurt by bad people all the time." His expression darkens once more. "Doesn't make it your fault."

"But it also doesn't mean I'm a good person."

"You are."

"How do you know?"

"I just do." When I don't immediately respond, he takes off his baseball hat and runs a hand through his thick dark hair before placing the hat back on his head. "Don't stress about something before you have all the facts. Not when you have other things to be worried about."

"Like who put me in that creek?"

"Exactly."

I take a deep breath. "Is it weird that I'm not scared?"

"You don't have anything to be worried about. You're protected here."

"I know that, but shouldn't I at least be a bit worried that whoever did it is going to realize the job isn't finished? That they're going to come for me? Aside from the confusion when I first woke up, I feel like I've been pretty calm about this whole thing." I laugh nervously. "I even asked the nurse if they could take me back to surgery and cut me open again, that way they could count the rings and tell me how old I am."

Elliot stares back at me, and for a moment, I wonder if

he's as horrified at the dark joke as she was. But then, to my absolute delight, he throws his head back and laughs. It's completely unburdened, a beautiful happy sound that brings a smile to my face.

"You asked nurse Jan that?"

"How did you know it was Nurse Jan?"

"Her name was written on the whiteboard in your room." He's still laughing. "Oh, I bet she just loved that joke."

"Not really," I reply with a laugh. "She looked honestly horrified."

"That's Jan. She's always been serious. Once, when I was fifteen, Bradyn and I were wrestling, and he broke my nose. It was a total accident, but while I was sitting in the emergency room bed, nose all bandaged up, I challenged Bradyn to a do-over. Jan gave us a thirty-minute lecture on safety and how being able to physically subdue each other wasn't what makes us men."

"Did the lecture work?" I ask, fighting another smile. He looks so much lighter now, unburdened compared to earlier.

"Absolutely not. We were back at it the next day. I had something to prove, you know? Younger brother syndrome and all that."

"Are you the youngest?"

He shakes his head. "Bradyn is the oldest, I'm next; then it's Riley and the twins. Lani is the youngest."

"The twins?"

"Tucker and Dylan. They're out of town right now."

"Wow, there are six of you?"

He chuckles. "Feeling sorry for my mom?"

"A little," I admit. Darkness settles over my mood. "I wish I knew if I had parents out there looking for me."

"I'm sure someone is," he says.

"Maybe. Do you think that whoever shot me thinks I'm already dead? Or do you think they're going to try to come for me again?"

"No one is going to get to you." The words are spoken with such anger that it leaves me breathless. It's completely contrasted to the laughter from mere moments ago.

I tilt my face up to look into his eyes, noting the storm raging behind his intense glare.

"No one will hurt you again," he says.

"I'm not worried," I remind him honestly. "Part of me hopes they come for me so I get the chance to ask some questions. They might be the only one who knows who I am."

"Lani told me she thinks it may have just been a hit-and-run. That someone accidentally ran you down then panicked and tried to finish the job."

"Your tone doesn't make me think you believe that," I say. His tone is too flat, too emotionless for me to think he actually believes that theory.

He shrugs. "My gut tells me there's more to the story. Either way, we'll figure it out."

I smile at him. "I know." Our gazes hold for a moment, and I'm captivated by the way he watches me. Does he feel this connection, too? Or is it one-sided since he's the one who saved me?

He turns away from me then stands, his mood shifting back to neutral. "We need to get you back inside before Lani comes looking for us."

I long to remain out here—to stay with him—but since I sense he's desperate to get away from me for some reason, I force a smile. "You're probably right. I'm getting tired."

He helps me to my feet, and we start toward the hospital.

A loud *bang* fills my ears, and my heart rate skyrockets. I rip my arm free of Elliot and whirl toward the sound, pain shooting through my abdomen.

And then another *bang*.

Suddenly, the prayer garden is gone, and I'm in the woods. It's dark. I'm running. Feet pounding against the wet ground.

Someone is behind me, but I can't see who. I have to get away though. I have to run. It all depends on me.

Calloused hands cup my cheeks. "Breathe."

The memory fades, and I stare up into Elliot's hazel eyes. "I—"

"It was just a car backfiring," he tells me. "Are you okay?" He pulls back and looks down at my abdomen. "You're bleeding again."

"What?" I follow his gaze down to the front of my gray sweatshirt, the fabric now stained with blood. "I—"

Elliot lifts me into his arms and rushes toward the hospital. We're just reaching the door when Lani comes out of one of the patient rooms.

"What is it?" she demands.

"Car backfired. It spooked her, and she lunged. Tore the stitches, I think."

"I'll get the kit." She rushes off, and Elliot carries me into my room. He sets me down on the bed.

"I saw something."

"It was just a car," he assures me.

"No." I look up at him. "I *remembered* something."

CHAPTER 6
ELLIOT

Mood already sour, I climb out of my truck and make my way up the short walk to the Jackson family's front door. Riley has been silent—thankfully—giving me time to figure out what I should do.

I'd been dead set on not taking this case until Lani pushed me into taking Jane Doe out for that walk. Spending time with her helped separate her from the memory of Renee since the only similarity they share is the red hair. But I can't figure out if that's a good thing or not since now I can't get my mind off of her or her terrified expression when that car backfired.

Riley's not wrong about the rest of them being busy. Since I don't have any current assignments, I'm the only one who can take the lead on this. But is it such a good idea to jump back into a missing person's case? Especially one where the woman in trouble looks a whole lot like the last one I lost?

It may have been three years ago, but that failure still haunts me.

We climb the porch steps, and Riley rings the doorbell.

Irene Jackson answers the door, her graying hair pulled back in a tight bun, her face already twisted in irritation. "What do you two want?" she demands.

"Ma'am, we were wondering if we could talk to you. Something happened that we think you should be aware of." Riley offers her a smile.

"Then talk."

"It's sensitive, can we come inside? Please? It will only take a moment." *Honey catches more flies,* I remind myself. The Jackson family has never cared for us, thanks to an old feud between our family and theirs. It started decades ago when my father showed interest in my mother. She'd been on a date with the Jackson patriarch, and ever since, he's claimed my father stole her away. Even though she's told us many times that there would never have been a date two.

Still, the feud grew and is apparently healthy and strong today.

"I only have a few minutes," she says, though she doesn't step aside to let us in.

"What is it, Irene?" The grumpy voice of the Jackson patriarch himself, Lester, sounds as he pulls the door from his wife. His dark eyes are hard as he studies us. "What do you two want?"

"As we were telling Mrs. Jackson, something happened that we would like you to be aware of. It will only take a few minutes of your time." I force a friendly smile even though irritation is clawing its way to the surface.

"Fine. Only a few minutes though. I have things to do." He pulls the door open farther and steps to the side to let us in. By the time we've made it through the door, Irene is already out of sight. "This way." He slams the door and stalks through the foyer down the hall toward a study. As soon as the door is closed behind us and he's seated behind his desk, he crosses his arms. "Go."

"A woman was found injured in the creek bed on our property." I watch closely, waiting for any sign that he's not surprised.

"That's a shame. What does it have to do with me?" Cool, neutral tone.

"We believe she washed down the river."

He arches a brow, cheeks reddening as he shifts his attention to Riley. "Are you accusing my family of something?"

"Of course not. We believe she may have been dumped north of your property and washed in."

"Then why are you here?"

"We were just hoping, if you don't mind, that you would allow us to trace the creek on your property as well. That way we could see if any clues washed down with her," Riley says.

"She wasn't hurt on my property."

"We never said she was," I reply, frustration growing. "As my brother said, we think it happened on the other side of your property. As you well know, there's a park over there with river access."

"Yet you want to search my land."

"We want to ride the creek line," I tell him. "Just in case there are any clues."

"I don't see badges on your chest. If I'm not mistaken, you boys aren't police."

"Getting a warrant takes time," I reply. *This is going nowhere.* "However, if you would rather the police comb your property, that's entirely fine with us. We're simply trying to save you the trouble."

"Unless you find something. Then I'll have to deal with two intrusions."

"Mr. Jacks—"

"No." He shoves back and stands. "I told you I would give you a few minutes, and I did. Now, if you don't mind, you can get off my property. Should the police show up with a warrant, I will do what I must do to comply. Until then—" He walks around the desk and pulls open the study door.

Riley and I both turn to face him, but we don't move. "Mr. Jackson," I start. "This woman has no idea who hurt her. We're just trying to help her."

A flicker of emotion moves across his face, but it's gone so fast I'm sure I must have imagined it. "That has nothing to do with me. Get off my property before I have you forcibly removed."

Neither Riley nor I say anything as we leave the house and make our way back toward the truck. I start the engine, but before I can pull out, Irene Jackson marches toward my truck.

"Great, so this isn't over," Riley mutters under his breath.

I roll my window down. "What can I do for you, Mrs. Jackson?"

"I heard what you told Lester. The woman is alive?"

"She is," I reply.

Her expression softens. "You can search our property for clues. But do not get caught. Lester is adamant you stay away from our land."

"Why do you think that is?" Riley questions.

Irene levels a glare on him. "He doesn't like you. I assure you, no one in my family had anything to do with harming the woman. But if it's possible you'll find something that leads the police to who did, then I don't want our family to stand in your way."

"Thank you." I offer her a smile. "I appreciate it."

"Warrants take time. If Lester is waiting for the police to obtain one, whatever was there could be gone." She steps back. "Come tonight after midnight, and steer clear of the house and barn. I'll make sure no one is out and about."

"We will," I assure her.

She nods then turns and stalks back toward the house.

"That was unexpected," Riley comments as we pull out of the gated drive.

"She was in an abusive relationship before she met Lester," I tell him, remembering a story my mother once told me.

"Man, I didn't know that."

"Yeah. My guess is she's looking at this a bit more personal than Lester."

He sighs. "Looks like a midnight operation is on the books," Riley says. "I was hoping to have sleep deprivation."

I chuckle at his sarcasm. It's hardly the first late night we've had. "We'll do a thorough check of the property then go from there."

"Do you think Irene is wrong and he's hiding something?"

"I don't know. But we're going to find out."

"I COULD GET in trouble for this, you know." Lani reaches into her purse and withdraws a plastic bag with the blood-stained clothes Jane Doe was wearing when we found her. She offers it to me.

"Which is why we appreciate you taking the risk," Riley replies with a grin. He takes the bag first and opens it then holds the clothes in his hand so his dog Romeo can catch the scent.

"We'll make sure you get it back," Bradyn promises as he takes the clothes and repeats what Riley did, this time with his dog, Bravo.

Tucker and Dylan, who only just returned a few hours ago, repeat the process with their dogs, Tango and Delta. Then Dylan hands it to me, so I kneel in front of Echo. Ears perked forward, he leans in and sniffs the dress. "We need answers, bud. Yeah, you got this." I pet him then stand and offer the clothes back to Lani.

She sticks them into the bag and shoves it back into her purse. "Anything you can find will help. Gibson said they've had no luck on the fingerprints or facial ID. They're still digging, but so far, our Jane Doe is a ghost."

Isn't that the truth? Red hair and hazel eyes swim into my memory. Cold, dead hazel eyes that once held such warmth. I shake it off. *Stay focused, Hunt. You have a living woman counting on you. There's nothing you can do for the dead.*

"She still hasn't remembered anything aside from running through the woods?" Bradyn questions.

"Not so far. Kennedy is with her now. She brought her dinner, and we're hoping that random, easy conversation will help jog something. Gibson has an officer stationed outside her door just in case running her prints alerted whoever shot her that the attempted murder didn't stick."

Bradyn nods then looks at the rest of us. "Let's pray and get this night on." He bows his head. "Lord, we ask for Your guidance as we search for any signs that can lead us toward answers. Please help us remain steadfast and quiet, and help us to find something that points us in the right direction, Lord. We ask this in the name of Jesus Christ, Amen."

A chorus of "Amen" follows. Then we're all grabbing our gear and heading for the door. Here's hoping the black tactical gear will keep us hidden tonight. Even though we have Irene's permission to enter their property, Lester explicitly told us no. Which means if he catches us, it'll be bad. I seriously doubt she'll take our side if we're caught.

Either way, it's a risk I'm more than willing to take if it means getting answers.

"I saw trees. Tall trees. It was dark, and I was running." I recall the memory Jane described to me. She hadn't remembered much, but it was enough to confirm

Lani's hunch that she was running from whoever shot her. And the trees eliminate all urban areas. Which, to be honest, is a good lead. We'd only suspected she was dumped in the creek; now we know she was there before being shot.

My gut tells me we'll find something tonight. Whether it's answers or something else, I'm not sure.

But something is in those woods. I *know* it.

CHAPTER 7
JANE DOE

"How long have you known the Hunts?" I ask then eat another salty fry. I learned something else about myself tonight—fries are one of my favorite foods. Crisp, salty French fries.

"About a year and a half," Kennedy replies. "I'm engaged to Bradyn. The oldest brother." She shows me a beautiful ring on her left hand, and the look on her face is one of pure love. "We're getting married in a day shy of three weeks. I'm counting down the hours," she adds with a bright smile.

"Three weeks? That's soon."

"It is. And I couldn't be more excited. Pretty much everything is done, so now it's just the waiting."

"I imagine that's hard."

"It is," she admits. "We've been through a lot, the two

of us. And I'm ready to make it official so we can start our lives."

"What do you mean you've been through a lot?" I immediately want to kick myself. "Sorry, that was intrusive. Everyone knows as much about me as I do, so I'm being nosy."

She laughs. "Not intrusive at all." Her expression falls a bit. "My best friend was murdered, and I got pulled into a pretty nasty fight. I actually ended up on the run and was hiding at the Hunt ranch. Bradyn and his brothers helped me get the proof I needed to clear my name."

"Oh, wow. That's—" I stare at her. "That is a lot."

She smiles. "It was. Bradyn came to me when I was at my lowest. And even though I'd made mistakes, he stayed by my side. What we have—I never thought I'd find it." Her eyes get a bit misty.

"That's wonderful." I can't help a pang of jealousy. Have I ever felt such love? Is there someone out there looking for me? Or was I all alone?

"It is." She wipes her eyes. "Oh, sorry, I'm a mess. The closer we get to the wedding, the more emotional I get." Kennedy laughs. "Let's talk about you."

"Well, I know that I like French fries. And being outside."

"That's something."

"Not much." Frustration ebbs at my pleasant mood.

"You don't seem like a bundle of nerves, given every-thing that's going on."

"No," I admit. "I'm not."

"So that's something too. You're strong."

"Or not worried about self-preservation," I reply with a laugh.

Kennedy shakes her head. "You are strong. I can see it."

"Maybe." I don't vocalize the same fear to her as I did to Elliot. But every hour that passes, I become more and more convinced that I must have been wrapped up in some-thing. I mean, why would I have that memory of running through the woods? What was I even doing out there?

"Well, we're all certain of it." She takes a bite of her cheeseburger and swallows it down with a drink of water. Silence surrounds us, and with it, I find my mind drifting back to the earlier walk I took with Elliot.

For a moment, he softens toward me, and I feel so comfort-able with him that it's as though we've known each other for years, not hours. "Kennedy, can I ask you something?"

"Absolutely. What is it?" She looks at me expectantly.

"What do you know about Elliot?"

She smiles softly. "Elliot Hunt is one of the most genuine, kindest men I've ever met," she replies. "He was the first to welcome me to the ranch, aside from Ruth and Tommy, of course."

"Tommy?"

"Elliot's dad."

"Oh, gotcha. So he's not normally—blocked off?" I try to find a way to put it that won't sound as though I'm being judgmental.

"Not usually." Her brow furrows. "Why? Did something happen?"

"What? Oh, no. He's been nothing but kind. He just seems like he gets a little distant. I wasn't sure if it was me or if that's just how he usually is."

"Oh no, it's not you. Elliot gets a bit wrapped up in his own head sometimes. And right now, I know he's focused on the case."

"Case?"

She cocks her head to the side, clearly expecting me to know what she's talking about. "Your case. He and the brothers are looking for the place you were attacked."

Fear sneaks up on me out of nowhere. My heart begins to pound, and suddenly the room might as well have had all the air sucked out of it. *They don't know what they're walking into.* It's the first thought that pops into my head, though I have no idea what it means.

The forest comes back, the tall dark trees passing by in a blur as I run for my life. "No, they need to let the police do it. The police—"

"Honey, calm down." Kennedy reaches forward and touches my hand. "Do you not know what they do?"

"What do you mean?"

"The Hunt brothers. They run a search and rescue company. Finding people is what they do."

That fear dissipates just slightly. "Search and rescue," I repeat, letting it soak in. That horrible sinking feeling remains, though. The fear that they have no idea what they're up against, and I can't even remember what it is so I can clue them in.

"Yeah." She squeezes my hand gently. "You don't have to worry about them. They're really good at what they do."

"But I was shot. Whoever is after me is dangerous. What if something happens to them because of me?"

"They were soldiers first," she assures me. "Special Ops. And you should've seen the place they pulled me out of." She offers me a smile. "They'll be just fine, okay? Besides, aren't you ready for some answers?"

"More than ready," I admit. Elliot's words come rushing back to me. He said that he'd been shot, stabbed— and he's still standing. They all are. So why can't I have more confidence that everything will be okay? What is this dread coiling in my belly? Fear—not for myself but for innocent men wrapped up in my nightmare?

"Then trust them," Kennedy says. "If there's anything to be found, they're your best bet."

———

THE SILENCE IS ECHOING as it surrounds me.

A sliver of light sneaks in from where the door is cracked, but aside from that, the room is cast in shadows. Kennedy left hours ago, but I haven't been able to sleep. Not while Elliot and his brothers are out risking their lives for me.

I didn't even ask them to. I wouldn't have asked them to.

Yet they went out anyway. What if they don't come back?

Closing my eyes for the millionth time tonight, I take a deep, steadying breath. Kennedy said they're good at what they do. Survivors. So I have to trust in that. It's not like I can call and ask them to back down.

The door opens, but since I don't want to argue with the nurse again about how I'm not interested in medication to make me sleep, I keep my eyes closed and my breathing steady. That way she can simply peek in and leave me to silently panic alone.

Soft footsteps carry farther into the room, and the door clicks closed.

What?

I open my eyes.

A man stares back at me. He's wearing the same blue scrubs as the nurses, but there's something hard in his eyes. Something that sets off an alarm within me.

"He—" I start to yell, but he's faster. He lunges across the distance and grips my throat with his hands, squeezing so hard I can't get a sound out. Pain shoots through my throat as all oxygen is cut off.

I thrash in the bed, adrenaline silencing the pain from my still-healing injuries. I raise my arm up and slam my fist into the side of his face. He loosens his grip just enough that I can raise my head and slam my forehead into his.

He stumbles back, releasing me, and it takes a moment for my vision to clear. I note the vase Ruth brought for me, and when the man charges again, I grip it and slam it into the side of his head. He falls backward, hitting the ground with a heavy thud.

I throw myself off the side of the bed. *I have to get to the door.* "Help!" I choke out, but the sound is raspy, barely over a whisper.

A hand grips my ankle and tries to drag me back. My fingers close over a chunk of the broken vase, and I cling to it. He flips me onto my back and straddles me, but when he reaches for my throat again, I use what little energy I have left and slice out with the glass.

His eyes go wide, and he stares down at me as he grips his own throat. Blood pours from the wound on the side of his throat.

I push him off of me, and he falls to the side, holding his throat.

"Help!" I scream again, this time louder.

The door is ripped open, and Lani races in. "Get security!" she yells. "And find out where that deputy is!" She rushes in and checks the man. I watch as she feels for his pulse.

"Did I kill him?" I can't move. I don't even have the energy to make myself sit up. Every inch of my body hurts, and when Lani turns toward me, I see the answer in her eyes. "He attacked me. I didn't have a choice." My voice is shaky as tremors take over my body. I can't stop shaking.

"I know you didn't," she says softly as she comes to my side. "You're okay, Jane, but I need you to breathe."

I try, but it's ragged, every single breath like acid in my throat.

The door opens again, and a man wearing a black security uniform rushes in alongside a deputy.

"I only stepped away for a minute!" he insists. "The nurse, he said he'd—" He stares down at the dead man.

"He's not a nurse," Lani growls. "Call Gibson. Now."

"I— I'm so sorry," the deputy says, his face twisted in horror.

"You're lucky she's not dead. Call Gibson *now*…before I have to."

"Okay." He steps from the room.

"Get me a wheelchair," she orders a nurse.

I close my eyes.

My body continues to tremble, tremors that cause my teeth to chatter.

"Breathe, Jane. You're safe, okay?"

I nod. *Breathe.* I can do that. Right?

CHAPTER 8
ELLIOT

The river roars beside us as we comb the park. It's long past dark, and we've already been at it for four hours. Tucker and Riley ended up splitting off and heading for the Jacksons' property line since, at this rate, we wouldn't have finished if all five of us stayed on the same path.

Bradyn walks to my left while Dylan is just behind, sweeping the area closest to the creek. This park is made up of over a hundred acres, most of them treed in the way Jane described in her memory.

Which means we have a lot of ground to cover.

Aside from trash left behind by people who can't be bothered to throw it in one of the trash cans lining the hiking trails, we've found nothing.

But that doesn't mean there's nothing here.

Echo tugs on the leash then lets out a single bark. "He's

got something," I say aloud, even though my brothers both know my dog's signals the same as I do. Reaching down, I unclip the leash from his harness. "*Voran*," I order. *Go on.* He takes off, rushing through the trees, and I follow, my brothers behind me. We sprint through brush a few hundred yards then come to a stop when Echo sits beside a tree.

He looks back at me and barks.

I withdraw my weapon as I come around the corner—just in case. But the moment I see a pair of bare feet sticking out from behind the trunk, I holster my weapon. "Echo found someone!" I call back to my brothers as I rush around.

My stomach plummets when the beam of my flashlight illuminates a woman leaning against the tree. Her hair is matted and dirty, and there's a red stain on the front of the man's white button-down shirt she's wearing.

Just like our Jane Doe.

Only, she's not lucky enough to have survived whatever was done to her.

Moving carefully, I reach forward and press my fingertips to her throat, checking for a heartbeat I already know I won't find. The body isn't quite cold yet, but there's no pulse.

"Calling it in." Bradyn steps away, and I lower my hand.

"She's gone." I study the woman. The white shirt is covering a dress that peeks out and rests right at her knees.

Unlike Jane, though, there are no defensive wounds on the body. Her feet aren't even dirty.

I stand, anger burning in my chest because I know exactly what this might mean. Two women dressed in the same outfit. Both left to die in the woods. Does Pine Creek have a serial killer?

"She's dressed just like Jane was," Dylan growls.

"I know." I turn back toward him. "She's been out here a few hours," I tell them.

"Which means, if the killer were here, he's long gone now," Dylan says, turning to study the trees.

"Why just leave her out in the open like this?" I question. "Why not bury the body? Or toss her in the creek like he did with Jane?"

"Could be he was interrupted," Dylan replies.

I stand, desperate for air. Flashes of that night, so long ago, assault my mind. *Stumbling over Renee's body in the dark. Landing in a pool of blood. Her face turned up toward me, eyes frozen wide.*

I make a fist and press it against my heart. *God, help me. Please help me.*

"You good, brother?" Dylan clasps a hand on my shoulder.

"I'll be fine." I suck in a breath, but when I turn back toward the woman, it's not a stranger I see. It's Jane. "One thing's for sure. This wasn't a hit-and-run. Which means

Jane was likely hit while she was trying to get away. I don't think she was an accident."

"I don't either," Dylan replies.

"Gibson is on his way. There was an incident at the hospital," Bradyn says, crossing the distance toward us.

Fear ices through the assault of memories. "What happened?"

His gaze is hard, his jaw set. "Someone tried to kill Jane."

AN HOUR LATER, I'm shoving through the doors of the hospital. It would have been sooner if I could've shown up here in full tactical gear and not had a mountain of questions to answer. So after I dropped all the gear and Echo off at my house, I sped here as fast as I could.

Bradyn said she was alive.

Lani confirmed it.

But until I have eyes on Jane, I won't believe it.

"We changed her room," Kira, a nurse working the emergency room desk says as she buzzes me in. It's after hours, but everyone here knows me, and Lani alerted them that I'd be coming through.

Even if she hadn't, only a bullet would have stopped me.

"Where is she?"

"Room four-fifteen," she replies.

"Thanks." I rush toward the elevator. But when it doesn't immediately come, I head for the stairs. I take them quickly, two steps at a time. By the time I've reached the fourth floor, there's a thin layer of sweat on my arms.

But it doesn't matter.

I fling the door open and head down the hall. Her new room is directly across from the nurse's station, and they all glance up as I stop in front of it. I can feel her there, a knowing presence just on the other side of the door.

With a deep breath, I knock.

"Come in," a raspy voice calls out.

I push it open and step into the dim light. Lani crosses over toward me and smiles softly then squeezes my arm before leaving without a word.

Jane is staring at the door when I come inside. Her eyes are rimmed with red, her throat bruised. There's a cut on the side of her head, and white-hot rage sears me from the inside.

"Hey," she greets, trying to force a smile.

"Are you all right?" I cross toward her, stopping only once I've reached her bedside. Closer now, I can see the handprints bruising her throat clearly. And it only makes that rage burn hotter.

"I'm alive," she replies. Her gaze darkens. "He's not."

"If you hadn't killed him, I would have," I growl.

She studies me. "Murder is not okay."

"It wouldn't have been murder," I reply.

"If you'd done it, it would have been."

She's right—obviously—but that doesn't make my statement any less true. Even as I know vengeance does not belong to us, I don't know that I would've been able to leash the rage within me at the sight of her damaged throat.

She could have died.

"You did good," I tell her. "Defending yourself."

"I don't know where it came from. Gibson said the man was twice my size, and he's surprised I survived."

"Gibson should have chosen someone better to protect you."

"It's not his fault. The deputy thought the guy worked here. He checked his badge and everything. It was just a mistake."

I clench my fists. "A mistake that nearly cost you your life."

"You're not wrong." She reaches up and touches her throat, fingers trembling. "I really thought I was going to die." Her eyes fill, so I step forward and take her hand in mine. Touching her feels right, and it calms the anger still waging war within me.

"I'm sorry. You should've been safe. I promised you that you would be safe."

"It's not your fault," she says. "I just—" Jane closes her eyes, and a tear slips free. "I didn't want to be alone. That's why Lani was here. I went from not being afraid to being terrified."

"Someone just tried to kill you," I remind her. "It would be foolish to not be afraid." I reach back with my free hand and tug the chair closer so I can sit. "I'll make sure you're not alone anymore, okay?"

She nods, tears slipping down her cheeks. "I'm so tired, but every time I close my eyes, I see him there. Standing over me, dark eyes full of hatred, his hands around my throat."

I have to take a moment to breathe as the visual settles over me, too. Then I reach forward and brush my fingers over her cheek. "Sleep, Jane. I'll watch over you, okay? No one—and I mean *no one*—will get to you while I'm here."

Her eyes flutter closed, and she nods. "I believe you."

"Good. Now sleep, Jane."

It's not two minutes later before her breathing softens and she's drifted off. In the silence and the dim light of the room, I take a moment to study her features. She's beautiful. A sharp nose dotted with freckles that dance on elegant cheekbones.

Who are you?

The door creaks open, and I glance back as Lani enters the room.

"Good. You got her to sleep."

"Where's the deputy who was supposed to be watching her?"

"Relieved from duty while Gibson decides what to do with him."

"He needs to be fired."

"As much as I want to agree with you, he made a mistake."

"That nearly cost Jane her life."

Lani rests her hand on my shoulder. "You'll get no argument from me." She yawns.

"You're tired, too."

She nods. "Been here since five yesterday morning. I pulled a double shift since the hospital is short-staffed. Then I hung around because Jane didn't want to be alone."

"Go ahead and go get some sleep. I'll watch over her."

"Yeah? You must be tired too. Did you find anything out there?"

"We'll talk later," I tell her, not wanting to get into it while Jane is sleeping only a few inches away from where I'm sitting. "Or better yet, call Bradyn and have him come get you so you're not driving."

"Nah, it's okay. I'm going to sleep in the on-call room. There's no way I have the energy to go home and do all the things necessary to sleep in my own bed." She chuckles, and I note the dark circles under her eyes.

Lani has always been a hard worker, but these extra hours are going to kill her if she's not careful. "Lani, call Bradyn. You'll feel better in your bed."

"Jane might need me."

"Then I'll call. Please, sis, get sleep."

She opens her mouth, presumably to argue with me, but closes it again and nods. "Bradyn's awake?"

"Yeah. He was talking to Gibson."

"Okay. I'll give him a call and have him come get me."

"Great. Sleep well."

"Call me if she needs anything, okay?"

I shift my gaze back to Jane. She's sleeping soundly, her red hair splayed out on the white pillow. "I will."

CHAPTER 9
JANE DOE

Elliot is still sitting beside my bed when I wake.

Sunlight streams in through the crack between the curtain panels, casting his face in a golden light. His gaze is on his phone, but my hand is still firmly in his. The heaviness of his calloused palm feels heavenly against my skin.

He lifts his gaze from the phone to me, and it holds mine. For a moment, the rest of the world disappears, leaving only the two of us. "How do you feel?"

"Sore," I admit, my voice still raspy. "I tore some stitches, and Lani had to fix them."

"How is your throat?"

"It hurts." I study him. "You stayed all night." I check the clock on the wall just behind him, noting that it's already dinner time. "And all day."

"I told you I would stay until you woke up."

"You must be exhausted. I'm so sorry."

"I'm fine. Don't apologize." He uses his free hand to type something on his phone then sets it down. "I let my brother know you're awake. He and Sheriff Lawson have been in and out all day, wanting to talk to you."

"Oh, okay."

A soft knock on the hospital door interrupts my response. "Come in," I call out. Elliot releases my hand, and I hate the sudden emptiness that fills me.

The sheriff, who'd introduced himself to me as Gibson Lawson on that first day, steps inside with a smile, alongside a tall, muscled man who looks a whole lot like Elliot. I remember him as one of the men I'd seen that day Elliot rescued me.

"Hey, Elliot," the sheriff greeted.

"Lawson." He nods in response.

Gibson shifts his attention from Elliot to me. "Hi, ma'am, I'm Sheriff Lawson, and this is Bradyn Hunt. Can we talk to you for a few minutes?"

"Sure. Bradyn, you're Kennedy's fiancé?"

He smiles. "I am."

"Bradyn and the other Hunt brothers are helping me on this case as consultants. I wanted to know if we could ask you a few questions?"

I look to Elliot, noting that he's not the least surprised they're here. Truthfully, he looks completely agitated at their presence. "Sure. Though I don't know how much help

I'll be; I still can't remember anything. As for the attack last night, that's been documented already."

"This isn't about the incident last night."

"You mean the attempted murder?" Elliot snaps.

Bradyn crosses his arms and shoots his brother a warning glare.

"Yes, it's not about that," Gibson replies, glaring at Elliot. "Though I am so incredibly sorry for what happened and want to assure you we're looking into how your attacker gained access to you."

"Thanks."

He nods. "As for not remembering, don't worry about that. This isn't about your past, actually. At least, not entirely." Gibson reaches into his pocket and withdraws his cell phone. After tapping on the screen, he turns it to face me. "Do you recognize this woman?"

I study the image. The woman's dark hair is loose around her face, and she's smiling brightly. There's no spark of recognition, though. "If I knew her, I don't remember her. I'm sorry. Who is she?"

"Her name was Rosalie Wallace. She was found dead last night in the same woods we believe you were attacked in."

I can feel the blood drain from my face. Everything goes cold from my toes all the way to the top of my face. I shift my gaze to Elliot. He knew? For nearly a full day, he knew someone else was dead, and he didn't say anything? Why? "What?"

"I know this is hard," Bradyn says. "But that's not all. She was wearing the same style white shirt you were found in, and underneath was a dress similar to the one you were wearing when Elliot found you."

I can hardly hear anything he's saying. It all sounds like I'm underwater, a loud echo surrounding me. Dead? She's dead? Another woman?

"I—I don't understand."

"Breathe," Elliot tells me. When he says it, we're no longer in this room but back in that garden yesterday. *"Breathe,"* he'd told me. *Just breathe.* But how can I when the walls are closing in? First, someone tries to kill me; then they find a woman dead in the same woods I remember being in?

"I know this is hard, especially after last night, but we needed to know if you remember anything," Gibson says.

"I— No." Tears roll down my cheeks, and I quickly wipe them away. "She died?"

"I told you both this was going to be too much." Elliot stands then faces both men and crosses his arms, standing between them and me like a wall of angry muscle.

"We needed to know," Bradyn argues. "You *know* that's how this works."

"This is too much for her after what happened last night. You should have let her have some time. Some—"

"We don't have time," Bradyn replies. "If we did, someone wouldn't have tried to kill her last night."

"It's okay," I tell Elliot then take a deep breath. And another. Letting the oxygen calm my nerves. "Do you think the man last night could have been the same one who killed her?"

"We're running him through the system," Gibson replies. "Based on first impressions, though, I'm thinking he was hired and had nothing to do with the woman in the woods."

"Hired? Someone wants me dead so badly they're willing to pay for it?"

"That's my best theory," Gibson replies.

"Mine, too," Bradyn adds.

Elliot remains silent.

Bradyn offers me a friendly smile. "We're going to figure it out, okay?" He and Gibson share a look. "I want to ask you something, and it's okay if you want to say no."

"What is it?"

"I would like to offer you a safe place to stay until we get all this figured out. We own a ranch here in town, and all of us have houses on the property. My parents have a spare bedroom, and they've agreed to take you in until this is all over. We can keep you safe there. But if you're not comfortable—"

"No," Elliot snaps.

Disappointment slams into me.

"No?" Bradyn questions. "It's her safest bet."

"I agree. But she's not staying with Mom and Dad. The stairs will be too much, and if someone is really after her, we shouldn't put them at risk too."

"Then what do you suggest?" Bradyn questions.

Elliot turns to me. "I have two spare rooms. You can sleep in one, and I'll see if Lani is willing to come stay in the other. That way, you have someone there to look after you. No one will come within a hundred feet of the house without us knowing about it."

I stare at him. I'd thought he was refusing to let me stay at the ranch, but instead, he's offering me a room? In his house?

"Well?" he asks.

"Yes. That would be great."

"Really?" He seems surprised.

"Yes. Maybe being out of this room will also help me remember something—anything that can help. I'm going crazy just lying here, and now another woman is dead. If I can help, I want to help."

Elliot nods.

"Okay. Great," Bradyn says. "I'll coordinate with Lani about having you checked out. Then we'll drive you out to the ranch."

BEING out of the hospital is the greatest feeling.

But the moment I think that, guilt crushes down on me. I'm only here because someone tried to kill me and another woman is dead. Because two other people lost their lives.

Even though I'm sitting in Elliot's living room while he prepares the guest rooms for me and Lani, I can still see the woman smiling out from that photograph Gibson showed me. There'd been so much life in her eyes, and now she'll never smile again. Emotion burns my throat. *Why can't I remember something that will help?*

The image of her has me wondering so much. Did I know her? Were we friends? Did she like being outside too? Did she have a family? Loved ones?

Do I?

I run my hands over Echo's soft fur as he lies beside me. Elliot's dog has been at my side since the moment we got back to his house. I smile as I run my fingers through his thick fur.

I like dogs.

Another thing I learned about myself.

Elliot comes down the hall and steps into the living room, wearing dark jeans and a black T-shirt. Colored ink snakes up both arms, and the muscles of his biceps flex as he lifts a hand to remove his baseball cap. "He's not normally so calm with people he just met."

I smile down at Echo then up at his owner. "He's a good boy." Echo's tail thumps in response.

"That he is." Elliot takes a seat on the other side of Echo. "The room is ready."

"Thank you so much for letting me stay here."

He nods. "My parents have stairs, and I imagine those would not be easy on your injury."

"You would be imagining right," I reply. He'd had to carry me up the two steps onto his porch earlier because moving is beyond painful right now. Reopening those stitches last night certainly didn't do me any favors.

"You're sure you're comfortable with this?" he asks. "We just met."

"And you saved my life then sat by my bedside all night so I could get some sleep. I feel safe with you, Elliot." Our gazes hold. "I don't know how to explain it, but I do."

"I won't ever hurt you," he says. "Or let anyone else hurt you."

I smile. "Thanks." Truth is, being here in his space, I'm more relaxed than I've been in—well—as long as I can remember. Not that that's a tall bar to meet. His space is warm and inviting with soft, muted colors balanced with an accent of hunter green.

It's peaceful.

"My mom is sending Lani over with dinner when she gets here."

"She was okay with staying here, too?"

He nods. "She crashes with one of us occasionally. She

has property here on the ranch too but hasn't started building her house yet."

"That's so neat. That all of you are so close."

"It's always been this way."

"You and Bradyn seemed a bit at odds earlier."

Elliot's jaw flexes, and he crosses his arms. "It wasn't Bradyn I was annoyed with."

"Gibson?"

He nods.

"What happened isn't his fault, either. Truthfully, I don't even blame the deputy. Everyone makes mistakes."

"A fast-food restaurant might forget to pack an order of fries. *That* is a mistake. Not letting a complete stranger into a guarded room where he can murder the woman inside. There's more to that. I know it. And Tucker is looking into it."

"Tucker?"

"One of my younger brothers," he replies. "Can I get you some water? Tea?"

"No, I'm okay right now, thanks." I rest my head back against the soft couch.

"You're sure?"

"Aside from being helpless, I'm fine."

"You're anything but helpless," he replies. "Last night should have taught you that."

"Sure, I survived last night. And I got away from

whoever shot me. But that woman didn't. Who knows how many others weren't so lucky."

His hazel gaze levels on me. "That's not your fault."

"I just feel like, if I could remember something—anything—then maybe I could tell you all something that will help."

He reaches out and brushes a strand of hair out of my face. I freeze at the contact, the feel of his fingers brushing against my cheek. It feels far better than a simple touch should. "We've found people with much less to go on." His tone is soft, his voice low.

"Thank you. For trying."

He drops his hand. "We'll get it figured out." Elliot turns his head to study the setting sun through a large picture window overlooking the ranch.

"It's beautiful out here."

"My favorite place in the world."

"Have you been to many places?" I ask.

He nods. "Far more than I wish I had. I need to go grab a shower before Lani gets here. Dylan is monitoring the perimeter of the house, so you're covered as far as safety goes. Are you sure you don't need anything?"

I hate that he's leaving already. "I'm totally fine. Thanks."

He nods. "I'll only be about fifteen minutes. Call out if you need something, okay?"

"Okay. Thanks."

He offers me another friendly smile then turns to head down the hall. Echo remains here with me, though his ears perk up as Elliot leaves the room. It's strange how empty it feels now that he's not sitting on the couch anymore.

I rest my head back again, my hand on the dog sleeping beside me, and close my eyes. As exhaustion pulls at my consciousness, I drift off to sleep, my thoughts on the handsome hero who burst into my hospital room last night, ready to go to war for me.

CHAPTER 10
ELLIOT

T*hree days later.*

"TUCKER AND DYLAN are heading out to wrap up their assignment this afternoon," Bradyn says as he makes a note on the tablet in front of him. "They'll be out of touch for a few days, but Elijah Breeth has agreed to help with any tech issues that might arise."

The former Army Ranger lives in Maine and works alongside our cousin, Silas, at a private security firm. He's also the only one who can come close to beating Tucker on a computer.

"Any word on Elliot's Jane Doe?" Riley asks then pops a piece of gum into his mouth and grins at me.

Irritation eats at my already frayed nerves. Something I can thank my lack of sleep for. "She's not my Jane Doe."

"You found her," he replies. "She's living with you."

An all-too-familiar vise tightens around my heart. "Doesn't make her mine. And she's not living with me. She's staying there so I can keep her safe."

"Fine. How is *the* Jane Doe?" Riley asks again.

"So far, nothing has popped up on any database anywhere," Bradyn replies. "Gibson said they cannot find a single record based off of fingerprints or facial ID."

"I even ran her photograph through a few places the local PD can't get into." Tucker crosses his arms. "And nothing. Not a driver's license, yearbook photo, or social media picture has gotten any hits."

Strange. Even the most elusive people have a minor presence online. Whether it's an old yearbook photo, passport, or membership card. She had to have popped up somewhere. It's not like she just blinked into existence. Unless… "Witness protection?" I ask, noting that Bradyn's fiancée actually spent some time with marshals up until three years ago. She ran away from them and spent nearly that entire time on the run before coming here to the ranch a year and a half ago.

"Nope," Tucker replies. "I got into contact with Frank Loyotta over at Find Me, and he helped me get in touch with his marshal buddy. No one matching her description is missing from their program."

"This makes no sense." I push to my feet and start pacing Bradyn's dining room. "What about the guy who attacked her?"

"Him, we do have answers on." Bradyn taps something on his tablet, and a mugshot pops up on the projector screen.

I glare at the man staring back at me. His hair is a bit long, brushing his shoulders, and his eyes are so dark they almost appear black, but aside from the orange jumpsuit he's wearing, he looks like any average man. Which is what would make it so easy to blend in when going after a target.

"Meet Christoper Dornan. Thirty-seven, on the FBI's most wanted list. He's been wanted for questioning in over twenty-two active murder cases all over the country. Yet somehow managed to evade everyone sent to bring him in."

"Until Jane put him down," Riley comments. There's clear pride in his voice. Pride that she was able to defend herself against a professional like Dornan.

"So he was hired."

Bradyn nods at me. "There's more." His gaze moves from me to Tucker. I know that look. He's afraid what he's about to say is going to set me off.

"What is it?" I demand.

"Well, as I said I would, I did some looking into the deputy stationed outside her door."

"And?" I growl, wishing they'd just get to the point.

"There was a large deposit—fifty-thousand dollars to

be exact—deposited into his account two hours before he took the shift."

Fury ignites in my veins. "*What?*" I growl. Even as I knew no cop worth his uniform would have stepped away so an untrained nurse would watch over a patient in protective custody, I still hate that I was right.

"Gibson arrested him and brought him in for questioning an hour ago. He swears that the man said he knew Jane and just wanted to talk to her."

"And the fact that he was willing to pay that much for alone time with her didn't set off any red flags?"

"Apparently, he got himself into some gambling debt and was desperate," Bradyn replies. "He's not getting out anytime soon. Gibson has him locked up."

"Let me talk to him."

"Absolutely not," Bradyn replies.

"Why not?"

"Because you'll rip him apart," Riley replies. "We don't have time to bail you out after you get slapped with murder charges."

I turn to him. "I could get answers from him."

"That's not our job," Tucker says. "Gibson is a good cop. He'll get whatever he can from the guy."

"Gibson is the reason that man was stationed outside Jane's room in the first place."

"Not his fault," Dylan says. "We've all made mistakes."

It's a jab.

And a low one at that.

But he's not wrong, and the comment did exactly what it was supposed to—it deflated my anger. I take a deep breath. "Fine. Anything on Rosalie Wallace?"

"Nothing new so far. She lived alone and worked for a shipping company. She handled transportation documents, some of them high-value clients. That's an angle to work. Gibson asked local PD to do some canvasing over at her apartment in Galveston, and he said they reported that no one recognized the photo of Jane Doe. As of now, they've found nothing linking them," Bradyn replies. "There was also no DNA on the body, and unlike Jane, she showed no signs of a struggle. They're waiting on the tox report to see if she was drugged."

Jane fought. Hard. The cuts and scrapes on her legs, hands, and arms, her bruised ribs, as well as the bruising on her face, are evidence of that. So why did this other woman not fight? Is it because she knew the killer? "Where's the shipping company located?" I ask.

"The Port of Galveston."

"A six-hour drive. So she was abducted out of Galveston and dumped here? How does that make sense?"

"Not sure," Tucker replies. "But I looked into hotel bookings, motel bookings, B&B's, and she wasn't staying anywhere within a hundred miles of where she was found. Not under her real name, at least."

More questions. A serial killer typically chooses

hunting grounds. They likely wouldn't have risked driving six hours with a kidnap victim in the car.

"It's not a bad drive. I'll head out first thing in the morning."

"There's no telling if they'll talk to you," Dylan says. "You're not police."

"No, but I might be able to show Jane's picture. If they're linked somehow, it's a lead to go off of."

"We can also have local PD go," Bradyn says. "They've already notified her employers that she was found. We can send over a picture of Jane, too."

I shake my head. "I want to look them in the eye," I reply. "If they have something to do with this, I need to be there."

Bradyn looks at our brothers then back to me. "You're sure you're up for this?"

"You made me lead on this case," I tell him. "So, yeah. I'm good."

"Okay. I'll let Gibson know what you're planning. Riley can stay at your place while you're gone to help keep Jane protected."

"Great."

"You're sure you'll be all right with Tuck and me gone?" Dylan asks. "Seems like there's a lot on the plate right now."

"We'll manage," Riley replies, shooting a grin at the twins.

We were hired to track down a man wanted for embezzling his clients' pension funds. Since Tucker can trace any digital signature, and Dylan is a punch-first-and-ask-questions-later type of person, they make an incredibly valuable team. Then there's the whole twin thing, which means they're even more on the same wavelength than the rest of us.

They'd spent the last trip doing recon, and now it's time to track him and close it down.

"Should only take a few days. We've got most of the intel we need, and we're pretty sure we know where we're going to find this guy," Dylan says.

"I bet we're back in two days," Tucker replies as he stands. "We'll check in before we head out."

"Sounds good, thanks. Let me know if you need anything." Bradyn stands, and we say goodbye to the twins and then to Riley as he walks out alongside them. As soon as it's just Bradyn and me, he turns toward me. "Want to talk?"

"I'm fine, big brother." Even though Bradyn is only a year older than I am, he's taken on a second father role for all of us. His leadership skills are far beyond anything any of us possess, and his time as an interrogator overseas gave him perceptiveness that no one else can match.

It's also one of the reasons I knew this conversation was coming sooner rather than later.

"Remember when you confronted me about Kennedy?"

"You were being an idiot."

He chuckles. "Fair enough. I see what you're dealing with, and I want you to know we can talk about it."

"There's nothing to talk about."

"You've had Renee on your mind since you found Jane in that creek. I can see it all over your face."

My stomach twists into knots. "It's in the past."

"Renee will never be in the past for you." Bradyn's candid comment hits me square in the chest. "Not until you're willing to forgive yourself."

"This isn't about Renee."

"Isn't it? You were pretty adamant at first that you wouldn't be primary on the Jane Doe case. Renee's sister, Jesse, was the last missing persons case you took on."

"Yeah. And it went sideways, didn't it?" Renee contacted us in hopes of locating her sister, who had been missing from her college dorm for three days. The police all claimed that Jesse would turn up. That, since she liked to take impromptu trips, that was all it was. But Renee had known differently.

And she'd been right.

"What happened to her wasn't your fault."

"It was my fault, and pretending I didn't miss important information is a lie."

Bradyn takes a step closer to me and crosses his arms. "It was not your fault," he repeats. "And bearing that burden is going to destroy you. It's already done damage,

Elliot. How much more are you going to let that case take from you? Your sanity? Your second chance?"

Emotion claws at my throat. "I'm choosing to learn from that mistake and not repeat it."

Bradyn reaches out and clasps a hand on my shoulder. "Good. It's been three years, brother. And it's time you moved forward."

***

"So do you think this means anything?"

I glance over at Renee as she holds up a slip of paper we'd found in the bottom of a shoebox beneath her sister's bed. Reaching over, I take it and turn it over in my palm. "Looks like half a phone number. I'll have Tucker run it. If there's something there, he'll find it." After taking a picture of it and sending the image off to my computer-whiz brother, I offer it back to her. "How are you holding up?"

Her thick red hair has been pulled up in a loose bun, but a single strand touches the top of her shoulder. Renee turns toward me, and her hazel eyes are red-rimmed from crying as we go through her sister's things. "I just want to know if she's okay."

"I know." I reach over and cup her cheek, running my thumb over her soft skin. "We'll find her."

She nods. "I know. I'm honestly afraid of what we'll find when we do."

"Let's get you home, okay?"

Nodding again, she buckles her seatbelt then leans back in the seat as I pull away from the dorm rooms. Every moment that passes, I grow more and more concerned that I won't be able to reunite Renee with her younger sister.

Not just because she's a case, though that certainly would be motivation enough, but because Renee's become important to me in just the short time I've known her.

I want to see her happy. And bringing Jesse back is the only way to do that.

Minutes tick by in silence, and before long, we've made the thirty-five-minute drive back to Renee's apartment complex.

After putting my truck into Park, I turn toward her.

"Are you sure you're okay?"

She turns toward me. "I will be. I just want the truth."

"I'll help you find it."

Renee smiles softly, though it doesn't reach her eyes. "You'll call if that paper means anything?"

"Absolutely."

She turns around in her seat and offers Echo a friendly pet on the head. "You're a good boy. Take care of him, okay?" she adds, smiling at me.

"I'll be fine. It's you I'm worried about."

Renee takes a deep breath. "I'm not the one in danger."

IT'S STILL dark outside as I tug on a pair of tennis shoes and head for the front door. Bradyn is on camera duty until seven this morning, so this might be my only chance at burning off some steam. Lani is asleep in the guest room, as is Jane. The house is quiet, but my thoughts are anything but. "Echo, *hier.*"

He falls into step beside me, and we bound down the porch steps. By the time I've hit the bottom step, I'm already running. The nightmares aren't new to me—Renee haunts me every time I close my eyes.

But this time when I woke, it was Jane I was thinking about. It was her lying on the living room floor, dead, because I'd missed the fact that it was her who was in danger. That Jesse was merely collateral damage for a deranged teacher's assistant who'd become obsessed with Renee after she'd visited Jesse at school.

I'd been so focused on returning Jesse to Renee that I missed clear indications that everything was not what it seemed.

And she'd paid the ultimate price.

Pumping my arms faster, I move through the dark, racing through the trees. If I can just run off this anxiousness, I'll be better. I have to be better. With me as primary, it's my call what we do. How we handle things. Which means, if something goes wrong—I shake that thought off. Nothing will go wrong. Not this time.

The dirt is soft beneath my feet, the creek roaring beside me as soon as I hit the trail I want to run. Echo keeps pace, running beside me, his tail wagging, tongue dangling out of his mouth. For him, this is joy. For me, it's therapy.

By the time I've reached the end of the creek trail, I've managed to run off the remainder of my nightmare. I sprint up a small hill then run down the other side, following the path around the bottom and back toward my house.

Muscles warm and exhausted, I'm feeling a whole lot calmer than I was when I left nearly forty-five minutes ago. Once I have a shower and coffee, I'll be even better, my mind set on the task at hand, which is making the drive to Galveston and meeting with Rosalie's employees at the port.

I come up the hill leading toward home, but as soon as I get close enough to have a clear vision of my house, I come to an abrupt stop. Bathed in the light of the guest room window, Jane stands, staring out into the darkness. Her red hair is loose around her face, delicate waves that fall well past her shoulders.

I can't see her eyes from this far away, but I know they're crystal green. The kind that seems almost too beautiful to be real.

I'm captivated by the sight of her dressed in a baggy

sweatshirt, bathed in the soft light of the bedside lamp. *Beautiful.* Attraction burns in my gut. What is wrong with me? Bradyn believes I was so afraid to take this case because of what happened with Renee.

And maybe that is part of it. But the truth is I know myself. I know how Jane makes me feel even though we just met. I know that, even as I cared for Renee, what I feel when I'm around Jane is more potent than anything I've ever experienced in my life.

And I know, with horrible clarity, that I will get too close and make a mistake that will cost this woman her life.

I'm lead on this case, so the rules have never been more important.

Work is work. Personal is personal.

And I can't afford to mix the two.

No matter how badly I want to.

CHAPTER 11

JANE DOE

For the first time since I woke up in that hospital bed four days ago, I managed to get a full night's sleep. It's four in the morning and still dark out, but I'm wide awake and feeling good enough that I'm ready to try my own route of getting answers.

Certain movements still ache, but I'm back on my feet and able to walk a few miles a day—with Lani or Elliot's supervision, of course.

My hope for today is that I'll be able to borrow a computer and just start googling stuff. Even though I'm fairly certain Tucker's research has been far more detailed than a web search, it'll feel good to do something. Anything, really.

The front door opens, so I head out of the room and down the hall. Echo jumps up off his bed, barely visible from the hall, and races toward me.

"Morning, boy," I greet, petting him happily before continuing down the hall and into the kitchen.

Elliot is standing in front of the coffee pot, wearing a tight zip-up sweater, shorts, and tennis shoes. His skin is gleaming in a thin layer of sweat, and the dark hair at his temples is matted to the side of his head.

"You look like you've already been productive."

He turns and offers me a smile. "Something like that. Coffee?"

"Yes, please." I take a seat on a barstool. "So, listen, I was thinking I could use a computer today. Start poking around on the internet and see if I can remember something?"

"Sure, I'll have Riley bring one over when he heads this way."

"He's coming over?"

"He's going to stay here tonight."

"Oh, why?"

"I'll be in Galveston."

Unease churns in my gut at the mere idea of this man not being right down the hall. Elliot feels safe to me. Not that Riley isn't, but Elliot is just—well—he's different. "Why are you going to Galveston?"

"To meet with Rosalie Wallace's employer. I want to know if it's possible something she was working on could have caused someone to target her. I'll also be showing them your picture. See if somehow you were involved too." He pours coffee into two mugs then offers me one.

"I should go too, then. Right?"

He leans back against the counter. "No. You need to remain here."

"But if I am involved, then maybe they'll be able to tell me who I am."

"Information I can get with your photograph."

"Sure. But if I'm there, it might open them up more," I insist. I *need* to go. I can feel it.

"Jane, it's safer for you here."

"I don't want to just sit around, Elliot. I'm just waiting for someone to tell me who I am, but I want to actively be doing something to figure it out too. Can't you understand that?" I can see from his expression that he does. "Please let me go. I promise to follow your lead. I'll take it easy."

"It could be dangerous."

"So was the hospital. Besides, I'll have you to keep me safe, right?"

He clenches his jaw. "I don't know. Lani might not approve."

"Lani might not approve of what?" Lani asks, yawning as she steps into the kitchen.

Elliot pours her a cup of coffee.

"Of me going with Elliot to Galveston to meet with Rosalie Wallace's employer."

"Oh, well…" Lani considers it. "Thanks," she says when Elliot offers her the mug of coffee. "I mean, as long as you're careful, I don't see an issue. I want to check your injury first, make sure it's looking good. But Elliot is skilled enough with medical emergencies that I trust he can keep you alive."

"See?" I turn to Elliot. "It could work."

He takes a breath filled with frustration. "I don't know. You literally almost died three days ago."

"But I'm still breathing," I insist.

"She's moving around really well and hasn't needed anything stronger than OTC pain meds since she left the hospital. Besides, it could help jog her memory, which would be excellent for her mental health and overall well-being. If you want to get technical about it." She grins at him.

Another wave of hope surges through me despite the glare Elliot shoots at his sister.

"That's a six-hour car ride," he tells Lani. "Can she really be sitting that long?"

"Just stop at least once during the drive so you can both stretch your legs, and it'll be fine. I need to go get ready for work; then I'll look you over to make sure you're good for the trip." She offers us both a smile then starts humming and heads down the hall.

"So? Can I come?" I ask, hopeful that Elliot will agree. It's a place to start. And, while it's possible there is no link between me and Wallace, it's still hope. A place to start.

Elliot studies me. "Fine. But you follow my lead, okay? If I tell you it's too dangerous—"

"Then I will do whatever you need." Unable to help myself, I cross over and wrap my arms around Elliot. He freezes against me, but I don't let go.

And when his arms come around me, I feel like I'm home. Safe. Warm.

Before I can lose myself in his embrace, I pull back and clear my throat. "I'll go get everything ready. When are we leaving?"

"In an hour," he says. "Is that okay?"

"Not a problem for someone who only owns, like, five borrowed outfits," I reply with a laugh. "I'm so ready to start doing something. Thank you for letting me come."

"Sure thing. I'm going to call Riley and let him know. Just be ready in an hour."

"You got it."

"So what made you start up Hunt Brothers Search & Rescue?" I ask then take a drink of the coffee we'd stopped for about half an hour ago. We've been on the road for three hours already, and so far, it's been far quieter than I was expecting.

Just silence and country music between us.

"It was Bradyn's idea," he says. "Since he joined the

service a year before me, he was out first. When he got home, he was restless, and in his search for something to do, he found a reward being offered for the return of a missing teen. He said he felt driven to help her, so he set out in search of the girl. Found her within forty-eight hours and returned her home safely."

"That's wonderful."

"It was," he agrees. "Anyway, he tried to turn down the reward money, but the mother insisted he take it and use it to help more families."

"And so, Hunt Brothers Search & Rescue was born," I finish.

He chuckles. "And so, it was."

Silence surrounds us once again. "It's great what you guys do. You're making such a difference in people's lives."

"I hope so. I know it feels good when we can do something good for someone else."

"What did you do when you were in the service? If you can share, that is."

He smiles, but it's empty. "I was good at getting into places without anyone ever knowing I was there." Since he doesn't elaborate, I imagine those places didn't leave him with the best memories, so I drop it.

"I wonder what I did. Before, I mean."

He casts me a sideways look before returning his attention to the road. "I'm thinking rodeo clown."

I snort, nearly spewing coffee from my nose. "Excuse me?"

He shrugs. "You're funny."

"Hold on a second." I turn in my seat so I can see him more clearly. "You think I was a rodeo clown because I'm funny?"

"That tree ring joke was gold."

"But a *clown*?"

He laughs, a deep, booming, joyous sound that once again takes me by surprise. The man laughs so infrequently you'd think he rarely felt joy. "Fair enough. Maybe not a rodeo clown. Though I could see you facing down bulls without batting an eye."

I grin, wondering if he realizes just how much I needed to hear that. "That's quite the compliment coming from a soldier like you, sir." He chuckles but doesn't say anything else.

After taking another sip of my coffee, I stare out the window. It's been miles and miles of smooth driving, just a flat road and no traffic. It's been easy to forget that we're technically going to try to find out why a woman was murdered rather than taking a vacation.

I take a deep breath. "Tell me something else you think about me. What have you observed?"

"You like your coffee black, which means you likely drink it on the go. That makes me believe you're a person who balances a busy schedule."

"So I'm motivated and brave, go on."

He smiles. "You also tend to dress in muted colors, so I'd say rodeo clown really is off the table of possible careers."

"You're the one who put it on in the first place."

"You're quick to trust some people but are cautious around others, which means you either have a great judge of character or aren't afraid of anyone hurting you."

"Which do you think it is?"

He meets my gaze for a moment then looks back out at the road. "Both." The way he says it leaves a heaviness in the cab of the truck. "I would guess that you're a good judge of character because you've had to be."

"Why is that?"

"Why would it be? You've been hurt. At some point in your life, someone betrayed you. But you refused to let it steal your light, so you turned that knowledge into a weapon of self-preservation."

I stare back at him, imagining all of the things he's saying. Is it possible he really read me that well? Or am I merely confused and acting out of character? "You have unpacked me so elegantly, Hunt."

He chuckles. "Bradyn is better at reading people than I am, but I do have some observation skills of my own."

"Do you all have your own special expertise? Or do you all train in everything?"

"As I said, Bradyn is great at reading people and situations. If he weren't prepping for his wedding, I would've insisted he come with us. There have been plenty of times his skill has meant the difference between life and death. Tucker is a master behind a keyboard, and Dylan moves faster and quieter than anyone I've seen."

"And Riley?"

"Riley could sell ice to a penguin," he replies with a smile. "I hate to admit it, but charm is his superpower. Just don't tell him I said it."

I laugh. "Your secret's safe with me. And you said you're great at getting into places without anyone knowing."

"I'm also handy with a lock. There's not much I can't get into."

"Color me impressed, Hunt. That's quite a skill."

He shrugs. "It does the job when it's needed."

"And how often is it needed?"

"More often than I'd care to admit," he replies. His phone rings, so he hits a button on his steering wheel. "Hunt. You're on speakerphone, and Jane is in the car."

"It's Gibson," the sheriff says, his voice coming through the speakers. "Hey, Jane."

"Hi," I reply awkwardly.

"What is it?" Elliot asks.

"We got the tox report back on Rosalie Wallace."

"And?"

"Her blood alcohol level was seven times the legal limit. Even if she'd have wanted to fight back, she wouldn't have had the strength."

"So they waited until she was drunk then killed her." Elliot casts a look at me, likely to check to see how I'm handling the information.

Truthfully, even as horrifying as it is, I'm trying to focus on the facts. "Were there any other markers on her body?" I ask.

"Nothing that would help us ID the killer. She had no DNA under her fingernails or anywhere on her body or clothing. Whoever did it was thorough."

Elliot lets out a frustrated breath. "Keep me posted if anything pops. We're halfway to Galveston."

"Sounds good. You'll let me know if you find anything?"

"Of course."

"Good luck."

The call ends, and Elliot is silent for a few moments. "How are you feeling?"

"Fine. Lani checked the injury before we left and said everything looked great. She sent me with some fresh bandages, which I've been told I have to put on tonight, and other than being afraid I'll mess that up, I'm good."

"You won't mess it up. Maybe you were a doctor."

I roll my eyes. "Maybe. And maybe I was a sometimes-broody former Special Forces soldier."

He laughs. "Given that you took down a professional hitman? It wouldn't surprise me."

CHAPTER 12
ELLIOT

The Galveston Port is home to cruise and cargo ships, and there is no shortage of either docked today. After we dropped our stuff off at the hotel, Jane and I had changed and headed straight here.

She walks beside me, studying everything, and I have to imagine the woman doesn't miss much. Our earlier discussion has had me wondering all day what it was she must have done to land her in that creek.

Honestly, I'm leaning toward cop or private investigator. With her self-defense skills, the way she acts, dresses—I'd bet my money she did something to help others. Social worker, maybe?

"Any of this jogging your memory?" I ask as I guide her down a walkway and toward the Port offices.

"Not really," she admits, frustration lacing her tone. "I wish I could say it was."

"Maybe once we get into the building."

She forces a smile. "Maybe."

I rush ahead and pull the door open for her then close it behind us. The offices are small, just an older building with a desk up front and a series of offices in the very back.

A woman with curly gray hair and black-rimmed glasses glances up from the book she's reading. "Hi, can I help you?"

"We're here to meet with Victor Fontana," I tell her. "I'm Elliot Hunt, and this is Jane."

"Great. I'll let him know you're here." She sets her book down then lifts the receiver of the phone next to her. "Mr. Fontana, your four o'clock is here." After a brief moment, she hangs it up. "He'll be right out. You can wait over there." She gestures toward a small waiting area tucked in the far corner.

"Great, thanks."

Without thinking, I place my hand on Jane's lower back. The moment my palm touches her, a jolt of attraction shoots straight through me. Especially when she hesitates a moment and leans into my touch.

Man, I'm in trouble.

Between the truck ride here and the time we spent talking, I'm opening up more and more to her. Which means those lines I was so careful to keep drawn are beginning to fade. Little by little.

Solve it quickly, Hunt. Then you can see what can happen from there.

"Mr. Hunt?"

I turn and greet a middle-aged man as he crosses over to us. "Mr. Fontana, thanks for agreeing to see us."

"Of course. Us?" he asks.

I realize that Jane is hidden from view, so I step aside. "This is—"

"Gena," he chokes out, eyes widening and face paling.

She looks from him to me then back to him. "Wait, you—"

The man turns and sprints from the building, moving so fast he might as well have left a cartoon-sized hole in the side of the building. I take off after him, shoving through the door and leaping over the yellow barrier that will take me toward the docks.

Boots slamming against the pavement, I push my body faster, closing the distance between us in a few short seconds. I throw myself forward, slamming my body into his and taking us both down to the grass.

"Wait!" he yells as I pin him to the ground. "Stop! You don't understand!"

"Then stop moving and tell me," I growl.

"I didn't do anything! It wasn't my fault!"

Standing, I pull the man up with me, keeping a hold on his arm as I tug him back toward the building. "How about we go and have a chat so you can fill me in, huh?"

"Talk," I order as soon as we're back inside and he's seated in a conference room alongside the woman who'd been working the front desk.

I flipped the closed sign, locked up, and took both of their cell phones. So for now, we're all alone.

"You know who I am?" Jane asks.

"Of course I know who you are. One doesn't forget someone who broke their nose."

Jane straightens, her eyes widening. "I broke your nose?"

Victor looks from her to me. "What game is she playing?"

"No game," I reply, glancing back at Jane, then turn my attention back to the worm in front of me. "See, someone shot her and left her for dead in a creek. She has no idea who she is or why that happened. But I'm guessing you can give us some answers."

He pales. "I don't know who shot her."

"Then why did you run?" she demands.

"Because you told me that, if anything happened to Rosalie, you were going to hunt me down and break more than my nose."

I turn to her, honestly amused. The more the guy talks, the more she makes sense.

"Why?"

The man lets out a sigh. "Look, Rosalie and I were a thing, okay? And she told you that she thought I was messing around on her, so you came down here to threaten me. The next day, Rosalie stopped returning my phone calls."

"So we were friends?"

"No. She barely knew you." He sneered. "You just showed up at her old place, flashing a smile, saying you needed her help with something."

"What did I need?"

"How am I supposed to know? She dumped me, and I didn't hear anything else about her until they called saying she got herself killed."

Jane's face reddens. "That's a callous way to talk about someone you cared for."

"She dumped me, remember?" he snaps. "Dumped me and left without a trace. She didn't even move out of her apartment. The landlord wouldn't give me much, but he said some woman with red hair came in and paid the rent up through two years."

"Two years of rent payments?" Jane looks at me. "That's no small amount of money."

"No," I agree, "It's not."

"I knew you were slimy from the moment I met you. Took a good, obedient girl like Rosalie and started putting thoughts in her head." Victor scowls.

"I think I'm understanding why I broke your nose."

He glares at her.

"You expect me to believe that you have no idea what Jane—Gena—needed with Rosalie?"

"No clue. You ruined my life," he snaps. "Took my girl and almost tanked my business in the process."

"And how did I manage that?"

"Ever since Rosalie left, clients have been leaving us. Big clients too. It stopped about a week ago, but for over a year, I lost people that *I* brought in. They all claimed to have found a better deal with another company."

I consider, piecing together what he's saying.

Jane comes here and recruits a woman who works for a cargo shipping company. She threatens the boyfriend when she finds out the woman wasn't being treated properly, but then the woman leaves anyway, not taking any personal belongings or breaking her lease.

Clients start dropping him.

The woman ends up dead, and someone tries to kill Jane.

"I'm not trying to get into trouble here. I just want to run my business."

"I don't know *anything* about any of this," the secretary insists. "I just work the phones."

She looks honestly terrified, but until local PD gets here to iron things out, I'm not letting either of them out of my sight.

"What's my last name?" Jane asks.

"How should I know? It's not like we exchanged business cards," he barks.

"Do you know?" Jane asks the secretary, who shakes her head.

"I only started working here a couple of weeks ago," she insists.

"Fine. Then where was I from?" Jane asks.

Victor glares at her, fury etched in every line of his face. "Even if I knew that, why would I tell you?"

I lunge forward and grip the front of his shirt, ripping him up out of the chair. "You're going to answer the woman. Now. Or I'm going to start breaking things."

Victor swallows hard. "Rosalie told me she'd met some woman out of Dallas who was going to change her life."

CHAPTER 13
JANE DOE

*G*ena.

If that's really my name, then why does it sound even more impersonal than Jane Doe? I've spent the last week going over everything in my head, repeating that name over and over again, but I might as well be talking about a complete stranger. Then again, I guess I kind of am a stranger to myself. *Ugh, how sad is that?*

"Are you all right?"

I glance over at Lani as she plops down onto the couch beside me. Elliot is out on the ranch handling chores, and Lani has a rare day off. Earlier today, she'd finally made me let her trim my hair, so it's all the same length for the first time since Elliot had to cut some of it to get me out of that creek.

Now she's prepping for her own hair appointment.

"I'm processing," I reply. It's not a total lie, but telling her that I'm slowly spiraling doesn't seem like the best thing at the moment.

"Tucker is still running Gena and your description through every database he can. If you're out there, he'll find you."

"We know I was from Dallas; that should help narrow the search," I reply, tone dry.

"That's what Elliot said he's hoping for too." She smiles. "Are you sure you don't want any coffee?" She worked an overnight at the hospital last night, so this is her third cup since she woke up two hours ago.

"Nah, thanks though. I may not know much about myself, but I do know that will keep me up well past when I want to sleep."

She laughs. "Honestly, I'm not sure it even does anything for me anymore. I really should give it up, but I just love it so." To emphasize, she kisses her cup.

Lani has such a comforting presence about her, and the woman can lighten any sour mood with just a few words and a smile. She makes a good friend. Especially since I'm living in a world where I don't feel as though I have many.

There's Elliot, sure, but my feelings for him are

anything but friend-based. Even if I don't fully understand just what it is that's blooming between us—at least on my side—I know that much.

"There really wasn't anything else at that shipping company?" she asks then takes a sip. "Nothing that's come up since you guys came back?"

"Nope. It was completely empty. Aside from some employee records we'd looked through. Local PD let Victor and his secretary go, and they're back to business as usual."

"But you did learn your first name, so that's good."

"Sure. If it really is my first name," I say.

"You don't think it is?"

I consider the question then evaluate the pit in my stomach. "Something feels off. I just can't put my finger on it. It could just be hope though."

"Hope for what?"

"That he was lying."

"Why do you hope he was lying?"

I take a deep breath. "I mean, he said that Rosalie met a woman out of Dallas who was going to change her life. Does that sound like a positive thing?"

"Changing someone's life can be a good thing."

"She ended up dead in the woods," I reply. "Seems to me like she would have been better off if I'd have left her alone." I stare straight ahead and out the window at the ranch. From here, I can see an empty round pen, a blooming garden, and—in the distance—the auto shed. Which is where Elliot currently is, trying to fix one of the old tractors.

"You don't know if you had anything to do with that," Lani says quietly then touches my arm.

"I also don't know that I didn't." I sigh. "I have no idea if I'm going to like the person I find once everything clicks back into place."

"Is that what you're worried about?" Lani asks.

I shrug then turn toward her. "Honestly, yes. There's a part of me that wants to stop looking for answers."

"You don't mean that."

"I really do. I've spent the last week going through everything, trying to come up with a scenario where I wasn't into something illegal, and I've got nothing. Every rock we turn over has me beneath it, looking more and more like a worm."

"Everyone has a past. Yours is a part of you. And if it was bad, you're not that person anymore. You *can* choose a different path."

But will Elliot still look at me the same? It's what I really want to ask but can't bring myself to. What if I was a killer? Or what if I worked for some horrible, evil person? What if I'm the reason Rosalie Wallace is dead?

The shrill tone of Lani's alarm cuts through the silence, and she stands. "Time to get ready!" She hesitates, her expression morphing into one of concern. "Are you okay? I can cancel my appointment. My hair can wait."

"No, you're good. Seriously. Go have your hair trimmed. You deserve it."

"Are you sure?"

"Positive," I reply with a smile.

She remains where she is. "Oh! You know what? Girls' night tonight. We can kick Elliot out of here, and he can go hang out with Bradyn. I'll call Kennedy and have her come over, and we'll hang out. Maybe watch a cheesy movie and paint our nails." She beams at me, the idea forming in her mind.

"Doesn't Kennedy have enough going on? The wedding is coming up fast."

"Which means she could use the distraction too. Come on, it'll be fun! I'll even call Emma and have her come over. Ooh, yes! I haven't seen her in forever!"

"Emma?"

"Dylan's ex. They were childhood sweethearts. She's super sweet. You'll love her. What do you think? Please say yes. I think it will be great."

With the way Lani is looking at me, even if I'd have wanted to say no, I couldn't. "Sure. Sounds great. I do feel bad about kicking Elliot out though."

She waves her hand in dismissal. "Nah, he'll be fine. They'll probably do some night training in the woods with the dogs or something. They like that."

I can't help but smile at the way she handles problems. The woman has an answer for everything. "Then that sounds great."

"Awesome. I'm going to go get dressed. I'll call the girls on the way to the salon." She squeals. "Oh, this will be so much fun!"

"I think so!" I call out as she heads down the hall.

Needing to do something, I push to my feet and head toward the window to look out. Elliot and I barely spoke last night or on the drive here today. I know that the silence was because of me. He'd tried to spark up a conversation, but my mind just continues reliving that moment over and over again.

"She met a woman from Dallas who was going to change her life."

I know where my thoughts go. Prostitution. Drugs. Murder. But even as those possibilities run through my mind, I reach up and touch the cross around my neck. None of those *feel* like me.

But if our past truly does define us, and I was involved in any of those things, then isn't that who I am? Will there ever be an escape for me?

"Hey there."

I turn, surprised that Lani is back in the room and already dressed in jeans and a blue T-shirt with the word "Waymaker" written in bright gold lettering, "Isaiah 43:19" underneath it. She holds out a leather-bound copy of the Bible. "What's that for?"

"I have a spare one I keep in my car. Why don't you use this one? Dad always said that the answers to all of life's struggles can be found amongst the words in red."

Warmth spreads through my chest, appreciation and emotion, as I take the Bible from her. I run my fingers over the gold lettering. It *feels* right. Familiar. Even as everything else around me is full of questions, holding this feels like home.

"Thank you."

Lani smiles and gently squeezes my arm. "You're welcome. All right, I'm out. Call if you need me. Elliot should be in soon, and you have the wonderful job of telling him he has to leave for the night," she adds with a wink.

I chuckle, shaking my head. "We'll see how that goes. Thanks for this." I hold up the Bible.

"You—" she starts then slings her purse over her shoulder, "are so welcome."

As Lani heads out, I take a seat on the couch then take a deep breath. "God, I'm not even sure where to start. I feel lost. Completely and utterly lost." A chill runs through me, and I take another deep breath. "Was I bad before? Did I do —" I trail off, tears stinging the corners of my eyes. "I don't know what I did before, but please don't let it have been horrible. Or if it was, please—please forgive me. Help me to not become that person ever again." I close my eyes, and a tear falls. "I want to be better. I want to feel like I do now. I want to do good for people." I tilt my face up toward the ceiling. "God, please don't turn your back on me."

I'm still reading when the front door opens and Elliot strolls in, Echo panting at his side. I glance up, my mouth watering when I take in the sight of him wearing dark jeans and a white T-shirt smeared with motor grease.

The man would look good in a garbage bag, I'm sure of it.

"Hey," he greets then heads into the kitchen to wash his hands.

Echo laps up some water then plops down on his bed.

"You get it working again?" I ask, leaving the Bible open but setting it aside so I can stand and head into the kitchen, too.

"I did. Took quite a bit, and I ended up giving the tire a good kick out of frustration." He smiles as he dries his hands. "But it's running again. For now."

"How old is it?"

"Older than me," he jokes. "It was the first tractor my dad bought for this place after my grandfather's finally became useless."

"It's neat that you're keeping it running for him."

He reaches into the fridge and pulls out a bottle of water then offers it to me. I'm not thirsty, but I take it anyway. "So, what have you been up to today?"

"Not much," I admit. "I made another list of everything we know so far then spent some time sitting on the couch. The last couple of hours, I've been reading."

"Oh? Reading what?"

"The Bible. Lani is letting me borrow hers."

His expression darkens just a bit. It's so faint I'm not even sure how I catch it. "Does that bother you?"

"No. Why would it bother me?" Elliot opens the pantry door and withdraws a bag of salt and vinegar chips.

"I don't know. That's why I'm asking."

"It doesn't bother me at all. If you can find your answers there, then I think that's great."

I study him further. "Elliot, what's going on?"

Without eating a single chip, he sets the bag on the counter and crosses his arms. "I struggle a bit in the faith department."

"Oh?"

"I know God is real. I know that Jesus came and died for our sins. What I don't understand is how He can forgive us even when we can't forgive ourselves."

His words hit home because that's something I've been struggling with. And I don't even know what it is I've done in my past. "I get that."

"You do?"

"Sure. Look, honestly? There's a part of me that wants to stop looking for answers. I can just find a job, start over, not even bother with ever learning who I really was."

His brow furrows. "Why?"

"Let's just go over what we know, shall we? I was shot and left for dead while wearing a party dress and a man's shirt. Then, someone tried to kill me again while I was in the hospital, and I knew enough to defend myself by taking *his* life. Then, a woman who thought I was going to change her life winds up having it ended instead. And to top it off, I broke a man's nose without hesitation."

"First of all, we don't know if you hesitated. Second, after meeting him, I can see how he deserved it. And while I agree our initial theory that it's a serial killer is not looking so solid at the moment, it's still a possibility that you were dragged into this and forced to bring her in. It happens sometimes with trafficking victims. They're often forced to be a part of the operation."

He's trying to ease some of the tightness in my chest. Unfortunately, it only has the opposite effect. "Then that makes me guilty. Besides, who knows what I was wrapped up in? What if I'm the killer? Or what if I did trap that woman into slavery? What if I promised her the world and instead trapped her in hell?" Tears blur my vision, but I can still see him clearly as he crosses over toward me, both large hands gripping my arms. "Even if I'd been coerced, I still could have said no. I could have refused."

"Even if that is the case—and I'm not saying it is— you're not that person anymore. You *can* choose a different path. But fear shouldn't keep you from the truth because it's a part of you."

"That's basically what Lani said."

"She's a wise woman, my sister."

That gets a slight smile out of me, but the tightness only increases. These people think so highly of me. What's going to happen when they learn the truth? "I'm scared, Elliot."

"I know you are. But you don't have to be. Whatever we find, we'll deal with it."

"And if I was a bad person? If I did truly horrible things? Will you let me turn myself in?"

A muscle in his jaw ticks.

"Because you need to promise me that you will. If we learn the truth before the cops do, you have to let me turn myself in."

"You aren't that person anymore."

"But if I *was* that person, then I deserve to be punished for what I've done. Especially if I was the one who got Rosalie killed."

"Jane—"

"I'm serious, Elliot."

He takes a deep breath and releases me before taking a step back. "Fine. I promise. But you aren't a bad person. No matter what is in your past, it's not as dark as you think."

"How do you know?"

"Because I do." He steps back. "Tomorrow, I want to take you back to the woods where we found Rosalie. I want to see if something jogs your memory. Do you think you'll be up for it?"

"Isn't tomorrow Sunday?"

"It is."

"Can we go after church?"

He stares blankly at me. "You want to go to church?"

"I do. You don't have to go with me if you don't want to. I just—"

"I'll take you." His tone is flat, and if I'm not mistaken, he honestly looks a bit nervous.

"Are you sure?"

"Yeah. It's—uh—been a while since I went."

"How long?"

"Three years."

I stare at him, shocked and saddened by his confession. "That's a long time to feel lost."

"You're no stranger to wandering aimlessly either."

"No," I reply with a soft laugh. "I'm not."

"Then let's be lost in church together. Then afterward, we'll head to the woods. Sound good?"

"It does."

"Great. It's a plan, then." He turns and heads down the hall. "I'm going to grab a shower. Then we'll go over the notes you took, and I'll check in with Elijah to see if he found anything."

"Oh, wait. Elliot?"

He stops and turns. "What is it?"

I remain where I am, rooted in my spot as warmth spreads through my body. It's ridiculous that his hazel gaze can stir such feelings within me. "I'm supposed to tell you to be busy tonight."

The corners of his lips lift in a smile. "Oh? Big plans?"

"Lani wants to have a girls' night, and she said I get to be the one to tell you that we're having it here." My cheeks heat. *Why did I think this wouldn't be that difficult?* "If you don't want to, I totally get it. Seriously, this is your house, and—"

"It's completely fine." He laughs. "I have some work I can do, anyway. I'll use my dad's office and beg my mom to cook me dinner."

"Are you sure?"

He comes down the hall, stopping just in front of me. "This will be the perfect distraction for you."

"But do I really need a distraction? We don't have any answers, and—"

"Exactly. We have no answers. Sometimes taking a step back helps you see more clearly. Maybe by not trying to remember, something will come to you." Elliot reaches up and brushes a strand of hair behind my shoulder. I freeze beneath his touch, every single muscle in my body going rigid for fear that even the slightest movement will have him dropping his hand.

"Okay. As long as you're sure you don't mind," I manage, though how I can even speak with the emotions warring within me, I'll never know.

"Positive." He drops his hand. "I'm going to grab a shower. Then, as soon as Lani gets here, I'll head out."

CHAPTER 14
ELLIOT

"Mom, this was great, thanks."

"You are so welcome." She smiles then starts to stand, but I shake my head.

"I've got it. You cooked; I clean. That's the deal, remember?"

With a sheepish smile, she sits back down. "Well, fine. But I really don't mind. I miss the days of taking care of you kids."

"You earned a break," I tell her.

"So true, honey." My father stands. "And since I also ate this delicious meal you prepared, I will help with cleanup." He retrieves the bowl containing a few leftover rolls then follows me into the kitchen.

"Well, there's no rule that says I can't make tea too, right?" My mom grabs her kettle and starts filling it.

I laugh. "Fair enough."

Working in silence for a few moments, Dad and I manage to finish half of the dishes before he finally lets out that sigh, the one I know means a difficult conversation is going to follow. "How are you doing, son?"

I dry a plate and stick it into the cabinet. "Fine. Why?"

He eyes me the same way he did when I was growing up and he'd suspected I wasn't being entirely truthful.

"Honestly, I'm doing okay. Staying focused on the case and hoping to find some answers."

"You're sure? If you need to talk—"

"Dad, I know. But there's nothing to talk about."

"She looks like Renee," my mother says from the corner.

I turn around and lean back against the counter then cross my arms. "She has red hair. That's where the similarities end."

"Jane is strong too, like she was."

"She still doesn't want to be called Gena?" my dad asks.

I shake my head.

My father's brow furrows. "Why not?"

"She told me that it just doesn't sound right. That until we know for sure, she wants to keep being called Jane."

"Interesting."

"She's struggling," I tell them truthfully. "With the weight of the unknown. I just want to find her some answers so she can move on with her life."

"Move on?" my mother asks. "You're ready for her to leave?"

The tightness in my chest constricts further at the mere thought of her leaving. Which makes absolutely no sense as I barely know the woman. "I'm ready for her to have her life back. Who knows who's out there waiting for her to come home? For all we know, she could have kids. A husband."

And that tightness becomes impossible to deal with. I reach up and rub the heel of my palm against my chest.

"Maybe." My father finishes washing the last dish and sets it in the drying rack. "It's a shame nothing has popped up."

"Gibson has run her through everything he can. He's trying to keep it relatively quiet, given the attack in the hospital."

"Understandable," my father replies.

"After church tomorrow, I'm taking Jane out to the park where we found that woman. I'm hoping it'll jog her memory a bit. Help her to—" I trail off because they're both staring at me like I grew a third arm. "What?"

"Church?" my mother asks, her eyes misting just a bit. I can see the happiness on her face, and it brings a fresh wave of guilt over me. "You're coming to church?"

I nod. "Jane wants to go. I said I'd go with her."

"That's great, son." My father grins.

"So great," my mother agrees. "You know what, I think

we need pie with our tea." She heads over to the refrigerator and reaches in to grab half an apple pie.

"I hardly think my going to church with Jane is worthy of pie."

"It absolutely is," my mother replies. "Three years, Elliot. We've been trying to get you back in a pew for three years."

More guilt. Not because I haven't been to church but because my mother has apparently been holding on to her concern for so long. "Mom, I'm working on it."

"We know you are. And we're not trying to be pushy," my father says as he heads toward the small round dining room table in the corner of the kitchen.

"You guys have been great about it. Truly." For two people who never miss a Sunday, they've been nothing but supportive as I took a step back. Even if they did continue talking to me about faith and forgiveness, it never felt uncomfortable. If anything, it was their support that helped me keep what little faith I still have alive. "I'm just still not sure about any of it. About where I fit into it."

"Do you want to talk about it?" my father asks. "Thank you, honey," he adds when my mother hands him a plate of pie and sets a mug of tea in front of him.

"Not particularly," I reply honestly. "But just know that I'm thinking about it." My cell rings, so I withdraw it and check the readout. After seeing Tucker's name pop up on the screen, I answer it. "What's up?"

"You still at Mom and Dad's?"

"Yeah, we just finished dinner, why?"

"I need you to come by before you go home. Sooner the better."

Unease churns in my gut. His tone is all business. Which is only typical of Tucker when something serious comes up. "What is it?"

"I found something you should see."

———

I HAVEN'T EVEN HAD the chance to knock before Tucker is pulling open the door. Tango is beside him, tail wagging happily, as Echo races in past me, and the two immediately start wrestling.

But even seeing the happy pups doesn't ease the dread in my belly. "What is it?"

"This way." He heads down the hall and into the home office directly across from the master bedroom. The window on the far wall has been covered by dark curtains while the wall to the left of it has a large projector screen mounted to it. On the wall opposite of the screen is Tucker's desk, adorned with three monitors placed side by side. His computer is humming loudly, processing whatever data he's been working on. There's a server tower tucked away in one corner and a laptop perched on a standing desk in the other.

Honestly, I don't know what half of the stuff in this office does, but I do know that, if anyone ever found out just what Tucker Hunt has access to, he'd likely be in a whole lot of trouble.

"So, I've been doing some digging. Checking surveillance cameras in and around Dallas and all that. After writing my own script, I was able to cross-reference Jane Doe's description with the processed data in hopes I would find a facial match."

"Just give me the Barney-style details, Tuck."

He nods. "Fair enough." After tapping a few keys on his keyboard, he retrieves a remote from beside him and turns on the projector screen.

I face it, and seconds later, a grainy image fills the large screen. Clearly taken by an exterior security camera, it shows three people standing in an alley. It's in black and white, so while it's hard to make out much in terms of the features, I can tell that there are two women, one with darker hair and the other with lighter hair.

They're arguing with a man who is clearly frustrated.

"What am I watching?"

"Just hang tight. Zooming in." Tucker uses a small device to enhance the image, zooming in on the three people.

And then the woman with darker hair turns toward the camera. "Rosalie Wallace."

"Bingo."

I hate that I already know who the other woman is before she even turns around. Which she does less than a second later. "Jane."

"Yeah. Took me quite a bit to find this one, and so far, the program hasn't found anything else."

"We already knew they were acquaintances. Based on what Victor told us at the docks."

"Yeah. But it's what happens next that I think you're going to want to see."

Jane waves her hand, and the man turns to storm off. She spins and lands a kick to the center of his back, throwing him forward into the dumpster. Rosalie jumps back and reaches into her pocket, withdrawing what looks to be zip ties.

As Jane pins him to the ground, Rosalie binds his hands behind his back. They're finishing securing him as a dark SUV pulls into the alleyway. Two men climb out and grab the third, throwing him into the SUV.

Jane crosses her arms and says something to one of the men then turns and heads back out of view of the camera. The screen goes black, but I'm already desperate to watch it again. So I can pick it apart and find some logical reason for what I just saw.

"Do we know who any of those men are?"

"I ran the two that got out of the SUV and got no matches. Whoever they are, they've managed to stay out of police and federal databases. As for the man they grabbed —that I have answers to. Unfortunately."

He taps on the remote again, and a crime scene photo populates on the projector screen. A man lies on the ground, eyes frozen open, a bullet wound to his chest. "That's the man they grabbed?"

"It is. Hector Frankfort. Known to deal drugs out of downtown Dallas. He'd been brought in for questioning quite a few times, but police haven't been able to get anything on him. He was found dead two days after that surveillance video was recorded. Police assumed it had something to do with him trying to expand his area. Doesn't look like they looked too hard for his killer, to be honest."

Bile rises in my throat as my conversation with Jane earlier echoes in my mind.

"Who knows what I was wrapped up in? What if I'm the killer? Or what if I helped trap that woman into slavery? What if I promised her the world and instead trapped her in hell?"

From the looks of it, Rosalie was right alongside her when that man was abducted. Was he another victim? Or was she herself being held against her will? As I told Jane, it's no secret that traffickers will sometimes force women and children to lure others in. Is it possible that Jane was a victim of the same circumstances as Rosalie?

"I'm scared, Elliot."

Her tortured tone still torments me. I'd told her that, no matter what the truth is, we'd deal with it. But how can I protect her from this? How can I shield her from the very serious implications that video places on top of her shoulders?

"And if I was a bad person? If I did truly horrible things? Will you let me turn myself in? Because you need to promise me that you will. If we learn the truth before the cops do, you have to let me turn myself in."

I'd made that promise to her. But now, as I stare down the barrel of a truth that would land her in cuffs or, at the very least, the opposite end of an interview table, I'm not sure that I'm strong enough to follow through.

"What do you want to do?" Tucker questions.

"Who else has seen this?"

"Just you and me, brother."

I study the image of a dead man last caught on video alongside Jane. All of the evidence points to her being an accomplice to murder. But every one of my instincts says otherwise.

There's more here.

There has to be.

"Bring Riley, Bradyn, and Dylan in so they can watch it. Then bury it. No one else sees this video, Tucker. Not even Gibson. Not until we have a better understanding of what's going on. I won't let her end up behind bars because some hotshot detective out of Dallas catches wind she might be a part of it."

"Might be? She's on camera."

"We don't know what's going on, though," I tell him. "It could be she's a victim in this too. Bury it. You asked what I wanted you to do. That's what I'm asking you to do."

Tucker clenches his jaw but nods. "If this is true though, then Jane isn't the victim we thought she was. And I hate saying this, but you need to consider the possibility that she's lying."

Anger flares within me, tightening my chest. "No. She's not."

"It's possible she does remember and just wants to avoid the truth."

"No," I snap. "It's not."

Tucker shakes his head. "I don't want to believe it either, but I just need to make sure you're looking at this from all sides. With her staying in such close proximity to us, we can't afford to take chances."

CHAPTER 15
JANE DOE

"And that's how I broke my nose," Lani announces as she leans back against the couch. "Elliot, a rock, and an old refrigerator."

"It just bounced right off of it?" Kennedy asks, tears in her eyes from laughing so hard.

"Like the old metal was a trampoline. Mom was *furious.* It's the one and only time I thought something might slip from her mouth she'd regret." Lani plucks a chip from the bowl in front of us. "Elliot was grounded for two weeks after that."

I smile off into the distance. Do I have any stories like that? Any siblings who accidentally broke my nose? This night should have been relaxing and wonderful, but instead, I'm feeling even more down than before.

Kennedy has shared stories about her life when she was

growing up. And Emma, Dylan's ex-high school sweetheart, has had her own fair share of tales from childhood. Yet, here I am, storyless. The only tales I can tell are ones from the last couple of weeks.

"How you doing?" Lani asks. "Have we successfully distracted you yet?"

"Absolutely," I lie. I hate that I do. I just can't bear any of them feeling guilty for something that's not even their fault.

"You sure?" Emma asks. "Maybe we should change the subject? Or watch another movie?" She's absolutely adorable, a petite blonde with pale freckles and bright blue eyes.

"I am totally sure," I reply.

"Okay, good." Lani turns to Kennedy. "How goes the wedding plans?"

The front door opens, and Elliot strolls in with Echo at his side. The dog runs happily toward me and rubs against my legs, so I reach down and pat his head.

"Hey, you weren't given the all-clear yet," Lani says.

Elliot smiles, but it's forced and doesn't reach his eyes. "Sorry, something came up. Jane, can I have a few words?"

"Sure." Nerves forming a pit in my stomach, I get to my feet and slip into a pair of shoes as I follow him toward the door.

"*Bleib,* Echo," he orders the dog, who lies down in place.

"Let's talk wedding," Lani says as Elliot closes the front door behind us.

We make our way down the porch steps in silence and toward the barn where Elliot worked on the tractor earlier. The air around us is heavy, weighted down by whatever is on his mind. Even as I want to ask if he learned something about me or if something happened, I keep my mouth shut.

He'll talk when he's ready.

I hope.

After stepping into the barn, he turns on the light then slides the door closed behind us. It's only then that he faces me. Arms crossed, his expression is all frustration. "I need to know if you're being honest with me."

"About what?"

His nostrils flare as he inhales sharply. "About all of it, Jane. Gena. Whatever you want to be called. I need to know if you really can't remember your past or if you're just hiding. If you are hiding, if that's the truth, then tell me what happened, and I'll protect you."

Elliot's accusation hits me square in the chest. *Lying? He thinks I'm lying?* "You think I'd make up the fact that I can't even remember my own name? Or whether or not I have parents and siblings out there?" I step forward, tears stinging the corners of my eyes.

"No. I don't. I just—" He closes his eyes and takes another sharp breath. "I need to know the truth, and every time we turn around, it's just more questions. Victor told us your name was Gena, but you're insisting it's not. That you should be called Jane Doe instead."

"Because *I* don't think Gena is my name!"

"Is it really that?" he demands, stepping closer. His gaze darkens. "Or is it because you know something about your past you'd rather pretend doesn't exist?"

Once again, his words land like a blow, and I step back. "I don't remember anything," I tell him, doing what I can to keep my tone low. "Being called Gena feels like I'm admitting to that being my life." I swallow hard. "And until we have all the facts, I need hope that there's more to my story than a woman who drags other women out of their safe, comfortable lives, only to have them be murdered."

His expression shifts slightly, and that frustration turns to something else entirely.

"What is it?" I demand. "You know something." I take a step forward. "What do you know, Elliot?"

He doesn't answer.

"What happened to 'we'll figure it out'?" I demand. "Hours ago, you told me that, no matter what it is, we'd get through it. Has something changed since then?"

"Of course not."

"Then what is it?"

He chews on his bottom lip then removes his baseball cap and runs a hand through his hair. "Tucker found a surveillance video."

"Of me?"

He nods.

"I want to see it."

"Jane, it's—"

"I don't want you to tell me anything else about it. I want to see it. Now."

He reaches into his pocket and withdraws his cell phone. I'm waiting for him to show it to me, but he fires off a text then shoves it back into his pocket.

"Aren't you going to show it to me?"

"We have to go to Tucker's. I don't want it getting out, so I had him bury it. He's the only one with access."

I push past him toward the door. "Then let's go."

Elliot's large hand closes around my arm, and I freeze. He holds me gently, but my skin heats to his touch. "I meant what I said, Jane. As long as you're honest with me, we'll get through this together."

I tilt my face up to look at him, our gazes holding. "I have been honest with you. And if I were to remember anything, you'd be the first person I'd tell."

His gaze drops to my mouth, and my lips part, heat traveling through my abdomen. Is he going to kiss me? Do I want him to?

Elliot forces his attention away and releases my arm. "Let's get to Tuck's. He's waiting for us."

I COULD HAVE WATCHED this video another hundred times, and I'd still be just as horrified as the first. Watching me take that man down only to have him kidnapped and thrown into the back of a dark SUV will haunt me. Of that, I'm sure.

"You said he's dead now?" I ask, turning to face the brothers. They were all here when Elliot and I arrived, and they'd all watched the video twice through.

"Yes," Bradyn replies.

"Two days after the timestamp of this video," Tucker adds.

"And when was that?"

"Five months ago." Elliot crosses his arms. He's been standing in the far corner of Tucker's office, not saying a word ever since we got here thirty minutes ago.

"Do they know who killed him?" *Was it me?* is what I really want to ask, but I can't stomach the likely truth that it was.

"No leads." Tucker clicks a button, and a mug shot shows up on the screen. "He was a drug dealer trying to expand his territory. The case was handed over to the DEA since they've been working the area for a couple of years now."

I turn back toward the image. "We need to have Gibson call them. Give them this video."

"Absolutely not," Elliot growls.

"They have to know that I was there," I insist. "That I had something to do with it."

"Except you can't remember a thing," he retorts. "They'll stick you in a cage and consider you guilty."

I gesture to the screen. "It certainly looks that way, doesn't it? You promised me, Elliot. You promised that you'd let me turn myself in."

He moves so fast I don't even have time to react as he eats up the distance between us in two furious strides. He leans in so close I can smell the pine-scented body wash still clinging to his skin. "We do not have all the answers yet," he growls. "Turning yourself in before we have the full story might ease the guilt you're carrying over what happened, but it's *not* a fast track to the truth."

I glare back at him, tension snapping between us like lightning.

"Before my office spontaneously combusts," Tucker starts, "with all the anger and tension between you two, I feel as though I should say that I agree with Elliot. This is just one video. I'm still looking for more. There's no telling what really went on in that alley. And it's not as though you abducted a kindergarten teacher," he says. "The man was a violent drug dealer. Wanted for murder and assault."

"It was still a life," I reply. Did I kill him? Did I pull that trigger?

"Tucker's not denying that," Dylan adds, speaking up for the first time since Elliot and I arrived. "But there could be more to this story. More to why you were grabbing him in the first place."

"Let's get the answers first." Riley rolls his shoulders. "After that, we'll let you do whatever you want with the information."

"Will you?" I ask, my glare focused intently on the warrior standing in front of me. His handsome features are hardened in anger, his jaw set.

"I promised I would." He pulls away, and I don't miss how those words really aren't a pointed answer.

After all, promises can be broken. And yet, how do I know that with this strong conviction?

CHAPTER 16
ELLIOT

A shrill scream rips me from a dreamless sleep.

Before I've even fully comprehended the situation, my hand closes around the grip of the pistol I keep in my bedside table, and I'm jumping out of bed.

Another scream.

Jane.

Adrenaline pulses through my veins, and I lunge out of my bedroom and sprint down the hall. I check the door, but it's locked.

Echo whines at my side.

"What's going on?" Lani asks as she stumbles from the room she's staying in.

Another scream.

I step back and kick the door in. Wood splinters, and I charge in, weapon drawn. But the room is empty except for

Jane, who is thrashing on the bed, arms and face gleaming with sweat.

Lani rushes in around me and reaches for her. "Breathe," she says. "Just breathe."

"Let me go!" Jane screams. She lunges to her feet, backing all the way against the wall. "He's going to come here! Don't you understand? He's going to kill me!"

Jane is standing near the window, eyes wide, hair wild around her face. She's wearing a pair of sweats and a sweater, her feet bare.

My sister is directly across from her, both hands held out. "He's not going to get you here," Lani says, her tone calm.

Jane shakes her head. "You don't understand. None of you do. I don't even understand. How can I? How can I keep everyone safe if I can't remember!" She's panicked, her night terror still clinging to her consciousness.

Echo cautiously crosses toward Jane and leans against her. I watch as she reaches down and touches his fur then collapses to the floor. He curls up beside her, head in her lap.

"I've got it, Lani. Can you make some coffee?"

"Of course." She smiles at Jane before leaving the room.

"Are you hurt?" I cross over and kneel beside her, scanning her for any injuries. I've seen men under the throes of PTSD attacks, Dylan being one of them. I've watched the horror in their eyes as they relive their worst days on the battlefield.

Is that what Jane was doing?

Reliving her nightmare?

"Not yet." She covers her face with both hands. Her shoulders begin to shake, and I rush forward, sliding to her side and wrapping my arms around her.

"How many times have I told you? No one is going to hurt you."

"I don't know how I know it, but he'll find me, Elliot. I —" She trails off. "I can't even remember his face. But the pain, I remember the pain." She chokes on a sob. "I'm losing even more of myself, and I already don't even know who I am. Oh, wait, no, I do. I'm a murderer. Maybe I deserve this. Maybe all of this is what should be happening."

Focus on the real problem, not the rationalization of it. So even as I want to tell her how ridiculous it is to think she deserves what is happening to her, I don't. "I won't let you get lost. You hear me? I won't let you lose anything else."

She leans against me, her head on my chest as she cries. I just hold on, cradling this woman in my arms.

I never want to let go.

But even as I'm terrified to hold on any longer, I push my own feelings aside and keep my arms around her. She needs this more than I need to let go.

Minutes tick by in silence until she's pulling away from me and wiping her eyes. "I'm so sorry. I lost it."

"Don't apologize. Did you remember something?"

She nods. "It's not much."

"Anything can help."

She takes a deep breath. "I was running through the woods again. A man was chasing me, but I couldn't see his face. Then I remember standing on the edge of a river. He was a shadow, but he pulled the trigger and there was so much pain." She touches her abdomen right over where the bullet tore through her.

"That's something."

"And then I woke up, and I had no idea where I was. Your poor sister—" She trails off and covers her face.

"Lani's fine. It's not the first time she's dealt with something like this." I scoot around so I'm facing her; then I reach out and take her hands, needing to feel them in mine to steady my own racing heart. "Tell me about the place you saw. Where you were shot. Was there anything special about it? Anything that stuck out?"

Her eyes go distant, and I can tell she's lost in the memory. "There was a sign. I ran past it."

Hope. "What did it say? Do you remember?"

"I don't remember what it said. It was made of wood. Looked old. I'm sorry, I don't remember anything else."

"It's okay." I force a smile. "It's not much, but it's something. Likely means you were near a hiking trail.

We'll figure it out when we go to the park tomorrow. There are some old wooden signs that mark different trails up there."

"I feel like I'm losing my mind. Like I *should* be out doing something but I'm not."

"You *are* doing something," I tell her as I release one of her hands and brush a strand of red hair from her tear-stained cheek.

She shivers beneath my touch, her shoulder slumping forward as though she can finally relax. "How can you do that?" she whispers.

"Do what?" I withdraw my hand, and her emerald gaze locks on mine.

"Calm the storm when nothing else can?"

***

"Is she better?"

"She's okay. It was a night terror fueled by anxiety. She's embarrassed, but she's okay."

"Oh, she doesn't need to be embarrassed at all." My sister offers me a steaming mug of coffee.

"That's what I told her." I take a drink, not even caring that it's hot enough to scald my tongue. "She'll be out in a few minutes."

"You're a great man, Elliot Hunt."

"I'm something," I reply.

Lani cocks her head to the side. "You doing okay, big brother?"

I turn back as my sister takes a seat in a chair at the kitchen counter. Unsure what else to do, I follow suit, sitting beside her. "Fine. Why?"

She studies me. "You never were good at hiding things."

"I'm tired, Lani. Exhausted, really. And frustrated that I haven't been able to help her."

Lani nods. "I know I kind of forced you into this by insisting you go up to the hospital, but I've been meaning to talk to you. About this. About her."

"What about her?"

She doesn't speak for a moment, clearly choosing her words carefully. While the rest of us have always struggled with the principle of being "slow to speak, quick to listen," my sister has mastered it. She takes after our father like that, despite being adopted. "I know you carry scars, Elliot. The weight of your past has been present in your life ever since Renee lost hers."

"It was a job. It went wrong."

"We both know it was more than that."

"It never got the chance to be more than that," I reply.

"But you wanted it to be."

Frustration twists in my chest. "Sure. But it didn't happen. Renee has nothing to do with Jane. They're two different people. Two different cases."

"I agree with you, I just want to make sure you're okay."

"I'm fine. I told you that."

"Mom said you're coming to church tomorrow?"

"Jane wanted to go. If she still does, we'll be there."

"Elliot."

"Lani." I push back from my chair. "I'll be fine, okay? But I need to make sure I help Jane get home. Otherwise, what good am I? Thanks for making coffee. I'm going to go check in on her." I stand and head for the hall, not strong enough to deflect any more of this heavy conversation. I'm lost. And my family sees it.

They've always seen it. Why am I surprised that they're trying to lead me back?

I HAVEN'T SAT in a church pew in three years.

Three long years of avoiding the one place I used to feel the most at home. And as I sit here beside Jane and my mother, I want to kick myself for waiting so long. Even though I've fallen—far—in my faith journey, there's a warmth to this small-town church.

"This world will tempt you in many ways," Pastor Ford says as he looks out over the congregation. He's been preaching here longer than I've been alive and is the one who baptized all of us Hunt kids. He's a man I know as well as I know my own father but haven't spoken to in any depth since Renee's death. "And you cannot face the temptation alone. God is the only answer. And those who seek will find." He smiles. "Let us pray. Dear Heavenly Father, thank You for Your gracious love. For walking alongside us as we don armor to battle our sinful nature. Lord, please continue to guide us until we see You face-to-face. Amen."

A series of "Amens" ring out through the pews, and the pianist begins to play.

"Go in peace, I will see you all next week." He smiles and waves then heads down the middle aisle to wait by the door so he can say goodbye to everyone as they pass.

I look over at Jane, who's been hanging on his every word ever since he greeted us an hour ago. She's worked hard not to meet my gaze ever since our argument last night. And to be honest, I haven't tried all that hard to engage her in conversation. She's so sure she was a terrible person, yet she's willing to throw herself into the flames before she even has all the answers.

How do I make her see what I do? How do I get her to see that throwing her life away on a half-cocked investigation would be a waste?

She stands, so I follow suit, filing in behind her and the rest of my family. Bradyn and Kennedy are already at the back of the church, talking to Pastor Ford's wife, Grace. They're smiling and laughing, all of them looking absolutely overjoyed.

Meanwhile, my stomach might as well be a den of vipers for how twisted up I feel.

"Good to see you, Tommy," Pastor Ford greets my dad with a handshake. "And you, Ruth. Those cookies you delivered were amazing."

"I'm so glad you enjoyed them." She grins, clearly delighted.

"And you must be Jane." He turns to Jane and offers her a handshake.

"Pastor Ford, that was—exactly what I needed."

"God's Word is what we all need." He smiles. "If you ever want to talk, my door is open."

"I appreciate that." She steps aside, and he turns to me.

"Elliot, good to see you."

"You, too, Pastor. I, uh—sorry I've been absent."

"No need to apologize." He shakes my hand. "I'm just glad to see you here. My door is open to you too. As you well know by now."

In the months after Renee's death, he'd reached out to me a few times. Inviting me to coffee and the annual men's retreat. But I'd declined every invitation, choosing instead to bury myself in my own pit of shame.

It was never supposed to last this long.

But one day turned into another. Then weeks, months, and years had passed.

"I know, thank you."

He offers me a kind smile. "See you next week?"

That pit in my gut grows. "Maybe."

"I hope so." He smiles then turns as an old friend of my dad's steps up to greet him. I follow my family out of the church, more than ready to put some distance between myself and the weight of what I'm carrying.

"Lunch?" My mother slips her sunglasses onto her face.

"Works for me," Riley says.

"Same," Tucker adds.

"I'm headed to the gym," Dylan replies. "Maybe next week." After kissing our mother on the cheek, he heads off toward his truck. I know how hard he's struggling with his faith—even if, unlike me, he hasn't missed a Sunday.

"Jane? Elliot?"

"We're headed out to the park," I remind her.

"Oh, that's right." She smiles warily. "Are you sure that's a good idea?" My guess is Lani mentioned the night terror Jane had last night, and my mom is worried about her.

"We have to start somewhere," I say. "And it's as good a place as any."

"We'll be careful," Jane replies, her tone soft. "I want answers, and I think they'll start there."

My mom's expression lightens. "Well, we'll see you both for dinner, then. I'm making enchiladas."

"Sounds delicious."

"Stay safe, son," my father says then wraps an arm around my mom.

"Will do. See you guys for dinner."

Both he and my mom offer me a hug; then they head across the street toward the diner while Riley and Tucker remain where they are. Bradyn and Kennedy are still somewhere in the church, my guess is talking to Grace and Pastor Ford about final wedding preparations.

"Are you sure you don't want us to come?" Riley asks.

"Nah, we'll be fine. The chances of him returning—and in broad daylight—are low. But I'll call at the first sign of trouble."

"You better." Tucker shoves his hands into his pockets. "You taking Echo?"

"Always," I reply. "We'll catch up with you guys later."

"Sounds good. Be safe, Jane."

"I will. Thanks, Tucker."

"Hey, I want you to be safe, too," Riley quips.

Jane laughs. "Thank you too, Riley. We will be."

My brothers head off for the diner, and I start toward the truck, Jane beside me. Once again, she's gone quiet. Her anger is apparently only geared toward me. *Yay.*

I open the door for her, and she climbs in; then I close it and head around to the driver's side to get behind the wheel.

"Are we heading straight there?" she asks.

"No. I need to grab a few things from the ranch first."

CHAPTER 17
JANE DOE

"We're going on horseback?" I study the small trailer attached to Elliot's truck as he walks a brown horse out of the barn. We haven't exactly been getting along since last night, but I feel like he should have elaborated a bit more on the 'few things' he needed to pick up.

"There's a lot of ground to cover. It'll be easier on horseback."

"I—uh—I don't know that I've ever even ridden a horse."

"Which is why I'm going to let you ride Cinnamon."

"Cinnamon. Is that Cinnamon?"

"No, this is Bobby. You met him the day we pulled you out of the creek." He stops in front of me. "Hold your palm flat."

I do as he says, and he reaches into his pocket and

plucks out a sugar cube, setting it on top of my hand. The horse takes it, its whiskers tickling my skin as it uses its lips to lift the cube.

"Hi again, Bobby," I reply with a smile, some of the unease I'd felt moments ago fading.

"It'll be easier this way. Especially with your injuries. Walking that far would be rough on you. Besides, you promised to do this my way. Remember?"

The sour mood I've been in since last night deflates at the knowledge that he thought ahead enough to account for my injuries when I know he could have done this on foot and saved himself trouble. "Fair enough. But if I fall, I'll never let you live it down."

And with that comment, the tension around us eases just a bit.

"I think you have that backward. If you fall off of Cinnamon, you have no business ever going near a horse." With an easy grin, he leads the horse into the trailer.

"So you don't think we need the backup of having your brothers along?"

He stops what he's doing and turns to me, "Are you okay with it just being us? I can call Lani—"

"What? Oh, no. It's fine. I'm just making small talk. Apparently, it's something I do when I'm nervous."

He grins, and my stomach twists into nervous knots. This time, having nothing to do with the horses. "I'll remember that. I'm going to grab Cinnamon and get her loaded. Then we'll be ready to head out. You have every-thing you need?"

"Yes. I think so."

He loads Cinnamon into the trailer then closes the main gate before crossing over to the passenger side of the truck and opening the door for me just like he's been doing every time I've ridden in the truck with him. "After you."

"Chivalry is alive amongst the Hunts," I joke, enjoying that it seems he's no longer frustrated at me either.

He chuckles. "We do have manners."

"Nice to know."

He shuts the door then opens the back so Echo can jump in. The dog sits happily in the seat, staring out the window as his owner climbs behind the wheel.

And because I can't leave well enough alone and just let a good mood be a good mood, I clear my throat. "Listen, Elliot, about what we saw last night—"

"I don't want to fight about it anymore," he says, putting the truck into Drive.

"I know, but if we take that footage at face value, then I'm not a good person. You could be helping a murderer, for all you know."

"I'm not taking it at face value because things are rarely black and white."

"But—"

"No." He pulls down the driveway. "If it turns out that you were a murderer, then I'll let you handle things the way you want to. But I still believe things are not always what they seem."

"Why? How are you so sure?"

Elliot stops at the stop sign at the end of his drive and turns toward me. "Because I know what I feel when I look at you, and I've learned the hard way to always trust my gut."

My heart flutters in my chest as warmth spreads through me. "And what you feel for me is that I'm innocent?"

A muscle in his jaw ticks. "Something like that." He shifts his attention back out the windshield and pulls onto the small two-lane highway leading away from the ranch.

All while my mind is still back there at that stop sign, trying so hard not to read into something that might not be there, even as I secretly hope it is.

———

I study both horses as Elliot finishes pulling saddles out of the trailer's small tack room and placing them on the animals. Nerves twist in my belly, but I do my best to keep them at bay. Honestly, I'm not even entirely sure it has a lot to do with the horses but more to do with the fact that we might very well find the place where I was shot.

I turn and study the tall trees surrounding us. This park has trails for bikes, hiking, and horses. According to Elliot, it spans nearly 300 acres and could take us days to look through. We may not even find the sign today, but I'm not letting go of the hope I have.

Twice now, I've had memories resurface of me running through trees. That *has* to mean something, right? And after that video last night, well, I've never been more desperate to get to the bottom of who I really am and why I seem to be wrapped up in not one but two murders.

"Ready?"

I turn back to Elliot. My heart leaps at the sight of him, standing there in jeans, boots, a long-sleeve button-down, and baseball cap. This time, it's not backward. He looks rugged and ready for whatever comes our way.

"Yes. Let's do this."

Holding Cinnamon's reins, he backs her up a few steps. "You have any idea how to climb on?"

"I'm guessing I put my foot in that handle?"

"The stirrup, yes." Elliot smiles. He's not mocking me, and for that, I'm grateful. "Put your foot there, grip the saddle horn here, and pull yourself up. I'll help if you struggle, okay?"

"Okay. Thanks." Reaching up to grip the saddle horn, I put my foot into the stirrup and pull myself up. My unused and still-sore muscles ache, but I'm able to get myself up and situated. The moment I'm on the horse, my nerves dissipate. The power of the animal beneath me isn't unfamiliar.

"You good?"

I look down at him and smile, feeling something missing slip into place. "I think I've ridden before. It feels —I like it."

Elliot smiles, his handsome grin stealing my breath. "You look like a natural." He hands me the reins then slips Bobby's bridle on and climbs on. Seeing him sitting in that saddle does something to me, unlocking yet more desire for the soldier who pulled me out of that creek.

Does he feel it, too? This connection sparking between us? Is that what he meant back at that stop sign?

"Let's head out. Does any of this look familiar?"

I look around as the horses begin moving. "Just the fact that they're trees," I reply truthfully. "But—" I trail off as we come around a small curve in the trail, and my gaze lands on a sign that had been hidden from our view before. My heart begins to pound. "That's what the sign looked like."

He follows my gaze. "A trail sign. Do you remember what it said yet?"

I close my eyes, searching the memory, but all I can see is the general shape and size of the sign. Everything else is a blur. "No, I'm sorry."

"No need to apologize. He taps the saddlebags behind him. "We've got food and time. We'll find it. Echo, *hier.*" The dog races into the trees before us, his ears perked, tail wagging.

"He won't run off?"

"Nope. He'll stay with us even if he ventures off a bit, following his nose." The horses navigate the trail easily as I study the trees around me, hoping to see something—anything that might jog my memory.

But so far, it's just a beautiful, serene outing with tall trees, bright sunlight, and chirping birds.

We continue in silence, with just the sounds of nature surrounding us, for what feels like hours, as Echo trots happily ahead. "Do you do this often?" I ask Elliot, who's riding beside me.

"Ride the trails?"

"Go out on horseback for a case."

"Not as often as I'd like. Most of our cases take place overseas or in urban areas of the States."

"Overseas?"

He nods. "We handle a lot of missing persons cases, and a lot of times, that takes us out of the country."

"Oh wow."

He nods. "It's a rough job, but I wouldn't trade it for anything. Even if things don't go the way we want all the time, I like to think we're making a difference."

"You are."

He glances over at me.

"I mean, I may not know much about what you do, but reuniting loved ones is a pretty fantastic mission."

"It doesn't always go as planned. Sometimes, we're too late." His tone is haunted, and it hurts my heart.

"Do you want to talk about it?"

"Talk about what?"

"When you were too late?"

When he remains silent, I worry that I've pushed him too far. That I've dug into a darkness he's trying to keep hidden.

"I had a client who needed to find her sister. The police wouldn't take her seriously since her sister was a party girl, but she insisted something was wrong. Said it was a gut feeling." He pauses. "We got close looking for her. And when she was counting on me to find answers, I was too late. She lost her life because the guy we were looking for was never really after her sister. He wanted her, and I missed it."

My heart breaks for him, the pain so evident in his expression. "Oh, Elliot. I'm so sorry."

"It happened, and I haven't quite been able to move past it."

"But it wasn't your fault."

"I missed something."

"Everyone misses something. There's never a perfect case. When things are cut and dried, it's rarely the full story. Isn't that what you've been saying to me this entire time?"

He cocks his head to the side and studies me. "Fair enough."

I smile softly at him. "I'm really sorry, Elliot. I can tell she meant a lot to you."

He stops Bobby, so I do the same with Cinnamon. "She looked like you. At first glance. When I saw you in that creek, there was a moment—"

And it hits me why he was so standoffish at first. Because I looked like the woman he couldn't save. "You thought I was her."

"It was impossible, of course. She's been dead for three years. But for just a moment." Anyway. "Aside from the red hair, you two really don't have a whole lot of similarities, but from a distance, it caught me off guard."

"Is that why you haven't been to church?"

He nods. "I couldn't face the guilt. I don't see how God can forgive me for something like that, and I have no idea how to learn to forgive myself."

I wish I could remind him that he didn't do anything wrong and have him actually believe me. But I know that, no matter what I say, he has to be the one to forgive himself.

"I'm truly sorry for what happened to her. But if you want my opinion, she was lucky to have you, Elliot. Even given what happened."

"Thank you."

I smile. "You're welcome. "So—" I turn my face and look out at the trees, and my gaze catches sight of a partially hidden sign. "Wait." I climb off the horse and offer Elliot the reins as I walk farther into the trees.

Like a magnet, it draws me in closer. The memory resurfaces again, this time slower. As though I'm currently living in it, the rest of the world fades away. My heart pounds, and I reach up to touch the sign.

"This is it."

"This is the sign?"

I nearly jump out of my skin when I hear him right behind me. I turn toward him and nod. Echo is sitting beside him, and Elliot has the reins of both horses in his hands with them lingering a few feet behind us, still on the trail.

"You're sure?" he asks.

"Yes. I—this is it, Elliot. I ran past this." Hope burns in my chest as I turn to look at him. "We found it."

He continues looking straight ahead, studying the brush around the sign. "Then let's head in. You okay to keep riding?"

"Yes. Absolutely." Truthfully, even if I weren't comfortable getting back on Cinnamon, I would have agreed to anything that meant getting closer to the answers I've been so desperately seeking.

He offers me Cinnamon's reins, and I place them over

her head just as he does to Bobby. "We can continue riding side by side for now, but if the trail narrows, I'll take the lead. Just keep an eye out for anything that might jog your memory, okay?"

"Okay."

We climb onto the horses, and Elliot calls out, "Echo, *hier.*"

The dog trots over to Bobby's side before he guides the horse down the trail beside the sign. I keep my eye on it as we pass by again, my heart racing with the very possibility of discovering what happened to me before I was dumped in that creek.

The brush is thicker through here, the trees closer together, and each step we take is like jumping back into that nightmare.

"This is definitely it," I tell him. "I remember all of this."

"Anything else coming to you?" he asks.

"No, not yet. But we're close. I know we're close."

We're only about half a mile down the trail before Echo lets out a warning bark. It's soft, an alert, and while both horses perk their ears, neither seems too bothered by the sound.

Elliot, though, goes completely rigid, his hand on the grip of the weapon holstered at his side. He turns around in his saddle, studying the trees.

Echo growls.

The hair on the back of my neck stands on end, and adrenaline surges through my veins. *Something is wrong.*

"We need to go," Elliot orders, his tone low.

"What do you think it is?"

"We're not the only ones out here."

I look around, searching for another person on horseback or a hiker. "It's a park. Isn't that normal?"

"Echo won't warn me unless there's an issue." Before I can ask what he means, he turns to me and his eyes go wide —panicked. "Get down!" He lunges off of Bobby and hits me with the full force of his frame.

A gun goes off.

We fall to the ground.

I land on my back, winded and dazed. But before I have time to catch my breath, Elliot is dragging me behind a tree. "Stay down," he orders. "Echo!" he calls out. *"Hier!"*

Another gunshot echoes through the trees. Wood splinters when it hits the tree beside us.

The dog rushes to Elliot's side and lays down, panting heavily. "Good boy." He pets the dog then falls backward.

"Elliot, what's—" Red blossoms on the front of his shirt, right above his heart. "No. No. No." Panic pulses through my veins. I rip my sweatshirt over my head and press it to his injury. He hisses in pain, but I keep pressure on it. *Dear God, please don't let him die.*

Echo whimpers, the hair on his back still standing on

end even as he nuzzles Elliot before turning to face the direction of the shooter. He growls low and deep, a warning of what's to come.

"Get back to the truck," he growls. "Take Echo. Do not run in a straight line. Stay behind the trees." He's breathless, barely able to keep his eyes open.

"What? No. I'm not leaving you."

"You have to," he tells me. "I can't keep up. But if you get there, you can call Bradyn—"

"You'll be dead before we get back."

He grabs my hand and holds on. "We'll both be dead if you stay."

How do I tell him I'd rather die than live in a world without him?

"Where's your cell phone?" I start searching his pockets.

"In my left pocket. But the service out here is spotty. That's why you need to get to the truck." He lies back, breathing through the pain.

"We'll make it work." I reach into the pocket of his jeans and withdraw his cell. The screen is shattered, the phone dead. "Calling isn't an option." I toss the phone to the ground.

"Jane, you have to get to the truck." His tone is strained, his breathing getting heavier.

I grip his face, blood staining my hands. "Listen to me, Elliot Hunt, I am *not* leaving you out here to die. Do you understand? Stop asking me to. I'd rather die here in this park than lose you. So *stop* arguing with me."

He clenches his jaw and nods. "At my back, there's a pistol. Grab it." He rolls over, groaning as he does. I reach behind his back and tug the firearm free, holding the cool steel in my hand. Echo remains at Elliot's side, ears perked.

Given what I've pieced together about myself, I'm betting I've fired a gun before. Even if I haven't, I refuse to go down without a fight. And if that means whoever is after me finishes the job, so be it. At least, I will have tried.

I creep closer to the tree, staying low. The horses are grazing a few yards from us now, their reins dangling from their bridles.

Why they haven't run, I'm not sure. But they're so close.

All we need to do is—

Another branch snaps. I grip the gun in my hand and peek around the tree. A man dressed in all black, a mask on his face, moves stealthily through the trees, every step bringing him closer to us.

And in his hands is a large rifle. The kind you'd see in a military movie.

My blood chills. I glance back at Elliot. He's breathing, but the rise and fall of his chest is labored. Whatever that bullet hit, it's done damage. And if I don't get him help soon, he's going to die.

Lord, please don't die.

I take a deep breath and raise the firearm.

The man comes into the sights, and I take another deep breath. As I let it out, I squeeze the trigger. The gun goes off, a clap of thunder that sends birds flying up from the trees. He stiffens and falls backward, but I don't waste any time as I lunge to my feet and sprint forward, my only thought on getting that rifle away from him.

He's lying on the ground, a bullet hole in the center of his chest. Blood pools to the surface, and he stares up at the sky, his eyes frozen open.

The rifle has fallen to the side, so I bend down and retrieve it then sink to my knees and check his throat. There's no pulse. *Dead.* I killed him. Just like the man in the hospital.

"Jane!" Elliot yells, his tone is pained as though he's clinging to whatever energy he has left to call for me.

"Here! I'm okay! Stay where you are! Don't move!" Quickly, I check the man's pockets. After withdrawing a wallet, keys, phone, and a knife from his boot, I rush back over toward the horses and slip the items into Bobby's saddlebags before sprinting back to Elliot's side.

He's pale. So pale. "He's dead, okay? We need to get you onto the horse so we can get back to the truck."

"Dead? How?"

"Apparently, I'm a good shot. Come on. Please, Elliot. Don't die on me." Echo whines louder, nuzzling Elliot again.

"I'll do my best." He groans as I help him to his feet, doing what I can to ignore the sharp pain from my still-healing side. Knowing it's life or death we're dancing around, I guide him toward the horse. I can heal later. He'll die if he doesn't get help now.

His legs are barely moving, every step labored with how weak he's growing.

"If I pass out, leave me and get help."

"Elliot—"

"You won't be able to get me back on the horse, Jane. And the longer we wait, the more likely it is I'll die. You have to leave me behind if I fall, okay?"

I look up into his hazel eyes then cup his cheek and nod. "I will. But I'm riding with you to make sure that doesn't happen." I slip Bobby's reins back over his head then climb into the saddle. After slipping my foot out of the stirrup so Elliot can use it, I reach down and take his hand.

Elliot, growing weaker by the second, takes a deep breath and then pulls himself onto Bobby's back. I pull as hard as I can, trying to offer what little strength I have until he's seated behind me.

I take his good arm and pull it around my waist then hold it steady. "Go, boy," I urge Bobby. The horse starts moving, galloping through the trees with Echo racing beside us and Cinnamon keeping pace slightly behind us. I hit the main trail, my mind focused only on getting Elliot to safety. Echo runs at our side, easily keeping pace with the horse.

Lord, please get us out of here. Please, God, save him. I need him. Please.

Minutes tick by, but they might as well be hours before we've reached the truck. As soon as we're in view of it, I stop Bobby. "Whoa, boy. We're here." But Elliot's not responding. Echo lets out a soft bark.

My chest aches. *Please don't be dead. Please don't be dead.*

"Elliot, I need you to hold yourself up long enough so I can get down, okay?"

Still nothing.

I can risk trying to climb down alone, but Elliot will fall.

Echo starts barking again, an alert as a large truck pulls into the lot, and I wave my hand. "Help!" I yell as the truck comes to a stop.

Bradyn Hunt and Kennedy jump out. The eldest Hunt brother's expression is one of terror as he sprints forward toward his younger brother. "What happened?"

"Someone was out there. They shot him. I can't get him down." Tears burn in my eyes, but I remain focused.

He has to live.

"We have to get him down, Bradyn. He needs help."

"Breathe, Jane," Kennedy tells me. "You're not alone anymore, okay?"

Bradyn reaches up and grabs his brother, pulls him down, and lays him out on the ground. He checks Elliot's pulse as I get down and rush to his side. "He's lost too much blood. I'm going to put him in my truck. You and Kennedy get him to the hospital, and I'll deal with the horses." Without waiting for a response, he lifts Elliot with a groan and carries him to the truck. "Where's the shooter?"

"Dead," I tell him. "His rifle is on Cinnamon's saddle horn."

I open the back door, and Bradyn lays Elliot on the backseat.

"God, please don't take my brother," he whispers, placing his hand on Elliot's stomach. "Please let him live. I ask this in the name of Jesus Christ. Amen." As soon as he's done, he pulls back and slams the door. "I'll handle it. Get him to the hospital."

"What if there was more than one?" Kennedy asks.

"I won't go in without backup. I'm calling Riley as soon as you leave. But if you don't go now—"

"We're going. He'll be okay," Kennedy says, gripping Bradyn's face and kissing him quickly.

Bradyn nods, but his expression is one of concern. Pain. "I'll keep Echo with me."

I nod and try to remain somewhat in control of the anxiety coursing through my body as I rush around to the other side of the truck and open the door. Carefully raising his head, I climb in and lay Elliot's head in my lap. I apply pressure to his wound and hold tightly while Kennedy gets behind the wheel.

She throws the truck into Drive and races out of the lot.

"Please don't die," I whisper. "God, please don't take him." With my free bloodstained hand, I reach up and hold the silver cross around my neck. *Please.*

CHAPTER 18
ELLIOT

I open my eyes slowly, the effects of whatever medicine I've been given keeping me hovering just out of reach of full clarity. Machines hum softly in the background, the beeping of a heart monitor the first sound I fully recognize.

"Welcome back, brother." Bradyn's voice is a welcome familiarity as he steps into my eyeline.

"Jane," I choke out.

"She's fine. A bit sore, but Lani checked her out. She's back at the house getting cleaned up. Kennedy had to practically drag her out to get her to leave."

"The shooter?"

"Anderson Jacobs. Former SEAL who was dishonorably discharged for killing three civilians in what was called a botched rescue mission. He's also dead."

"He's dead?"

He nods. "A .45 caliber round to center mass will do that. You had to do it, brother. He was going to kill you both."

"Me? I didn't shoot him."

Bradyn narrows his gaze in confusion.

"Jane did." I close my eyes, recalling the moment of panic when I heard a gunshot and couldn't see her. "I couldn't even move."

"From the bloodstained grass to where he was found was a good distance. Not many could have taken that shot. We assumed it was you, and she's barely spoken since then."

First, she takes down a trained killer while injured; then, she makes an impossible shot. I'm afraid of what it means once we've pieced it all together. *What if she really was working on the wrong side of things*? I dismiss the thought. No, it's just not possible.

I suck in a breath, but my chest burns. "What's the damage?"

"It missed your heart by seven millimeters. Went clean through, but you lost a lot of blood. You've been out for two days." He takes a seat on the edge of the hospital bed and covers my hand with his. "You almost died, brother."

"I didn't though."

"Because Jane managed to get you to the truck."

"How did she get me down?"

"There was a pit in my stomach," he says. "A nagging feeling that something was wrong, so I figured I'd drive out and just make sure. She was trying to figure out how to get down without you getting hurt when we got there."

"It's good you showed up when you did."

"It was God," he replies simply. "No other explanation. He knew you needed me, and He guided me there." Bradyn lets out a breath then squeezes my hand and stands, crossing his arms. "Gibson is running the shooter through so we can get some more information. But the rifle he used was military grade. Expensive. My money is on a professional hit."

"Just like the hospital. When I realized we weren't alone—" The fear claws at me again, as though I'm reliving the moment. "All I saw was her dead on the ground."

"You saved her."

"This time. But what happens if I'm too late again?" I let my fear in for only a moment. "What if I lose her, too?"

Bradyn crosses over and clasps a hand on my uninjured shoulder. "We're going to make sure that doesn't happen, brother. No matter what we have to do."

BY THE TIME BRADYN LEAVES, I've seen every member of my family—including Lani, who gave me a doctor speech about how I nearly died and need to start carrying a clot-stop kit in my saddlebags if I'm going to be out risking my life.

But the one person whose presence I'm craving hasn't been here yet.

I can't help but worry that she's shaken by what happened. After all, I failed her. I got shot, and she was forced to take someone's life to save ours. It's another stain that will never wash off. While I hadn't been there to protect her at the hospital, I should have been able to in those woods. It was my job.

The door creaks open, and the very woman who's been on my mind all day steps into the room.

I let out a breath when I see her, my chest warming at the mere sight of her standing there—alive. Bradyn told me she was okay, and I believed him, but believing and seeing are two totally different things.

"How do you feel?" she asks, coming into the room.

"I'm sorry."

Her gaze narrows on me, and she stops beside the bed. "For what?"

"I let you down. You counted on me to protect you, and you had to do the protecting."

She reaches out and takes my hand in hers. My stomach twists when she touches me, a piece of my heart coming back to life after being unused for so long. "You saved me, Elliot. You took a bullet that was supposed to be mine.

How could we have known that someone was out there waiting?"

"I should have suspected it. I should have—"

"Done exactly what you did." She takes a seat at the edge of the bed. "Elliot, you dang near gave up your life for mine."

"And you had to take a life. Again."

Her emerald gaze is locked on mine, and her response is without hesitation. "And I would do it, yet again, if it means you live."

We'd joked about her being a broody Special Forces officer, but I'm thinking a soldier isn't that far off. This woman has the heart of a warrior.

I swallow hard, trying to understand just how she's gotten so far under my skin in such a short amount of time. "It's a weight. Every death."

"Something I think I am adept at carrying. Whatever that might mean."

"You made a near-impossible shot today."

"The more I learn about myself, the more I believe that I should just turn myself in." Her expression is tortured, her shoulders slumped.

"Or what if you're prior military? What if you love to hunt? There are plenty of different explanations that have nothing to do with you being a bad person. If you were a bad person, you would have left me to die. You didn't."

"I would never leave you to die."

"Which is exactly how I know you're not a bad person. You asked me when we were on our way to that park, and I told you it's my gut. I *feel* it, Jane. You are not what you think you are. And I'm going to prove it."

Her eyes mist. "I was so scared, Elliot. That you were going to die before I could get help."

"I didn't."

"Because Bradyn arrived just in time." She smiles. "I may not be able to recall Bible verses or a single moment aside from this past Sunday spent in a church, but I feel my faith." She presses her hand to her chest. "I felt Him when we were in the truck. A wave of calm settled over me, and I just knew you were going to be okay." She reaches forward and brushes her fingertips over my hair.

My heart beats faster.

"I'm so glad you're okay, Elliot." A tear slips from her eye and trails down her cheek.

"I—"

A knock on the door interrupts me, and Jane turns away as Gibson steps into the room, a man I've never seen at his side. "So sorry to interrupt, but—"

"Nova!" The man sprints toward her, a wide smile on his face. But Jane takes a step back and throws up a hand. He stops, and his expression falters. "It's me, Nova."

"I don't know you." Jane looks from him to me then back to him. "Do I?"

Gibson smiles tightly then reaches into his pocket and

withdraws a photograph. He offers it to Jane, and she takes it from him. A soft gasp leaves her lips before she turns and shows the image to me.

Pain that has nothing to do with the bullet that ripped through my body yesterday, nor the hours of surgery to repair the damage, shoots through my chest. The image is of Jane, her hair braided over her shoulder, a black dress hugging her form, as she sits at a table before a man who's down on one knee, a velvet box in his hands.

"You're her fiancé." The words are poison on my tongue.

"I am," he says, eyes full of tears. "Nova, I never thought I'd find you. I thought—"

"I don't know you," she insists, shoving the photo back into Gibson's hands. "I don't remember you." She backs up closer to the bed, so close her hand brushes against where mine still lies.

I want to tell her to stay with me, but if I do, what was all of this for? She wanted to learn who she was, and this guy can tell her. Which is something I haven't been able to do. "He is who he says he is?" I ask Gibson.

He nods. "We ran him through the system just to be sure."

I look to Jane—Nova. "If he is your fiancé, he might be able to help you."

She turns toward me, emerald eyes wide. "I don't know him."

"Not anymore. But you did before. He can help you fill in the blanks."

Another tear slips down her cheek, and she closes her eyes. Then, after a deep breath, she turns back toward the man who'd come in. "What's your name?"

"Brett Grammer," he replies. "I'm a detective with the Dallas Police Department."

"You're a detective?" I can hear the hope in her voice. The draw of the fact that maybe, just maybe, she's more than she thinks.

He nods and smiles, tears of his own filling his eyes. "Yeah. You are too, Nova."

"I am?"

He nods. "Detective Nova O'Conner. It's how we met."

She glances back at me. It makes sense, of course. The way she spoke about cases when we were in the woods, the way she'd handled that gun, her cool demeanor even amid danger.

Her ability to protect herself.

I was right. She is a warrior.

Even the surveillance video in the alley can be explained by this new revelation. She could very well have been undercover when that was taken. Rosalie could be another cop she brought in, or a CI. Her attention shifts back to Brett. "My name is Nova?"

He reaches into his wallet and withdraws a plastic ID then hands it to her. She studies it, reading the name on the front, then shows it to me. The driver's license photo is her all right. Smiling. "It feels right. I guess I'm not so bad after all," she says.

"I told you."

Her smile doesn't quite reach her eyes as she turns away from me. "My name is Nova?"

He nods. "Nova O'Conner. I've been looking for you ever since you disappeared. If you give me some of your time, I'll tell you everything."

She turns back to me as though to ask permission. My gut twists into knots. I don't want her to leave. Not until I know for sure this guy is really who he says he is. Photographs can be manipulated, after all.

"I want to talk in here. Elliot's been helping me. Whatever you say to me, you can say to him, too."

Brett's dark gaze shifts from her to me. I can see his frustration, but he does what he can to hide it. "Okay. Of course." He moves farther into the room and offers me a wave. "Thank you for saving her. They told me what you did. How you took that bullet for her."

"Any idea who was after her in the first place?"

"Unfortunately not. Nova and I were both on assignments. Undercover," he says. "When her handler said she hadn't checked in, I abandoned my assignment and rushed back to Dallas. They wouldn't give me any information, so I've been tracking her as best I can. I just happened to be passing through town when someone at the café mentioned a Jane Doe just dropped a Hunt brother off at the hospital." He smiles at Jane—Nova—and I can see the love in his eyes. It breaks me. "I just knew, Nova. I knew it was you."

"No one can tell you who was after me?"

"No. I can't even get a clear answer as to what job you were on. Someone wiped all the files. Everything is gone."

"Even her identity," Gibson, who's been silent this entire time, says. "We couldn't get a hit on anything when we ran her name through the system."

"They did a thorough job," Brett agrees. "But now that I know you're okay, we can figure it out. We'll figure it all out." He takes a step closer. "Please? I just want to hold you a minute."

She hesitates for a moment.

Don't do it, I long to tell her. *Please don't pick him.* But he's her fiancé. She already did. And married or not, she's with him.

"Okay." She straightens and holds out her arms. He wraps his around her and buries his face in her hair, holding her close. Jealousy churns my stomach.

"I missed you so much, honey. So much. But I have you now. I have you, and I'll never let you go again."

Releasing her, he takes a step back. "Can we get some coffee? I have so much to tell you."

"I—" She turns back toward me.

"I'm fine." I force a smile. "Go."

"But—"

"I'm fine, Jane—Nova," I reply, using her actual name. "Go and learn about yourself."

"I'll be back," she assures me. "And I won't leave the hospital."

Will you? "I imagine I'll still be right here."

CHAPTER 19
NOVA

"You don't remember anything?" Brett questions then takes a drink of the coffee in front of him. He says we're engaged, but when I look at him, I feel…nothing.

"No. I don't. I mean, I have bits and pieces—mainly me running, but that's it."

"Tell me what you remember." He reaches across the table and covers my hand with his. It feels wrong. Unfamiliar. Not like when Elliot brushes my hand. Why is that? I barely know Elliot, and I was supposed to be marrying the man across from me.

I withdraw my hand, and he looks heartbroken. "I'm sorry. I—"

"Don't apologize. It's okay. What we had, it'll come back." He pulls his hand back and wraps it around the paper cup of coffee on the table, though he doesn't lift it to his lips. "Tell me what you remember. Maybe the two of us can piece it together."

"Um, I remember being in the woods. Running through the trees. The same ones we were attacked in two days ago."

"Where you nearly died." He shakes his head. "I'm so sorry I wasn't there to protect you. That I couldn't keep you safe."

I can't figure out why, especially since Elliot literally said the same thing to me mere minutes ago and it didn't bother me, but hearing that come out of Brett's mouth annoys me a bit. It's unfair to him, of course, but it's the truth. "It sounds like it's my job to be in danger."

He smiles. "It is, but that doesn't mean I can't try, right?"

"I guess not." I take a deep breath. "So, tell me more about myself. Do I like animals?"

"You love them. You grew up with horses and always talked about us getting a few acres outside of the city so you could have them again."

"Really?"

He nods.

"What about family? Do I have one?"

His expression falters. "Your dad died when you were young, and your mother passed a few years ago. You were an only child."

My heart aches for people I don't even remember meeting. For the siblings I'd fantasized about having. "So I have no one."

"You have me," he replies. My stomach twists. "And I promise you, no matter how long it takes, I'm going to make you remember what we had." He reaches into his pocket and withdraws a diamond ring then hands it to me across the table. "It's yours."

"Why do you have it?"

"You left it at home before you left for your assignment. I got it out of the safe to carry it with me. So that I wouldn't feel alone."

I study the ring, noting the way the light shimmers off the diamond in the center of a white gold band. Shouldn't I feel something for it? Shouldn't it jog my memory at least a little? Staring at it now, I don't feel even a glimmer of recognition.

"It's okay if you don't remember it," he tells me. "You will."

"And if I don't?"

"We'll make new memories." He reaches over and covers my hand again. His demeanor shifts, the joy on his face fading away. "There was a time when I walked away from you because I was afraid of what we were becoming. Things were moving so fast, and I wasn't quite ready for it." He takes a deep breath then lets it out. "But when you took me back, I promised I would never give up on us again. And that's what I'm doing. Nova, I will *never* give up on what we had. Not even when you can't remember it."

STANDING outside Elliot's hospital room, my stomach might as well be full of stones. Nerves twist and churn through me, eating me up from the inside.

Which, of course, is ridiculous. But after leaving his bedside to talk to Brett—my *fiancé*—I try the word on, but it doesn't fit nearly as well as I feel like it should. Shouldn't I feel something? Anything?

Honestly, it feels an awful lot like the name Gena did, which Brett assured me was likely my undercover name. If I hadn't been shown picture after picture of the two of us together, including an image of me pinning an award on his uniform, I don't think I'd believe it.

But the evidence is there. Staring at me in the face. And unlike the surveillance video, there's no misreading this. No interpretation needed. Even the cell phone videos taken of me decorating a Christmas tree in my apartment, the two of us laughing together as we were on vacation—they all speak of a happy relationship.

Then why can't I feel anything?

Before he left to book a room at the local inn, Brett assured me that time would bring it all back—my feelings, what we had—but as I stand here, I'm not so sure. With everything I feel for Elliot after only a short time of knowing him, I can't imagine I would *ever* forget. From the very first moment I laid eyes on him, something felt—right.

Doesn't that mean something? Or is my infatuation with the handsome soldier only born out of him rescuing me?

I take a deep breath and raise my fist to knock.

"Come in." His deep voice wraps around me, making me feel a whole lot calmer than I have all afternoon. I push the door open and step into view of the bed.

Elliot looks almost surprised to see me, though his walls go back up, carefully slipping into place like a mask. "I didn't expect you to come back tonight."

"Why not?" I cross the room and set a paper cup of coffee on the bedside table. "Coffee. I thought you could use some."

"Thanks." He clears his throat. "I figured you'd be asking your fiancé everything you could."

He's putting distance between us. Is that because he feels the same? Or because he figures his job is done now that we know who I am? "I asked questions, he answered; then he went to book a room."

Something flashes over Elliot's features. "You'll be leaving my guest room then? I bet you're excited to get back to normal."

"Actually, if it's okay, I'd like to stay around a bit longer. Kennedy invited me to the wedding, so I don't want to miss it. And we still don't know who tried to kill us yesterday. Or who's after me now."

"A lot of pieces still missing," he agrees.

"Exactly." I take a seat in the chair beside his bed. "And —" I trail off, unsure if I should say what's really on my mind.

"What is it?"

"Have you ever been in a situation and not felt sure how you ended up there? Like, the choices you made led you there, but the outcome just doesn't feel right?"

He nods.

"That's what it feels like when I'm around Brett. It doesn't feel—like I imagine love does."

"Love is built on moments," Elliot replies. "If you can't remember those moments, it would be hard to feel it."

Except I feel something for you that I don't feel for him. "So you're not a believer in love at first sight?"

He smiles, but it doesn't reach his eyes. "I wouldn't say that." He doesn't elaborate, and I hate the way my heart warms at the thought that he might be talking about me. Which, of course, is ridiculous. "Maybe with losing your memories, it's just going to take time to feel the same way again."

"Maybe." I force a smile. "Brett says he thinks that it'll come back."

He clenches his jaw. "I'm sure it will."

I take a drink of my coffee then study him. For

someone who's built like a linebacker, Elliot somehow looks so fragile lying there, attached to machines monitoring his vitals. Still so unbelievably handsome that I can hardly tear my gaze away.

Shame burns my cheeks. I'm supposed to be engaged, and here I am, checking out the cowboy who rescued me. Before I knew I was attached, it was different, but now I know. Now the barriers between Elliot and me must remain standing. At least, until I figure out what I'm going to do.

"Are you okay? How are you handling the news?" Elliot asks, tearing my attention back to him.

"Some of it makes sense."

"Like the fact that you're a detective out of Dallas? I'd say that fits with the expert shot and cool demeanor you showed Sunday."

I laugh. "It also eased my panic that I was some kind of horrible person who attracted horrible attention. Though I can't explain the surveillance footage just yet."

"You were likely undercover even then," he says then flashes a smile that churns my insides. "I always believed in you."

"I know you did." Our gazes meet and hold. "Thank you. For everything you've done for me."

"You don't have to thank me."

I lean forward and touch his hand. "I want to, though. You risked your life for me, Elliot. I know you were probably just doing your job, but—" I trail off and sit back, withdrawing my hand. "Thank you anyway." It's wrong to fish. To hope he tells me that what's between us is more than a job, but I can't help it.

Elliot takes a deep breath then nods. "You're welcome. But again, you don't need to thank me."

My stomach falls, a flame of hope that I'm not the only one feeling this way dying down. "Well. I'm going to keep thanking you because it's important."

Silence settles around us, alongside a heaviness of things unsaid. "So, what else did he tell you? Do you have family?"

The knot of grief I've had in my stomach twists again. The fact that I can feel grief for the people who raised me, yet I can't feel anything for the man I'm supposed to be pledging my life to, has not escaped me. But I choose to bury that fact for now. "My dad passed when I was a kid, and my mom died a few years ago. I was an only child and have no other close family."

"Oh, Nova, I'm sorry."

"Thanks." I smile. "I can't even picture their faces, but I feel the loss. That's weird, isn't it?"

"Not at all."

"I also love animals and grew up with horses."

"After seeing you ride Cinnamon, I could have told you that." He grins at me, a playful smile that lessens the darkness of my pain.

"I thought you said Cinnamon was easy to ride."

"She is, but you still could've looked like you didn't know what you were doing."

"I didn't?"

"Nope. A natural from the moment you climbed into that saddle."

"I had fun."

"Then when I get out of here, maybe we can go back out. This time, within the safety of the ranch."

I laugh. "I'd like that." Neither of us mentions the fact that it's likely an impossible plan. One made with no real follow-through. "Has there been any more information on the shooter? Aside from the fact that he was a former SEAL?"

"Not that I've heard. Though, given that I'm in here, Gibson will probably tell Bradyn first. He'll call when he hears something."

Silence stretches between us. "Want to watch something?"

He arches a brow in surprise. "You're staying?"

I turn toward him. "Given what we've been through, I'd say we were friends, right?"

Something shifts in his hazel gaze. "Sure. Friends."

"Then, as your friend, I would like to stay and watch a movie. If that's okay with you?"

"The company would be nice. I'm not a fan of hospitals."

"Why not?"

He shifts his gaze from mine back to the television. "Spent more time in them than I care to remember."

Feeling the shift in his mood, I back off. "Then let's distract you with some mindless entertainment." I turn on the television and flip through the channels, hardly paying any attention at all to what I'm passing as my sole focus is on the man sitting beside me.

N *ine days later.*

With Bradyn and Kennedy's wedding mere days away, I've thankfully escaped the constant hovering of everyone in my family checking to make sure I'm okay. The hospital discharged me after two days, letting me come home to recover, though Lani made me promise I'd let her check in on the injury to make sure everything was healing right.

A small price to pay to be back in my own bed. My own space.

It's been a week since I was discharged. Seven long days of having to listen to Nova tell me about a relationship she doesn't remember and I frankly don't care to know about. Not when it should be me with her. Not some arrogant detective out of Dallas.

Still, as she said—we're friends. And having her here is worth the pain of listening to her work through her lack of feelings for Brett Grammer.

I place a red push pin on the cork board, right over the spot on the map where I was shot. There's another where we believe Nova was shot, a third where the body of that woman was discovered, and a fourth where that dealer's remains were discovered.

There's a yellow one in the place where Rosalie used to work as well as the location where that surveillance video was recorded.

It's complete chaos. Aside from the park, there's no pattern.

Something doesn't feel right.

I just can't place my finger on it, and I've been staring at it for over a week now, trying to get the pieces to make sense.

Now that we know Nova is a cop, there's a lot more information at our fingertips. Tucker was able to get into the Dallas PD files to confirm there is a Nova O'Conner. In fact, the only thing they didn't erase was her hitting a home run and bringing the department's softball team to victory. Something that was likely missed only because there's no accompanying photograph.

Once more, though, I'm left with more questions than answers.

Who erased her, and why? Was the mission she was working on so sensitive that the department erased her?

"Morning." I turn to see Nova standing in the doorway of my office, two cups of coffee in her hands. She sets one on the table and smiles at me. The sight of her standing there ignites the desire that's been growing out of control. Gone are the borrowed clothes, replaced with short boots, dark jeans, a white T-shirt, and a red leather jacket. Her red hair is braided over her shoulder, her eyes bright and wide.

She's stunning.

Perfect.

Everything.

But she's also taken. Engaged. Yet, I can't get her out of my head.

Echo raises his head as she steps farther into the room. His tail thumps heavily against the floor.

"You look different," is all I can manage to say. "Nice."

"Brett drove back to Dallas yesterday and grabbed clothes. He left them with your mother, and she dropped them off early this morning."

"She did? When?"

"You were in the shower," she replies.

"Oh, gotcha. And where is Brett now? Are you going into town to meet him?"

She shakes her head. "He's taking work calls now. He said he'll be by later."

Brett. They've spent a lot of time together over the past nine days. Every one of them like a dagger twisting in my gut. *And why wouldn't they spend time together?* They're engaged, after all. It still hurts, though. Still burns. Like acid on the skin. "Good."

She smiles. "Oh! Hang on." Nova leaves her coffee on the desk beside mine then steps back out of the room, only to return with a file box. "He also picked this up for me, too. It's from the precinct I work at. They said that it's every case I've been working over the last few years. Apparently, the one that nearly ended with me dead is confidential, and they need additional approval to get me the information on that. They did confirm that their technical team was responsible for wiping me from the face of the earth though." She chuckles. "Something about deep cover and all that."

I cross the room and lift the lid. "Have you looked through them?"

"Not yet. I thought we could do it together." Her green gaze shifts to my arm. "How are you feeling?"

"I'm fine."

Nodding, she moves farther into my office and studies the board as well as the stacks of notes and Post-its everywhere. "Are you sleeping?"

"What?"

She turns toward me. "You look tired."

"Gee, thanks?"

Her smirk is a knife in my heart. "You know what I mean."

"I've been busy."

"You need rest, too. You made me go to sleep last night, but there's so much added to this that I can't imagine you got much yourself."

"I need to figure out who's after you so we can stop them." It's the truth, though my motivation has a lot more to do with the fact that I need her gone so I can stop hoping she'll choose me instead.

Because every day that passes with her engaged to Brett is pure torture for me.

"Hopefully these will help with that." She studies the box again. "I don't remember if it is, but that seems like a lot of files."

"You must be a busy detective."

She leans back against my desk and folds her arms. "I talked to my captain on the phone. He said I'm one of his best."

Pride swells in my chest. "I'd bet on that." But there's something else behind those emerald eyes. Something that looks like a whole lot of pain. "What is it?"

She shakes her head. "It all just feels so alien to me. I'm being told who I am, but I can't remember any of it. Brett said he's trying to get through the red tape and get his hands on those confidential files, and my hope is that they'll jog something in me. Almost like I'm trying to fit into a precut shape of my life that I no longer fit into. If that makes sense?"

Because you're not supposed to be with him. "It's just going to take time," I assure her. "You've already had some memories resurface."

"But not enough. It's one thing to be told something about yourself; it's another to know it." The brokenness she tries hard to hide surfaces. "I feel lost, Elliot. I'm being told that I was all these things. That I loved Brett. But—"

"But?" I ask, hating myself for needing her to continue. It's wrong. I know it's wrong.

"I don't feel anything for him." She reaches into her pocket and withdraws a diamond ring.

It might as well have been a venomous snake for how much dread seeing it brings me.

"When I look at this, I see nothing but a ring."

"It is a ring."

She smiles and shakes her head. "I mean, I don't feel a promise. I don't see a future. I don't feel attached—at all."

Even as I know it's a mistake, I move closer. "Everything will come back to you. You just need time."

"Time." She takes a deep breath and smiles. "I suppose you're right." Pushing off of my desk, she shoves the ring back into her pocket and claps her hands. "Shall we get to it, then? There's a lot of files in there, and any one of the people listed in them could want me dead."

<hr>

"ALL RIGHT. It's time for more coffee." Standing, I roll my neck and good shoulder. "You want some?"

Nova looks up from where she's sitting at my dining room table that's currently covered in open file folders and used-up notepads. "What time is it?"

"Seven-fifteen."

"Really?" Quickly, she gets up. "Time got away from me. I, uh, I promised Brett I'd meet him at seven thirty for dinner."

The words grate against me. "Gotcha. Well, you better get going then. I can keep up with this." I head into the kitchen and add fresh grounds to the coffee bin before pressing start.

"Why don't you wait for me? I'll be back in a few hours. Then we can keep at it—"

"Nah, I'll be fine. It'll give me a chance to get some more done before calling it a night."

"Elliot."

I turn, surprised to find her standing right behind me, close enough that I can see the flecks of copper in the emerald. She stares up at me through thick, dark lashes, and I have to grip the countertop to keep myself from reaching for her.

From feeling the silky strands of her hair against my fingertips.

Everything in me is screaming to close the distance. To take her into my arms and capture her lips with mine. Maybe then she wouldn't leave to be with him. Maybe then she'd choose me.

Before I lose what little self-control I have around her, I take a step back and retrieve a clean mug from the cabinet. "You should get going."

She's silent for a moment. "Promise me you'll at least eat dinner? I haven't seen you eat anything but chips all day."

"I will," I assure her, though I'm not entirely sure that's something I can carry through on.

"Thanks. I'll see you later?"

"See you later."

With a final smile, she grabs her purse, pets Echo on the head, and heads out of the house. When the door finally closes, I grab the coffee mug and throw it as hard as I can across the room. It hits the wall and shatters.

Echo jumps up from his bed and rushes in to investigate, all while I'm barely catching my breath.

Why me?

Why do this to me?

Steal one love, give me another, then keep her just out of reach?

I kneel down and start retrieving broken pieces as the guilt of what I did sets in. Trying to control things I can't control will always get me into trouble. Something I know better than most.

The door opens, and Bradyn comes in. He eyes me curiously but doesn't say anything as I retrieve the broken pieces and stick them into the trash. When I grab the broom, though, he crosses the room and grabs the dustpan, holding it while I sweep the pieces in.

"Feel better?" he asks.

"Not even close."

"Then let's talk. Sit, I'll get us coffee."

Because years of experience has taught me that arguing with my older brother is futile, I take a seat on a barstool at the counter while he fills mugs with coffee. "I'm losing it," I tell him.

He hands me a mug. "So I can see."

"It doesn't make any sense. I haven't even known her that long. She's been with us—what—two weeks? But she's under my skin. More so than even R—" Guilt burns my insides at the comparison.

"It's okay, Elliot. I know you're not comparing the two of them."

"I thought I'd fallen for Renee," I tell him. "It wasn't at

first sight, but every moment we were together, we grew closer."

"I know."

"I cared for her." I meet his gaze, and the guilt on my shoulders presses down harder. I want to crumble beneath it. "But it's nothing compared to what I feel for Nova. And I barely know her."

Bradyn comes around the counter and sits beside me. "Do you remember when Kennedy was taken and you came in and prayed with me? For me? Even with the struggles you've had, with avoiding church, you stuck to your faith and made sure I carried it forward."

"You needed it. We needed it."

"Exactly. You told me that I was in love with her before I was even able to admit it to myself."

"It was easy to see."

"Just as it is now."

"Things are different. Nova's engaged. God brought her to me, gave me a second chance, then stuck it just out of reach."

"God doesn't work that way. You know that. Everything is in His timing."

"She's engaged, Bradyn."

He takes a deep breath. "I know, brother. And maybe she's meant to help you move past what happened with Renee. And if that's the case, then your second chance is still to come. You can't lose sight just because you can't see His plan."

I know he's right, but that doesn't make it sting any less. Because I *want* my second chance to be Nova. I want her to be my forever. My partner. More than I want to draw my next breath.

Bradyn turns and studies the table. "Looks like you've been losing sleep. Maybe Nova should stay at Mom and Dad's until—"

"No. She stays here until we solve this."

"Are you sure that's wise?" I know he's just trying to help, but it angers me that he's assuming I can't handle it.

Then again, he did just walk in right after I shattered a coffee cup against the wall.

"Lani is still staying here, and for the most part, all Nova and I do is work on the case. There hasn't been much personal conversation. I'll be fine. I just need to get this figured out. Something's not sitting right, but I can't figure it out."

"Then maybe an extra pair of eyes will help. Come on. I have a few hours before I need to get back."

"Shouldn't you be getting beauty sleep? You are marrying a woman way out of your league the day after tomorrow."

He laughs. "She'll be beautiful enough for the both of us. Come on, brother. I'll call Riley, Tucker, and Dylan. Let's get some work done."

CHAPTER 21
NOVA

Sweat beading down my skin, I sprint as hard and as fast as I can, coming up over the hillside with my heart feeling as though it might beat right out of my chest. Pausing for a moment, I work to catch my breath then turn back and look at how far I came.

I smile, feeling strength through my exhaustion.

There haven't been many good days lately. But today—today has been good. Peaceful.

"Gena, my darling. There you are."

All peace vanishes at the sound of the male voice behind me.

Forcing a smile onto my face, I turn to face Ivan. He's tied his dark hair back at the nape of his neck and is still wearing the same clothes he was when I left early this morning. White cloth pants and an oversized linen shirt. "Sorry, Ivan, I was out for a run."

"I see that. Feel better?" He holds out a hand, and I reach out to let him take mine. As it does anytime his fingers brush against mine, a shiver runs up my spine.

"Much. Thanks."

"Another restless night, I'm sorry for that. I fear our current predicament has given us quite the runaround these days."

"You could say that." He tucks my arm through his and together, we walk back toward his sprawling mansion. Set in the middle of 300 acres, it's a compound surrounded by guards.

Guards that I lead as his head of security. Or so he thinks. "We'll find the mole," I tell him. "They can't hide forever."

"No, of course not. Not from you." He stops walking and turns me to face him. The man has made it no secret that he's attracted to me, but that's a line I won't cross. Ever. Not even for this assignment.

The silver cross beneath my shirt is heavy against my skin, a reminder of the darkness I've already had to look past in order to get to the greater good of why I'm here.

Sometimes you have to let the monster close. That way, when you strike, he doesn't see the blow coming. And this man is a monster all the way to his shriveled black heart.

I smile at him then start walking again. "I'll get showered and start handling the interviews. Anything else I can do for you today?"

"You can start with Patterson."

Dread coils in my belly, but I force the mask to stay in place. "Why?"

Ivan's dark eyes grow even darker, turning murderous. "We both know why. Stop pretending you don't suspect him too." When I don't respond, he reaches up and runs a finger over my cheek. "You're too smart not to see it, my darling." His finger leaves my skin crawling in its wake. "Start with him. If he's not the mole, you can let him live. But if he is, I fully expect his body dumped by nightfall. Okay?"

I have to force the bile back down to avoid vomiting all over the cloth shoes he wears everywhere. "Of course. I'll see to it that it's done."

I SHOOT UP IN BED, sweat pouring down my face. After throwing the covers off, I rush out and head down the hall. Elliot's bedroom door is open, but his room is empty. So I slip into a pair of tennis shoes and head out the front door.

I sprint out into the early morning air, thankful that the sun is already rising over the horizon. Rushing toward the path that would take me to the barn where Elliot spends most of his early mornings, I continue to go over the memory in my head. Over and over again.

I was there in that memory. It was so vivid—I slam into

a hard chest, and a man groans as a large hand goes out to steady me. "Easy, you okay?"

"Yeah, sorry, I—" I trail off as my gaze meets Elliot's. He's not dressed for ranch work as I thought he'd be, but rather in shorts, a tight sweatshirt, and tennis shoes instead of boots. Echo happily trots alongside him, tongue hanging out of the side of his mouth. "Wait, are you supposed to be running?"

"Says the girl who took a six-hour road trip to Galveston days after being shot." When I don't respond, he smiles softly. "Lani said it was fine as long as I went easy on myself. I did."

"Uh-huh."

"That why you're out here? To yell at me for exercising?"

"Huh? Oh, no!" I grin at him even though the memory was anything but pleasant. "I remembered something. I don't know what it means, but I remembered something."

"What did you remember?"

"Can we go back inside? I want to write it down before I forget." I'm jazzed, energized by the memory. Does this mean the others will soon follow? Does this mean I'm close to unlocking everything?

"Sure. Let's go." He gestures toward the house, so I turn and head back inside.

"Want some coffee?" he asks.

"Yes, please."

"Great. Talk while I make it."

"Okay. So, I was out for a run—in the memory, not this morning," I add when he turns to eye my pajamas curiously. "Anyway, I was feeling peaceful and exhausted but in a good way. And then this man showed up."

He presses a button and turns to fully face me. "Brett?"

I shake my head. "In my dream, his name was Ivan. He was wearing these oversized linen clothes, and he had long hair that was pulled back in a ponytail."

"Ivan."

I nod.

He starts toward the table. "Keep talking. What else did you remember?"

"I think I was undercover. He called me Gena and told me that I needed to take care of finding a mole. He told me to start with someone named Patterson. But I think it upset me. I remember feeling a pit in my stomach like it was not good he wanted me to start there."

Elliot uses his good arm to shuffle through a stack of folders then straightens and studies the folders. "There aren't any labeled with an Ivan."

"Maybe it was the one I was working on? They said those files were locked up, right? What if he's the one who shot me?" Realization dawns. "What if he realized I was the mole? That I was the one informing the police?"

"Easy, Nova," Elliot says. "Just breathe."

"I can't. This is another piece. This means that we're

getting close!" I step into the kitchen and stretch up to grab two mugs then pull them down and fill them with steaming coffee. "Maybe this means everything is going to start coming back." I turn to offer him a mug then lean back against the counter with mine.

"Maybe." He smiles, but it doesn't reach his eyes.

"What is it?"

"Rough night," he replies.

"You were supposed to get sleep."

"I tried. My mind wasn't cooperating." He takes a drink of the coffee, and I note dark circles beneath his gorgeous hazel eyes.

"Talk to me."

"There's nothing to talk about."

"Elliot." I eye him.

"There's that detective stare," he says with a laugh. "But I'm not a perp, and this isn't an interrogation."

"No, but you're my friend, and I'm worried about you."

He takes a deep breath and sets the coffee mug down. Reaching up, he undoes the sling and sets it aside then carefully stretches his injured arm. "Look, I've got things in my past that make it hard to sleep sometimes."

"Renee?"

"Some of it is her." He doesn't elaborate though as he leaves the kitchen and heads toward the table that has been serving as our workspace since I brought the files in yesterday.

Because I need to busy myself, I pull out the used coffee grounds and carry them to the trash. When I open it, broken pieces of a mug are sitting on top of the trash. "What happened?"

"I dropped it."

"Elliot."

"What?"

"You can talk to me."

His nostrils flare in anger, eyes hardening. He looks so frustrated, so angry. Is it me? Did I do something? "Look, I —" Someone knocks on the door, cutting him off. He crosses over and pulls it open. "Can I help you?"

"Is Nova here? Your mom said she was."

Brett. Horrible timing. My stomach plummets.

"Sure, come in. I guess you're roaming the ranch in the early mornings now." He holds open the door, and Brett strolls in. He smiles at me, but that smile fades when he notices I'm in my pajamas.

"What's going on here?" he asks, gaze traveling from me to the table. "Late-night work session? I thought you were staying at the main house."

"No," Elliot replies. His demeanor has shifted, and I can tell the last thing he wants is Brett here. "She's been staying here with me and my sister so I can make sure what happened at the hospital doesn't happen again."

Brett looks from me to him then back to me again.

Before someone starts peeing to mark their territory, I clear my throat. "I remembered something last night."

"You did? That's great. What is it?" Brett moves into the kitchen and crosses his arms.

"Some man named Ivan. He was asking me to look into something. Does that ring a bell?"

Brett considers then shakes his head. "Not that I can remember. But like I said, you were undercover, and I haven't been able to get my hands on those files. It's entirely possible that's from your last case."

"That's what I was thinking too." I glance over at Elliot, who's turned his back on us and is studying the Post-its on the wall. Though, if I had to bet, he's not paying any attention to them.

"Great. I'll do some digging. Maybe we can uncover the truth so you'll finally be okay coming home." Brett reaches out and takes my hand.

"I need to get to work. Feel free to let yourselves out." Elliot crosses toward the front door, calls Echo, and shuts it behind him.

"Why do I get the feeling I walked in on something?" Brett asks. "Is there something I need to know, Nova?"

"Of course not. Elliot's just had a rough morning is all." I try to offer a smile to ease what is clearly jealousy flaring to life. "Come on, I'll get dressed, and we can grab some breakfast so we can talk more about what I remembered."

CHAPTER 22
ELLIOT

"You doing okay?" Tucker drops into a chair beside me.

I take a drink of the sweet tea in my glass as I watch Bradyn and Kennedy dancing on the makeshift stage that will serve as the ceremony area and the dance floor for the reception tomorrow.

"Doing fine. Why?"

"Maybe because you're over here sulking, which, big brother, is very unlike you."

I shake my head. "I'm not sulking. In case you forgot, I was shot a few days ago."

"You've been shot before." Tucker crosses his arms. "And if I remember correctly, less than a day later, you got yelled at by the charge nurse for being down in the children's ward, chasing monsters out from beneath beds."

"It was a necessary job. Someone had to do it." I eye

him, grinning. "What is it, Tuck? Do you have a monster I need to get rid of?"

"No thanks. I've been successfully chasing my own monsters away for years now."

I laugh. "Look at you, all grown up."

"Spill, Elliot. You're out-sulking even Dylan." He gestures toward his twin, who is currently dancing with our sister while she laughs at something he said.

"I'm just tired."

"Not sleeping?"

"No."

"Well, maybe this will help. I know Mom said no work at the rehearsal dinner, but—" He reaches into his pocket and withdraws his cell. Once unlocked, he turns it around and shows me a photo of the man Nova described.

"You found him?"

"Ivan Davis. Arms dealer located here in Texas."

"How did you find him?"

"I have friends in high places." He grins. "Anyway. My guess is he's who you're looking for. He's not the type to get his hands dirty, but he is the type to hire it out. And he has the funds to do so."

"Then if we can trace proof of payment from him to the guy who attacked her or the one who shot me, we might be able to find something."

"Already on it," he replies. "I've got things running as we speak."

"Thanks."

"It's my job." He studies me, his bright blue eyes so like our mother's. "Is the redhead what's bothering you?"

"Excuse me?"

Tucker shrugs. "I noticed she's not here. You're sulking. I can put two and two together."

"She's engaged."

"So I hear. She remember him?"

"No. But her memories are coming back little by little."

"Then that's what's bothering you."

"Please, Tucker, tell me what's bothering me."

"She's going to remember him and go home." Never one to beat around the bush, Tucker just blurts out exactly what he's thinking.

Unfortunately, he's not wrong.

"I want her to get her memories back."

"Do you?"

I turn toward him. "What's that supposed to mean?"

"You care about her."

"She's a client."

"No. You may be able to lie to her and convince yourself, but you forget who was there when you found Renee," he says. "I was right there beside you, and I remember that broken look on your face. You cared about her, and she was a client too."

"So you're saying, because they look similar, you think I'm treating Nova like I did Renee?"

"I don't think it has anything to do with what she looks like. Not anymore. It's how she makes you feel. You care about her," he repeats. "On a deeper level than just her being a client. I've seen the way you look at her. And even as you cared for Renee, you never looked at her that way. You're falling for Nova. As in, willing to do something stupid kind of falling."

I could deny it. I should deny it. But Tucker will just continue to argue with me. "She's engaged. And I need to figure out who shot her and get them put away so she can go back to her life and I can refocus on mine. I won't do anything stupid."

"Good." Tucker reaches out and clasps a hand on my good shoulder. "I'm sorry. For what it's worth."

"Thanks."

He squeezes my shoulder gently then gets up and heads over toward where our mother is dancing with our father. After he cuts in, I decide that sitting here and bringing the mood down is not the best way to celebrate my brother's impending nuptials. The last thing I want to do is bring down his night.

With that in mind, I leave the outdoor area where we'll be holding the ceremony and head toward the barn. Bobby sticks his nose over his gate and whinnies, so I walk over to offer him a sugar cube from the container we keep in the barn. "Hey, boy. I'm hoping to be back to riding soon. We'll be back out before you know it."

He eats the cube, so I pet his face, running my hand over his long nose.

As she always does, Nova haunts my mind. Surfacing to remind me just how fast I fell for a woman I barely know.

Bootsteps just outside the barn have me turning my head. I'm assuming it's Bradyn or Tucker, coming to chase me down. Instead, Brett walks into the breezeway.

"Brett."

"Evening, Elliot. I saw you come in here; hope it was okay that I followed."

"I didn't realize you were coming to the rehearsal dinner."

"I wasn't. I just dropped Nova off and wanted to come in to talk to you."

Here we go. I turn toward him. "What is it I can do for you?"

He reaches into his pocket and pulls out his cell phone then crosses the distance between us. Turning the camera so I can see it, he shows me an email from his captain.

Ivan Davis was found dead this morning. I need you and Nova back ASAP to work this. I'll have the files on my desk first thing Monday morning.

Knots twist in my gut, and my heart sinks. She's leaving. "Guess you'll be headed back to Dallas then."

"We are. Nova wants to stay for the wedding, so she'll be doing that while I get things ready, but I'll be picking her up Sunday morning, and we'll be going back."

I nod. "We'll keep trying to trace a payment from Ivan to the shooter in the park, the attack at the hospital, or the deputy who was paid off to look the other way."

"No need. I have local PD on it. They'll be working directly with us. You can send me whatever you have, and we'll handle it from here."

So he's going to try and mark his territory. "We've been working this case."

"And now you're not needed." He takes a step closer. "Look, I get that you were military and you run this search and rescue business now, but Nova doesn't need your help. She has me. Not to mention the fact that we're both actual cops. Let us handle it, and I'll call you if we need any runaways tracked down."

I've never been known to have a temper, but right now, I want to throw him through a wall. "If Nova tells me to drop it, I will. Otherwise, I'll keep working this thing until it's done."

He shakes his head. "You just aren't getting it, are you? Nova may not remember me now, but she's *my* fiancé. We'll be getting married—soon—and I won't have some cowboy getting in the way of that."

"Jealousy isn't a great color," I tell him. "Again, I'll be asking Nova what she wants. She asks me to drop it? Fine, I'll drop it. Until then, I hope you have a safe trip back to

Dallas." I gesture toward the exit. "You can get off my property now."

"She's not interested in you."

"I never said she was. I just don't take too kindly to men trying to intimidate me on my own property."

Brett turns to leave but pauses by the door. "I am grateful you saved her, but I think you've let that get to your head. Leave the heroics to those with badges." He doesn't wait for a response before leaving. I turn, hands balled into fists, as I fight the urge to slam them through the nearest wall.

Why am I so full of anger? Of pain? *God, I need help. Because I don't know how to move forward alone.*

"Are you okay?"

"I need a minute," I tell Lani.

"I just saw that tool leaving here, so I wanted to make sure he didn't take a cheap shot at a guy who got shot recently. Of course, I don't actually think you needed backup; I was just looking for a show."

"I'm fine." I turn to face her.

"Elliot. That guy is a jerk, and clearly, he made you mad."

"He told me to drop the case and leave it to the real cops."

Color floods her cheeks. "I'm sorry, how is he still walking?" She turns to leave. "I'll be right back."

"Don't bother with him," I tell her. "He's not worth it."

She whirls on me. "He comes onto *our* property and says that to you, and you won't let me rip him a new one?" The woman is slow to speak most times, but when she's angry, it's like gasoline on a fire.

"No." I smirk, a calmness settling over me. "Let him have his perceived victory over me. I don't need to prove anything."

"You're darn right you don't. What a jerk. You guys have saved more people than he could ever dream of. And you have a lot of friends in law enforcement."

"It'll be fine, Lani. I'm letting it go." I take a deep breath, her flare of temper calming my own. "So I take it you're not a Brett fan?"

"Ugh. Not even a little." Lani reaches out and pets Midnight as the mare sticks her head over the gate. "My guess is Nova will realize what a jerk he is and be done with him."

"She agreed to marry him before."

"Doesn't mean she still feels the same way. We all know a good knock on the head can sometimes be just what we need to think clearly."

"A little knock on the head? She was shot and nearly died."

Lani smiles. "I know, and that's not how I meant it. I just—I've seen the way she looks at you."

My little sister has always been perceptive. She would've made a great addition to our team if she hadn't followed her own calling into medicine. But even I think she's off on this one. Nova hasn't made any indication that she feels anywhere near like I do.

"I saved her."

"Sure, but that's not how she looks at you." Lani steps forward and wraps both arms around me.

"Then how does she look at me?"

"Like she wants you to keep saving her."

CHAPTER 23
NOVA

Dressed in a navy-blue dress and heels I somehow—thankfully—know how to walk in, I make my way up the porch steps and into the main house. Ruth is standing at the counter, her back to me, staring out the kitchen window.

"You look beautiful," I say as I walk into the kitchen.

She turns toward me, eyes misty, and smiles before running her hands over the front of her floral dress. "You're too kind. And quite the image yourself, if I do say so."

"Thanks." I return her smile and walk over to stand beside her. "You okay?"

"I'm just trying to figure out how I'll keep from crying at the ceremony when I can't keep from blubbering right now."

I wrap my arm around her shoulders, and she leans against me. Over the past month that I've been staying on the ranch, we've grown quite close, and I like to imagine that my own mother was just like Ruth Hunt. Warm and welcoming. Maybe I'll remember one day. "You're the mother of the groom. You're allowed to cry."

She sniffles and dabs at her eyes with tissues. "I'm so happy for Bradyn and Kennedy. She's so lovely, and they're going to be a wonderful family. But—"

"It's still a goodbye," I finish. "I get it."

She smiles up at me. "You are such a sweet girl too." Reaching up, she gently cups my cheek. "Would you like some coffee? I'll be heading over to Bradyn's to help Kennedy and her mother soon, but I can make a pot before I go."

"No, that's okay. I can make some if you don't mind." Elliot was already gone when I got up this morning, and since sitting around his house was making me depressed over the fact that Brett is taking me back to Dallas tomorrow, I'd needed to get out.

"Not at all. Help yourself, sweetheart." She starts toward the door then turns. "I hope you know that you're welcome to stay here on the ranch as long as you want. You don't have to leave tomorrow."

I swallow hard, emotion burning in my throat. "I know, thank you."

She smiles again. Only this time, I see something hidden behind it. "You're more than welcome. I'll see you soon."

"See you soon."

She leaves the house, and I start the coffee pot, breathing deeply as the scent of freshly brewed coffee fills my lungs. I close my eyes and try to stay focused on what matters about today.

Bradyn and Kennedy.

Not me, my forgotten past, the fact that Brett is making me leave tomorrow…and especially not the feelings I have for a handsome cowboy I have no business wanting.

We hardly spoke after he left the house yesterday. I'd fallen asleep on the couch, waiting for him, and woken up covered in a cream-colored blanket. Whether it was him or Lani who did it, I'm not sure.

He was so tense yesterday, and the moment Brett walked in the door, Elliot's mood went downhill fast. It's honestly something I get. Truthfully, I don't care to be around Brett much either. Which, of course, is horrible, given I'm apparently supposed to be marrying him.

I look down at my bare ring finger, trying to imagine what it would look like to wear that ring. It just doesn't feel right. None of it feels right. The pictures he shows me, the videos taken of us on trips…it all feels like someone else's life.

Not mine.

This ranch. The quiet. The Hunt family. *They* feel real.

Brett believes that, by going back to our normal life, my memories might be jogged. It's the only reason I agreed to go. Because leaving this place feels an awful lot like leaving my home.

I'm only glad he's not coming tonight.

It'll give me one more chance to say goodbye to everyone.

Elliot's handsome face swims into view. Gorgeous hazel eyes that chased away my fear from the moment I first saw him.

Tears burn in my throat. How am I supposed to say goodbye? How am I supposed to let go when it feels as though my heart might be ripped right out of my chest?

I reach up and touch the silver cross around my neck, letting my fingers trace the cool metal. "Lord, I need Your strength right now. I need Your help. Please." A tear slips down my cheek, and I quickly wipe it away.

Tonight, I'll be happy. I'll enjoy myself, celebrating people who I've come to care for.

Tomorrow is the time for tears.

LANI OFFERS me a bottle of water then turns to survey the dance floor. Her obsidian hair, which was pinned to perfection an hour ago, is now down around her shoulders. "Whew! That was fun." She beams at me. "Are you going to dance?"

"I don't even know if I can."

She waves her hand in dismissal. "Everyone can dance if they have the right partner."

"While I appreciate your faith in me, I'm going to save everyone here the trouble. Just in case."

She rolls her eyes.

"You know, Sheriff Lawson has been by this table at least half a dozen times in the last thirty minutes."

She perks up. "Really?"

"At least," I tell her. "And I noticed more than once that his gaze found you across the dance floor and he looked rather frustrated you weren't here."

Her smile becomes radiant, and she sets her bottle of water down. "Well, I think I should go let the man offer me a dance."

"I think that would be kind of you." Watching as she heads through the crowd, I can't help but appreciate what a beautiful ceremony it was.

Blooming flowers all around, a soft breeze chasing away any stagnant heat. It was truly stunning. The kind of wedding anyone would be lucky to have. The reception has been just as lovely. Great food, music, dancing. A perfect evening.

My gaze lands on Elliot.

He's avoided me all night with his gaze barely passing over me as he walked Lani down the aisle as best man and maid of honor. And now he's across the floor, talking to his father and Pastor Ford, who oversaw the ceremony.

Maybe I should just go.

Before I can act on that thought though, Riley stops in front of me, a wide grin on his handsome face. "You look like you need to dance."

I laugh. "I'm not sure that's a good idea. I could be a terrible dancer."

"It's a good thing that I'm impeccable on my feet then." He reaches out.

"Are you sure you know what you're risking? Broken toes are a hazard."

"Worth it." He smiles and tugs me to my feet when I slip my hand into his. He guides me onto the floor and takes my hand with one then places his other hand on my hip. We start moving to an upbeat country song, and he leads me, guiding my every step. "See? Natural."

"I guess it's better than I thought it would be."

He chuckles then pushes me out and spins me, bringing me back in. "Are you having an okay night?"

"Oh yeah. The ceremony was beautiful."

"It was," he agrees. "I may not be much for weddings, but this one was quite perfect."

I arch a brow. "Not much for weddings?"

"Nope."

"Really? You seem like such a romantic. Your dog is named Romeo, after all."

He laughs. "I have a no-settle-down policy. And it's one I intend to stick to."

Given what I know about the Hunt brothers, it's seriously surprising. Especially since they literally come from two people so in love that, even though they've been married forty years, I can still see the same affection on their faces as was on Bradyn and Kennedy's tonight.

"Well, maybe one day you'll change your mind."

He grins and spins me again, bringing me back in. "So I hear you're heading back to Dallas tomorrow?"

I take a deep breath, feeling that pit in my stomach grow. "Uh, yeah. Brett thinks it'll be good for my memory."

"Does he." The tone of his voice catches my attention more than the words.

"He does," I say. "Why? You don't agree?"

Riley shrugs. "I want to know what you want to do."

"I want my memories back. I want to remember everything so I can—" I trail off.

"So you can what?"

"Make my own decisions." I force a smile. "There's a lot that feels out of my control right now. Like another person backed me into a corner, and now I have to decide if I want to stay in it or leave."

Riley nods. "No one can force you to stay in a situation you don't want to be in. If it's not right, it's not right." He spins me again, and the song ends. His gaze lifts to someone past my shoulder, and he grins. "And speaking of right. Look who is right on time. I'll see you soon." He leaves me, heading off the dance floor.

I start to follow, confused by what he means, but a man clears his throat behind me. "Care to dance?" Elliot's voice washes over me, and my heart flutters. Like, stupid love-story flutters.

I turn toward him and raise my gaze to meet his. "Sure, since Riley took one for the team and we now know I don't have two left feet."

Elliot smirks and takes my hand in his good hand then places the other on my hip. The hold is light, but the weight of his touch pins me in this moment. And I never want to leave. "It's a good thing I don't either."

A slow song begins to play, a smooth love song that has my pulse beating faster. We start moving, and with Elliot so close, I can't think straight. He's everywhere, in my mind, my heart, a steady reminder that I really, *really* don't want to walk away.

Even though I feel like I have to.

"You look beautiful," Elliot says. "I wanted to tell you that earlier but haven't had the chance."

My stomach flips. *What is wrong with me?* "Thanks. You clean up quite nicely yourself."

He grins, and I practically melt right here. A puddle on the dance floor. I move in a bit closer, wanting so badly to just stay right here in his arms. Maybe it would all just fade away if he held me.

The dilemma.

The guilt.

Because even though I'm supposed to marry Brett, Elliot is who I wake up thinking of. It's his face on my mind as I fall asleep.

Tears burn in my eyes, so I let myself rest my cheek against his chest, the steady beat of his heart music to my ears.

CHAPTER 24
ELLIOT

I've never been much of a dancer. I know how, sure, but I could've gone the rest of my life without taking another turn on the dance floor. Yet, this single dance has changed that. Cradling Nova, as we sway to the music, is what I want to do for the rest of my life.

Late-night dances in the kitchen, an early morning spin around the living room. Every minute of every day filled with her. The fact that she's leaving tomorrow is a knife twisting in my gut. Pain that I can't seem to get away from, no matter how much distance I tried to put between us today.

Even still, the mere sight of her in that blue dress is driving me absolutely wild. She's curled her hair and left it loose around her shoulders, and with us this close, the silky strands brush against the hand that's holding hers.

I'm intoxicated by what I feel for her.

Driven mad by the bitter truth of our situation. Because Nova was never even mine, yet I know her leaving tomorrow is going to leave me a broken man.

The song ends, and even though I want nothing more than to remain right here, I pull back, and she lifts her head from my chest. When she looks up at me, tears are glittering in her emerald gaze.

I'm instantly aware of how very close we are. Did I step on her? Is her injury still bothering her? "Are you okay? What is it?"

She smiles. "I'm fine. Weddings apparently make me emotional. Let's add that to the 'getting to know myself again' column." She withdraws her hand from mine. "I just need some water."

Without waiting for me, she pushes through the crowd. I follow, helpless to deny the pull I feel. After plucking a bottle of water from the table, she heads toward the barn and slips inside.

"Nova, what is it? Did I say something?" I don't know how I could have since I didn't say a word, but I hate seeing her like this. Eyes wide and full of tears. "Did I hurt you?"

"No, of course not." She crosses her arms. "I'm just—" She lets out a breath. "I don't know how to say it. I'm horrible enough for thinking it."

"Tell me." I rush closer.

She shakes her head, keeping her eyes closed.

I feel helpless, lost, because I want to fix what's wrong. So, I offer up the only thing I know that always makes me feel better. "Want to go for a ride?"

"What? Seriously?"

"You said you wanted to go before you left. So let's go. Right now."

"Elliot, we're at your brother's wedding."

"Actually, we're in the barn."

She smiles slightly, and the knot in my chest loosens. "Even if I wanted to, I can't go in what I'm wearing."

"Sure you can. We'll ride double. Come on. Let's do it."

"Are you even cleared to ride?"

"We'll sneak out the side, Lani doesn't have to know."

"Elliot—"

"Please, Nova."

She swallows hard and stares up at me. "You know what? Let's do it."

"Yeah?"

"Yeah." She smiles, and I don't wait for her to change her mind. Moving quickly, I pull Bobby from his stall, run a brush over his brown hair, and then slip a bridle over his head.

"What about the saddle?"

"We don't need it." I jump up onto his back and swing my leg over then reach for her.

Joy shining in her eyes, she kicks her heels off and

reaches up for me. I tug her up, setting her in my lap so her legs are off to the side, her back against my chest.

We walk slowly out of the barn, veering off to the left to avoid the celebration that will likely be going on well into the night. With the music in the distance, we ride beneath the bright moon and a blanket of stars.

Alone with her, I can breathe again. The future can wait; all the unknowns no longer matter. Because she's here.

We reach the creek, so I help her down then climb down behind her and tether Bobby's reins to a nearby tree.

"It's so peaceful out here." She stands on the edge of the embankment, bare feet in the soft grass.

"Sometimes I come out here late, just to get some quiet."

"I see why." She smiles, but it's hollow. Broken.

"Tell me what's wrong." My stomach twists into knots.

"You bring me all the way out here so you can threaten to make me walk home if I don't answer?"

I grin. "The thought may have crossed my mind."

She smiles. *Man, I love to see her smile.* "I'm just trying to decide what I'm going to do."

"With?"

"The rest of my life."

A flicker of hope dances in my chest and those knots loosen. Does she feel it, too? Is there a chance? "What do you mean?"

She sighs. "Brett says we have this whole life back in Dallas. I apparently have an apartment with a great view that he was planning to move into after we're married. He shows me these pictures and videos, but when I see them, it feels like I'm watching someone else's life. Not mine." She takes a deep breath. "I want to remember, but I'm afraid that if I do—"

"You still won't feel the same way as you did back then."

She tilts her beautiful face up, and moonlight dances across her cheek. "Exactly. How am I going to explain that?"

She's hurting, and it's water on that flame of hope. Because as badly as I want her to know how I feel, the last thing I want is to cause her more pain. "Maybe you'll get those feelings back."

"I'm afraid of that, too," she admits.

"Why?"

She steps back. "Because I imagine the guilt I'm feeling will get worse."

"What guilt?"

Nova looks up at me through thick lashes, and I have to catch my breath to avoid being swept away by the intensity in her emerald gaze. "The guilt for doing this." She reaches up, grips the front of my jacket, and tugs me down, slamming her mouth to mine. I do what I've wanted to since the beginning and bury my hand in her thick hair, pulling her close as she opens beneath me, and lose myself in the kiss.

In this absolute heaven-on-earth kiss, everything falls into place. Every single situation that has led me to this moment worth the pain because it led me to her.

She grips the back of my neck, tugging me closer still.

Everything feels right.

Perfect.

And then she pulls away, leaving us both breathless. "I knew it."

"Knew what?"

"That this was going to be a mistake." She pulls away, tears streaming down her cheek.

"A mistake?" The words are a blade to my heart.

She turns back toward me. "Only because I don't know how I'm supposed to walk away from you."

"Don't."

"Elliot—"

"No. Don't walk away. Don't marry him." I move in closer. "We can finish this case together. We can find out what happened to you. Then we can start over."

"I have a life, though. A home in Dallas. A job."

"You have a home here." I move in closer. "A place here. With me."

"But Brett—"

"Can go back to Dallas. I'll take you there so you can get your things."

Her eyes fill again, the tears spilling freely down her cheeks. "I said I'd marry him. Don't I owe it to him to see if those feelings can come back?"

Her words are a bucket of ice-cold water on my head. "This was a test then. Kiss the cowboy and see if you see the stars? Get a taste before you run back to your life?"

"No," she insists, crossing the distance and placing her hand on my chest. "This was me confirming that what's between us is real. Not just a figment of my imagination because you rescued me."

I cover her hand with mine. "Then stay."

The heartbreak is evident in her eyes. "I can't. I have to know about my life. I have to know why I made the choices I did. Even if they don't end up being what I want, I *need* to know. Can't you understand that?"

I pull away, anger and grief battling for control over me. I haven't even lost her yet, and it already feels like she's gone.

"Can you understand?" she repeats. "Can you please see it from my side?"

"I did. Until that kiss. All you just did was set me up to lose you all over again." I head back toward Bobby.

"I'm sorry."

I whirl on her. "I've been fighting my feelings for you since I first saw you in that hospital bed. I kept telling myself it was only because of how much you looked like Renee. That my infatuation would fade the more I got to know you. But it didn't. It just rooted deeper." I pause, needing to catch my breath. "Then I realized that it has nothing to do with the fact that you look like her and everything to do with *you.* With who you are. A woman who would stand beside me on a battlefield and take an impossible shot because it was that or death."

She closes her eyes, and the tears spill down her cheeks. "I'm so sorry."

"You can keep your apologies," I tell her. "Because even if you are sorry for that kiss, I'm not. I'm only sorry you're making the wrong choice." I turn back toward Bobby. "We need to get back to the reception."

She doesn't follow me right away, and I don't wait to untether Bobby and climb onto his back. It's only then that she walks toward me and reaches up to give me her hand.

As I pull her up onto the horse, all I can think about is the fact that we never should have left that dance floor.

There, things were simple.

Swaying to the music, there was still a chance.

"Here we are. Home sweet home." Brett unlocks the door to my apartment and pushes it open then steps aside so I can enter first. The walls are off-white and undecorated, the couch a plush leather with a red-and-black plaid blanket over the back.

There's a small television in the corner and a fireplace that looks as though it's never held a fire. There are no pictures on shelves, no plants anywhere in sight, and the only appliance sitting on the laminate countertop is a coffeemaker.

He shuts the door behind him and flips the lock. I know it's just for safety, but this place with the doors locked—with him—feels an awful lot like a cage.

"Is it familiar?" he asks hopefully as he sets my duffel bag down.

I shake my head, and his expression falls. "I'm sorry, I don't mean to keep letting you down. I know you want me to remember."

He walks over and takes my hands in his. "Don't apologize to me, Nova. Even if you never remember a thing, we're going to get through this, okay?"

I force a smile and nod. He leans in and kisses my cheek. The action makes my stomach churn. I hate it. I hate all of this.

Why does it feel so wrong?

Because Elliot is what's right.

Tears burn in my vision, so I pull away and move around the room, looking for anything that might jog my memory. If I can remember, it will make the pain worth it. Hopefully.

"Are you getting hungry?" he asks. "I was thinking about grabbing something from that taco truck you love. It's right around the corner. We can eat in and talk? Maybe watch one of your favorite movies?"

"Sure. That sounds good. Thanks." It doesn't, but I'm in desperate need of space.

"You got it, honey. I'll be back in a few. Look around, and get reacquainted with your home, okay?"

"Will do."

He offers me a smile then leaves, locking the door behind him. Finally alone, I can breathe again, so I move into the kitchen. I go through the cabinets, looking at the small assortment of dishes behind the wooden doors.

The bathroom is no more personalized than the rest of the apartment, with a white shower curtain and an empty toothbrush holder.

Did I not have any personality? Because looking at this place now, none of it is what I would have chosen for myself. "On to the bedroom," I whisper to myself then head down the short hall.

The queen-sized bed is perfectly made up, the pale-blue comforter without a single wrinkle. Two pillow shams in the same color sit in front of two other pillows covered with white cases.

There's a Bible on the bedside table, so I cross over and raise it, running my fingers over the golden inlay with my name. *Nova O'Conner*. It's the only thing in this apartment that feels even remotely familiar.

I close my eyes as tears threaten to spill. *Lord, why can't I remember any of this? Why does it all feel so unfamiliar?* Reaching up, I touch my fingers to my lips. That kiss last night has haunted my every waking moment. Even as I tried to sleep last night, Elliot was on my mind.

The anger on his face when he'd accused me of using him.

At first, I couldn't imagine why it would feel like that. But it hit me after I'd climbed into bed. I *had* used him. I'd used him to gauge my feelings. To test the truth of them. I'd wanted to apologize, but by the time I got up this morning, Elliot was already gone.

Since he wasn't there when I went to bed, I honestly wonder if he even came home.

Guilt burns a hole through the shame, so I set my Bible aside and reach into my jacket pocket to withdraw the cell phone Brett had given me.

I scroll through the contacts, but when I realize that I never got Elliot's number, my heart falls. Then I see Lani's name. I tap the contact without hesitation because, if I can't apologize to Elliot, at least I can ask his sister to deliver my message.

"Hey, stranger. Tired of Dallas already?" she asks, tone cheerful.

"Would it be pathetic if I said yes?"

"Not at all. What's going on?"

"None of this feels familiar, Lani. You should see this place. There's *no* personality. No color, no pictures. Just blank walls and plain furniture."

"Really? You strike me as a splash-of-color type of person."

"Apparently, the old me did not agree." I take a seat on the bed. "The only thing that I found that feels even remotely familiar is a Bible with my name on it."

"It'll come back, Nova. You just have to be patient."

"And if it doesn't?" When she doesn't respond, I

continue, "What if I have to keep living this life even though it's not what I want?"

"You don't have to do anything you don't want to," she tells me. "And if your memories don't come back, you make new ones. The way you want to make them."

The memory of Elliot's hands buried in my hair assaults me. The feel of his lips on mine, my arms around his neck. "I don't know if that's a possibility anymore."

"Why not?"

"It doesn't matter. Could you do me a favor though? If you don't mind."

"Sure. What do you need?"

I hesitate. "Can you tell Elliot I'm sorry? He'll know why."

"Of course." She doesn't press, doesn't ask for more. And for that, I'm so grateful.

"Thanks."

"You're welcome. And hey, maybe you have some personality somewhere and you just need to find it."

"Oh?"

"Yeah. Maybe you were a diary girl."

I snort. "A diary girl?"

"Sure. Check all the places one might hide one. Maybe you'll find some secrets that will illuminate the splash-of-color girl I know is inside."

Laughing and completely certain I'll find nothing, I set

the Bible down and stand. "Okay. Let's see, where would one hide a diary?"

"Umm, check under the bed first. Shoeboxes. Beneath the mattress."

"You have experience with this."

"Five older brothers," she replies. "I was constantly moving it. Check. Quick. I only have another fifteen minutes before my next appointment."

"On it." I set the phone down on top of my bed then bend down and search beneath the bed. There's nothing. Not even a speck of dust, despite the fact that I've apparently been gone for quite some time. "Nothing under the bed," I say aloud.

Since it's not on speakerphone, I can't hear what she's saying, just muted mumbling. I raise the mattress and find it empty, too. Lifting the phone again, I survey the room. "Nothing there either."

"Hmm. Let's think. If I were a super-awesome detective, where would I hide a diary with all my secrets?" she says aloud.

My gaze lands on the bedside table, and a memory surfaces. I can see myself tipping it over and taping something to the bottom. "I don't believe it."

"What? Did you find it?"

"Maybe. I remembered something. Hang on." Setting the phone down on the bed, I crouch in front of the table. After moving the Bible to my bed and setting the lamp down on the ground, I pull the nightstand out and tip it, feeling up beneath the bottom.

My fingers brush something smooth, so I feel around until I find an edge.

Using my fingernails, I pry it away and pull it out.

"It's not a diary," I say aloud. "But—" I open it, and my blood chills. "Oh no." Surveillance photos of Brett are stacked inside, along with notes in my handwriting.

Has he gone dirty?

Not behaving the way he used to.

Money popping up out of nowhere.

Midnight rendezvous with Ivan on September 27th, 2024 at 7:00 p.m.

"No," I whisper the word, unsure how I'm supposed to believe what it is I'm seeing. If this is true—then I've not only let the monster close. I've literally given him the keys to my cage.

"What is that?"

I stiffen at the sound of Brett's voice. *Play it cool, Nova.* Forcing a smile, I turn toward him. "Nothing. Just some random stuff I found in the drawer. Did you get the food?"

His gaze narrows. "Come on, Nova. You can be honest with me." His tone is different and has me backing away from him, getting as close as I can to the bed.

"You're not my fiancé, are you?" I whisper.

"Sure I am." He smiles, but it's carnal. "Show me that folder, and I can help you fill in the blanks."

"No. You can't have it."

He closes his eyes and shakes his head. Both hands clench into fists at his sides, and when he levels his gaze on me once more, the façade he's been putting on since we first met slips away. Finally, the monster is visible within the man. And I was such a fool not to see it before. "We can do this the easy way or the hard way, Nova. Don't make me hurt you again."

"Again? You're the one who shot me."

"Nova, don't make this harder than it has to be. Give it to me, or I'm going to take it."

"I dare you to try," I growl, anger surging through my fear.

He betrayed me. At my weakest moment, when nothing felt real, he tricked me. And I was too foolish to see past it.

"Fine. Have it your way." He charges, and I toss the folder onto the floor then slam my fist into his face. He stops and wipes blood from his lip. "I always did like to play rough."

Fear chills me, but I know, if I give up now, I'll die. Here in this apartment, there's no escape. It really is a cage.

He swings, and I move, but not fast enough. His fist catches my shoulder, and I fall backward, hitting the wall. Brett snarls and lunges for me, but I roll out of the way, and he puts his fist through the wall. I grip the bedside table and swing it—hard. It hits him, so I grab the folder from the ground and sprint down the hall.

I have to get out.

If I can just get—

A hand closes around my hair and rips me back.

I scream.

My head slams into something hard.

And everything goes black.

CHAPTER 26
ELLIOT

The white house in front of me shouldn't be nearly as intimidating as it is. I've faced down killers on a battlefield, enemies both stateside and abroad, yet sitting here staring at a blue door is bringing me far more anxiety than any battle has.

I told myself that coming to Dallas right after Nova did was a mistake, but when I woke this morning in Riley's guest room because I was too afraid to go home and face Nova, I had a feeling in my gut that I needed to do this. That it was finally time to try to put the past behind me.

So, here I am.

Staring at a blue door from the safety of my truck.

"Just do it, Hunt." Before I can talk myself out of it, I push the door open and head up the steps. Pretty purple and pink hydrangeas are blooming in pots on either side of the door, and the sight of them makes my heart hurt.

Jesse's favorite color was pink.

Renee's purple.

I raise my fist and knock, seriously hoping no one is home. But seconds later, the door is pulled open, and Renee's father, James, steps into view. "Sir."

"Elliot. Finally made it to the door?"

I swallow hard, embarrassment heating my cheeks. I'm a coward. An absolute coward. "May I come in?"

"Absolutely." He steps aside and lets me through.

The living room still looks exactly the same as it did the last time I was here, the only thing missing: Renee smiling from the floral-printed couch. Something sweet fills my lungs, the aroma of baked goods wrapping around me.

"Who is it?" I hear Susan call out.

"Elliot Hunt."

"What?" She steps out of the kitchen, brown eyes wide. They're the same shade as Renee's. Her hair the same bright red, though now there are strands of gray woven through.

"Hi, Mrs. Young."

She smiles softly. "Come, have a seat. Would you like something to drink?"

"No, thank you. I was hoping I could have a few minutes of your time." I take a seat on the couch. "I know it's out of the blue, and I'm sorry for that."

"Not a problem, honey." She takes a seat beside her husband on the couch across from me.

Leaning forward, I clasp my hands together. "I'm sorry that I haven't reached out before now. I'd say it's because I've been busy, but that's a lie. The truth is I'm ashamed."

"Of what?" Susan asks, gaze narrowing.

"Of failing you. You lost both of your girls because I was distracted." Emotion sears my throat. "I let my personal feelings cloud me, and I missed signs."

"Oh, honey." Susan leans forward and covers my hand with hers. "We've never blamed you, Elliot. No one saw his true intentions. No one could have possibly seen that he was after Renee."

"I failed. You hired me to help, and I let you down."

"You brought our girls justice," James replies. "Because of you, he's serving two life sentences in prison without the chance of parole."

A tear slips down my cheek. "I should have seen it. I should have stopped it."

Susan squeezes my hand. "We've seen you outside the house every year on her birthday since we buried her."

"You have?"

"Your big truck isn't exactly a discreet white van," James quips.

I chuckle. "Fair enough. I wanted to be here. To apologize. But I couldn't get myself out of the truck. The guilt over my failure and the pain of losing her—of losing them both. It's weighed on me every single day."

"You got out of the truck today," Susan replies. "And

that's what matters." She stands. "I'm going to go get us some coffee."

"I would be lying if I didn't admit my anger after we lost them," James says. "The fury I felt at both of my angels being so brutally ripped away." He closes his eyes a moment, and when he opens them, they're full of tears. "But my anger was never at you, Elliot. And if I had known you were struggling with that, well, I like to think I would've reached out myself."

"It wouldn't have changed how I felt," I admit.

"Renee cared for you," he says. "And we all know that you did your absolute best. It was you piecing together the puzzle that brought him to justice. Without you putting it all together, he might have gotten away."

"I just can't help but think that if I'd have just realized it sooner—"

"Things don't work that way," he says. "It's taken me three years to get to where I am today, and I certainly still have bad days. But I know that God has a plan. He can take even the darkest circumstances and make something good come out of it."

"What good came from their deaths?" I ask, vocalizing a question I've been too afraid to ask myself.

He smiles. "Come here. I want to show you something." James stands and heads down the hall. I follow, doing my best to keep my focus straight ahead and not on the photographs lining the walls.

We head into the first room on the right, a bedroom that used to belong to Jesse. It's now been turned into an office with a bulletin board and a desk. James sits down behind it and opens his laptop. After a few moments of typing, he turns it to face me.

"What's this?"

"The good," he replies. "Susan and I started a nonprofit that helps educate college students on self-defense and recognizing red flags before they become deadly. We've had no less than eleven girls, in the two years since we started, come to us and tell us that it was this class that helped them get out of dangerous situations."

Pride swells in my chest. "This is fantastic."

He smiles. "It's still a work in progress, but we're doing what we can to expand our reach. We have an anonymous tip line where people can report things they've seen, in hopes we can intervene and offer help."

"Mr. Young, this is—"

"James," he interrupts. "It wasn't just them who inspired us. What you and your brothers do is amazing. While we're not trained like you are, Susan and I knew we wanted to do something—anything—that might keep other families from going through what we did." He takes a deep breath. "I would rather have my daughters back, Elliot. But this feels like a good thing."

"It's a great thing," I tell him. "You're honoring them with this."

He smiles, and tears glisten in his eyes. "That's all I want." He shuts the laptop and stands. "Now, let's go have that coffee."

FEELING LIGHTER than I have in years, I climb into my truck. I'm just turning over the engine when my phone rings and Lani's contact pops up on the screen. "Hey, you won't—"

"Elliot, you have to get to her!" Lani's panicked voice washes away all the peace I'd had only moments ago.

"Who? What's wrong?"

"Nova! He's attacking her. I could hear the whole thing. He—"

Fury coils in my belly, a viper poised to attack, even as fear laces my blood. "Who hurt her?"

"Brett. He's hurting her, Elliot."

My hand clenches on the steering wheel. *I'm going to tear him apart.* "Where is she?"

"Her apartment. But I don't have the address."

"I'll get to her." I end the call and phone Tucker.

"What's up?"

"Get me Nova's address now," I demand. "She's in danger. I'm already in Dallas, so text it to me."

All humor from his tone is gone when he replies, "On it."

Lord, please let her be okay.

Seconds later, a text comes through with Nova's address. *Nova, please hang in there. I'm coming.*

CHAPTER 27
NOVA

"Come on," I urge as I try to twist and break the zip ties currently binding my wrists to the arms of this chair. If I can just get a wrist free, then I can work to break the others binding my ankles to the legs of the chair. Unfortunately, the arms have no give, and the zip ties are secure. No matter how raw I rub my wrists, there's no getting them loose.

I shift my gaze around the dank basement, searching for anything I could use to get free. It's empty, though, except for the chair I'm sitting in. Tall brick walls surround me, and the concrete floor beneath my chair is covered in plastic.

I close my eyes and suck in a breath. I will *not* go down like this. Did I really escape the first time only to die? My thoughts drift back to Elliot.

His handsome face.

Strong arms holding me as we danced.

Tears blur my vision. I'll never get the chance to apologize. To tell him that I want more. That leaving him on that ranch was a huge mistake. And not just because the man I trusted turned out to be the same one who put a bullet in me in the first place.

No. I will not die like this. "This is going to hurt." I take a deep breath then jerk my body to the right. The chair rocks a bit.

I do it again—this time harder. Then again. It falls over, hitting the ground with a heavy thud, right with my head. Pain explodes behind my eye. I try to jerk my arm, hoping that if I can just crack the wooden armrest, I'll be able to break it free the rest of the way.

A small crack.

Hope.

Then a door opens. "You just can't leave well enough alone, can you?" Brett asks as he hoists my chair back up.

I glare at him.

"Nothing to say? That's a first. Normally you're quite chatty." Crossing his arms, he leans against the wall across from me. "Fine. You can just listen. I searched your entire apartment, tearing everything apart, and found no sign of the evidence you stole."

"What evidence?"

"Don't play cute with me. I know you remember now."

"Excuse me? What gave you that impression?"

"The folder you found tucked away beneath your night-stand. Great hiding place, by the way. I didn't even notice it when I'd searched the place."

"Just because I found one thing doesn't mean I remember anything."

"Sure it does." He crosses over and leans down, placing both hands on my legs to hold himself up. "And you're going to come clean, Nova, or things are going to get really messy."

"How about you tell me what it is you think I stole? That way, it might jog my memory."

He glares at me. "Nah. We'll get to the bottom of it one way or another." He pushes up, and the door opens behind me again, scraping against the floor as it does.

"This is such a pleasant, albeit unexpected, surprise."

Ivan. I recognize his voice, though it's not until he steps into my line of sight that I realize I'm not imagining it. "You're dead."

He smiles, and the sight of it makes my skin crawl. "No, I'm not. But I appreciate the concern. Brett, give us a minute."

"But, sir—"

"Give. Us. A. Minute," he orders, glaring at Brett.

Brett looks from him to me then back to him, and nods before leaving the room. It's not until the door scrapes and closes that Ivan crosses his arms and studies me.

"I don't remember anything."

"Yes, Brett filled me in on your predicament. Here's the thing though. I've learned that even those who can't seem to remember a thing can be motivated under the right circumstances."

Fear gnaws at my insides. "So, what, you're going to torture it out of me?"

"If I have to," he replies. "I'd really rather not. The idea of hurting you is distasteful."

"Why is that?"

"You know I always favored you. When I found out that you were protecting Brett, I was absolutely appalled. Heartbroken, even. You were my most trusted ally, someone I'd hoped to eventually build a future with, and you broke my trust."

I protected him? "What do you mean, I protected him?"

Ivan arches a brow. "You really don't remember, do you? Shame. Well, since you're such a captive audience, how about I fill you in? I suspected Brett—rather Patterson, as I knew him—and you buried it. Nearly had me convinced that I was overreacting, and it was a complete coincidence that my rival knew exactly when we were moving product and was able to intercept and steal from me."

"If he stole from you, then why is he alive?"

"Because he traded me important information in exchange for his life."

"What information?"

He takes a step closer. "That I had not one, not two, but three other untrustworthy people in my ranks. Including the woman I'd allowed close enough to learn far too much about me."

"Me?"

He smiles, a carnal grin that chills me. "You were one of them. The other, if you remember, *was* your old partner. I'm surprised you don't remember his death. You were present for it, after all." He laughs, and my stomach twists as a wave of grief washes over me. For once, I'm happy I can't remember. "The man actually cried when I put a bullet in him. Pleaded for his life."

Tears sting my eyes even as I can't remember his face. "You're a monster."

He doesn't even bother responding. "And Chelsea—or rather Rosalie—well, she didn't say much. Though Brett's the one who carried out that order. He was supposed to deliver her body to the same rival who stole my product. A gift from me to him since she'd double-crossed me and was also feeding him information in exchange for payment." He takes a deep breath and studies me. "However, after you were found wearing one of his shirts, he thought it best to use her to throw the cops off the trail by making them think it was a serial killer." He grins. "It did the trick since he sent photographs instead of a body deliver."

"You're sick."

"No, I'm practical. A businessman," he replies. "Then

there's you,… According to Brett, you didn't take payment, and somehow that makes you worse. I hate a moral cop. Believing you're so high above everyone else."

"If you needed evidence, why kill me?"

"Brett was sure it was at your apartment. He was certain we didn't need you. By the time we realized he was wrong, it was too late. But then, wasn't it handy that your beautiful face graced the screen of my computer after you were found in that creek? How fortuitous." He smiles, and I can all but picture venom dripping from his teeth.

I glare back at him, trying so hard to keep on a brave face. "I don't have what you're looking for. And even if I did, I don't remember."

Ivan shrugs. "Whether you remember or not, you're a loose end, Nova O'Conner. And loose ends have to be clipped." With no warning, he slams his fist into my jaw.

My head whips back, and pain shoots through the side of my face and down into my neck from the force of the blow.

Ivan grips my legs, squeezing so tightly I have to choke on a cry as pain shoots up through my thighs. "It's all up to you, Nova. We can do this the easy way, or the painful way."

I glare up at him, blood trickling from my mouth. "Do your worst," I growl as rage burns through the fear. If I die here, it won't be whimpering and pleading for my life. I won't give him the satisfaction.

Ivan releases me and takes a few steps back. He studies me, likely gauging whether or not he believes I truly don't remember. What he doesn't realize, though, is that it really doesn't matter whether I remember or not. Clearly, *past* me wanted to make sure that evidence was well hidden. There's no way I'd tell them where to find it.

Not even to save my own life.

Lord, please. Please help me. Please. I wish I could touch the cross around my neck. Wish I could feel it against my fingers. I lean on Him now though, praying for a rescue I'm not sure is headed my way.

"You're not leaving this place until I have those files in my hands," he tells me. "And since we have time, how about we see if we can jog your memory?"

CHAPTER 28
ELLIOT

Blood stains the carpet in her bedroom.

It's not a lot but enough that I know someone didn't walk out of here uninjured. Since we haven't heard from her, my money is on Brett abducting her. Fear tries to claw its way to the surface, but I need a clear head, so I beat it back down.

I missed something—again. Blinded by my own feelings, I'd been unable to discern my dislike for Brett as anything more than jealousy. Now I know it was more. That the distrust I carried for him meant something.

I'm just too late—again.

I can't lose her.

God, please don't let me lose her.

"The place was wiped clean at some point before this attack," Dylan says.

"You think someone cleaned up after tossing the place?" I ask.

He nods. "There's not even dust under the bed. If she were gone for as long as Brett claims, there should have been a dust bunny or two. Couple that with the missing personal items, I'd say a lot of it got destroyed and he had to replace what he could in a hurry."

"I just got off the phone with the captain of their precinct," Gibson says as he strolls into the apartment. Even though we're nowhere near his jurisdiction, he'd offered to come with us anyway to lend a hand with local police. "Brett hasn't made contact recently, and the captain never spoke with Nova."

"She said she talked to him." I recall how proud she was when she'd told me what he'd said about her being the best he had.

"It must have been fake. Brett set it up."

"The pictures?"

"Those were real," Gibson replies. "According to the captain, Nova and Brett were engaged for about a year before she called it off. That was right before she was placed undercover along with her partner, Sam Calloway. He was found dead shortly before you found Nova in that creek. Shot to death."

My stomach churns. Will Nova's body be the next one that washes up?

"Did they not think it was strange that Brett hadn't checked in?"

"He stopped checking in about a week ago." Gibson crosses his arms. "The captain said he's a good detective. Relatively quiet, but he had a jealous side, which is what led to him and Nova splitting. Despite the fact that Sam was engaged himself, Brett kept accusing Nova of having an affair."

"I could've told you he was jealous," I growl, recalling how he'd confronted me in the barn. What I wouldn't give to be able to go back and tear him apart right there. What if that's why he took her? What if that's why he's hurting her now? Because of me? "Does he know of anywhere he would have taken her?"

"He sent me an address," he replies, holding up his phone. "I asked him to send uniforms over for us, and he agreed."

"She won't be there," I reply. "He'll have taken her somewhere hard to find."

"Family?" Bradyn asks. He postponed the honeymoon he and Kennedy were supposed to be going on tomorrow and has been by my side since arriving an hour after I did.

"None. Guy had no ties to anything or anyone but Nova."

I survey her bedroom, trying to imagine what happened here. Her cell phone is still lying on the bed where she'd left it, her Bible beside it. I cross over, lift the leather-bound book into my hand, and run my finger over the name engraved on the front.

God, I can't do this alone. I know I need You. Please don't let me fail again. Please guide me toward her.

As I turn the book over in my hands, I note a photo that's stuck to the back leather. Peeling it off, I stare down at a surveillance photo of Brett and Ivan shaking hands. My blood runs cold.

He was in on it.

Is he the one who shot her? Did he do it for Ivan? Is he the one who handed her over?

My thoughts are going a million miles a minute as I run through everything we know. Brett told us Ivan was dead.

He showed me the email from his captain.

But if he never spoke to the captain, then that means Ivan is likely still alive. Alive and looking to tie up any potential loose ends. And I let Nova leave with Brett, my pride too wounded to even bother fighting for her.

"I got them!" Tucker yells from the living room.

Keeping the Bible and photograph in hand, I rush out of the bedroom and join three of my brothers and Gibson in the living room. Tucker is seated at the small dining table, and he turns the computer around to face us, showing off a traffic camera image.

Even though it's grainy, I can make out Brett's face as he drives.

Got you.

"I tracked the vehicle when it went through some toll booths. He exited at Highway 75 and was headed north."

"Back toward our neck of the woods," Gibson replies.

"I don't see Nova," Dylan says, leaning in to study the picture.

"She's in there," I reply. "And I think I know where they're headed." I toss the photo down on the table. "Get me an address for Ivan."

"On it," Tucker replies.

"I'll make some calls," Gibson offers as he heads for the door. "I shouldn't be here while Tucker breaks laws anyway."

"Love you like a brother," Tucker calls out as Gibson leaves the room.

Their banter is not unusual, and normally it lightens even the darkest moods. But right now, it's frustrating, especially when I feel so absolutely helpless to do anything but wait for answers. I step out onto the balcony and breathe in the fresh air while still clinging to the Bible.

"You okay, brother?" Bradyn steps up beside me.

"I knew better than to let my feelings get in the way."

"You have to stop blaming yourself for making mistakes. Having feelings for Nova didn't cloud your judgment. Brett fooled all of us. He's a cop. He has a badge. Tucker even looked into him and found nothing suspicious. None of us—even me—got a read on him as being anything more than what he claimed to be."

"You weren't there when he confronted me after your rehearsal dinner."

"No, I wasn't," Bradyn agrees. "But I doubt he held up a sign that said he was a dirty cop."

"He told me to drop the case and let the 'real cops' handle it. I thought he was just being a jealous fiancé, but he was trying to keep me away because he knew we'd find something." I shake my head angrily.

"It's not your fault," Bradyn tells me. "And we're going to find her."

"I won't stop until I do." I rest my gaze on his. "And, Bradyn, I can't be sure I'll let him survive if I get my hands on him."

"Guys." Gibson peeks his head out. "Brett's apartment was empty, but Tucker has a confirmed address for Ivan's place. Ready to head out?"

"Absolutely." I keep the Bible in my hand as I walk out of Nova's apartment. Blood is pounding in my ears as I climb behind the wheel and set the Bible on the console between me and Bradyn, who's climbed into the passenger seat.

He plugs the address into my GPS, and I pull away from Nova's apartment, my mind on one thing. Rescuing her and destroying anyone who gets in my way.

I'm coming, Nova.

CHAPTER 29

NOVA

My head hurts, but I'm alive. Even if I am a bit more bruised than I was a few hours ago.

"It doesn't have to be this hard," Brett insists as he kneels in front of me. "Come on, you have to be hungry. Thirsty?" He reaches up and brushes some hair behind my ear in what I'm sure he believes to be a tender gesture.

In reality, it only churns my stomach.

"I'm fine. Pretty comfortable, actually." I force a smile.

He shakes his head. "You always were stubborn. Seems that part of your personality didn't leave when you lost your memories."

"You mean when you tried to kill me?" I ask.

"You didn't leave me a choice. I know you can't see it now, but you will."

"When? After I'm dead?"

"That's just it, though." He smiles. "If you hand over the evidence, you don't have to die. We can go to Ivan together, plead for your life."

I stare at him. Is he really that stupid? That he believes Ivan isn't going to kill him, too, the moment he has those files? "You can't really think Ivan is going to let you live."

"He's already assured me he will. And a seat at his right hand with the paycheck to prove it."

I literally cannot tear my gaze away as I search his expression for a sign that he's making this up. That he doesn't truly believe things will work out that way. There's none. He actually believes every word of what he's saying. "Brett, Ivan is going to kill you. I may not remember anything, but I *do* know that."

He shakes his head. "You're wrong, and it's going to cost you your life." He slides to his knees beside me. "Come on, Nova. Don't do this. We have a second chance."

"Are you kidding me?" I glare at him. "Do you seriously think there would *ever* be a chance for us?"

A muscle in his jaw flexes. Should I be taunting a violent man when I'm tied to a chair? Probably not. Then again—his rage might be just what I need. A partial plan forms in my mind.

"We worked before. We could work again."

"I doubt it," I deadpan, trying to channel all of my anger into this one interaction. If I can just make him angry enough, then he might get violent enough to break the chair for me. That is if I survive the assault. *One problem at a time.*

Brett grabs a folding chair he'd carried down earlier and sets it up in front of me then sits down in it. "We were in love, Nova."

"You were in love. I was too foolish to see the monster behind the man."

His expression darkens. "We were in love," he repeats. "You asked me out first, did you know that?" he asks. "Walked right up to my desk and told me to meet you at Gio's."

"Who's Gio? Another psychotic friend of yours? Was it a double date?"

"An Italian restaurant," he replies. "It was also where I proposed." I don't respond because I'm not even remotely interested in hearing the rest of that story. "I almost didn't go, but you were so—fiery," he says with a smile. "A ball of flame that I just couldn't help but be drawn to."

My stomach churns. "That was in the past."

"It's not, though. You were so happy to see me again. To sit across from me in that café and talk about our past."

"And how much of that was the truth, I wonder?" Are my parents really dead? Do I really have no friends?

"Oh, all of it." He scoots closer. "Every word of it was the truth."

"Seems to me you omitted a whole lot of information. You know, like how you're a murderer and partnered with the same man who ordered my death and killed my partner."

"Killing you was the hardest thing I ever had to do. I threw up afterward. I couldn't eat, couldn't sleep."

"Probably because you were busy tearing my apartment apart, looking for the evidence you needed."

"I loved you, Nova. You may not believe it, but I loved you. I gave you a chance before you took off into those trees. You chose not to take it."

"What chance was that? Hold still and you'll make it quick?"

"I didn't want to kill you. I came here, to this place, to try to win you back. All of this started because I was desperate to get close to you again."

Interest piqued, I decide to bite. "What is that supposed to mean?"

He stands and begins to pace. "You were working this case with Sam." He turns to stare at me. "I knew Sam was weak, and I was worried he would break and get you killed. So I initiated contact with Ivan, hoping to get inside his organization so I could protect you." He sits back down in the chair and faces me. "When you first saw me, you were, admittedly, less than pleased, but we worked together to gather that evidence. Evidence you then stole from me."

"And then you tried to kill me. I know the end of the story."

"You don't even know half of it," he snaps. "Your

precious Sam nearly got you killed. I was so furious that I knew we couldn't wait any longer to get the evidence, so I broke into Ivan's office. Then I used what I found to tip off his competition so he'd be distracted. That way, I could get you out."

"Except you got Sam murdered. And not just Sam, but also the woman Ivan was seeing at the time, and—oh yeah —me."

"But you didn't die. Don't you see? We're meant to be together. We have a second chance. If you give me that information, I can buy our freedom with Ivan. Then, we can leave and start again."

"Let me see if I can make this any clearer for you." I lean forward as far as my bindings allow. "I have no interest in ever, *ever* being anything to you except the woman who puts you behind bars."

Brett's expression twists, turning furious in the span of a heartbeat. "Why is that? So you can go play cowboy?"

That's right. Get mad. "Excuse me?"

"I saw the way you were looking at him. Standing in his house in your pajamas." He shakes his head. "You'd already decided you wanted him, didn't you? It didn't matter that we were engaged. That you'd promised to share your life with me."

"I'm sorry, didn't you just say you plunged headfirst into *my* case to win me back? Which leads me to believe we weren't actually engaged."

"We were," he insists. "You gave it back to me right before you left. Told me it wasn't the right time."

"Well, seems *past* me wasn't completely blind." I straighten in the chair, wishing the arm of the chair was loose enough to get free.

"Where's your cowboy now?" he sneers, making a show of it by looking around the room. "I don't see him now. If he's so good at finding people, then why hasn't he come looking for you?"

I swallow hard, feeling the heartache all over again. *Because I didn't give him a reason to.*

"Ahh, there's the pain. I see it all over your face. Perfect." He leans in closer. "Now, how about we try another route? Either you tell me where I can find that evidence, or I'm going to go start taking out my frustrations on those hicks you were bunked up with. Maybe I'll start with their mother."

The blood in my veins turns to ice, and I stiffen. All desire to anger him dissipates because it's no longer just me in the crosshairs. "You won't touch them."

"Won't I?" he asks, leaning in even closer. We're only a breath apart. "I know the property now. I know where the parents sleep. All it would take is slipping in there, and no one would even know until Mother Hunt wasn't downstairs making breakfast."

"You will not touch her." My gaze drops, and I note a

dagger sheathed in the top of his boot. That's what I need. My ticket out of here so I can warn them.

"Maybe I'll bring you pictures. No one will ever even know it was me picking them off one by one. Not until your precious cowboy is left. I'll let him see me. Right before I drive a dagger into his heart."

I snap. Rearing my head back, I slam it into his. He roars in anger, practically exploding out of his chair. *Perfect. Use that temper. I only need one chance. Just one.* "How dare you!" He lifts the chair I'm tied to and throws it. I hit the ground with a painful thud, my entire body taking the brunt of it.

But it's exactly what I needed. Adrenaline shooting through my system, I rip my arm free from the broken armrest then kick my leg out.

He lurches toward me, but I roll, bringing what's left of the chair with me.

"You're going to pay for that!" he bellows.

I swing the chunk of wood still attached to my free wrist as hard as I can. It hits him in the side of the head, and he stumbles back. Using my free leg, I swipe out and knock him to the ground then slam that same foot into his face.

Bone crunches, and he falls still, eyes rolling back in his head.

Heart pounding, I drag myself closer and rip his dagger free then slice the two zip ties still attached to the chair from my wrist and ankle. The others can wait. Right now, I need to get out of here before he wakes up or Ivan discovers me.

Now free, I search Brett's pockets. Grabbing his gun and a set of keys, I creep toward the stairs. Pain radiates through my body from its impact with the floor, but I focus on freedom. I can't stop now. No matter how badly it hurts.

The house above is dark with only a lamp turned on at the end of the hall. There are no doors open, so I keep moving, not wanting to take any time trying to clear them. I descend a flight of stairs and sprint toward the front door.

Shoes thudding against the smooth tile, I reach the front and rip it open.

An alarm screeches, but I don't hesitate. I hit the lock button on the key fob in my hand and race toward the car that beeps, moving as fast as my aching body allows.

Every muscle in my body hurts, every inch of me burning, but I push on because I have to. They have to know he's coming. That he's planning to make them pay for my mistakes.

They have to know the truth.

I jump into the car and speed out of the driveway, racing as fast as I can down the road. With no idea where I am, all I can do is open the digital map on the dashboard and type in Pine Creek.

My vision wavers, but I blink rapidly and roll the

window down so the cool air will hopefully help keep me alert long enough to get there.

I'm coming.

BY THE GRACE OF GOD, I manage to make it onto the ranch. The gate is locked, though, so I get out of the car and make the walk up the drive. Adrenaline waning, my body begins to shake, but I continue putting one foot in front of the other, focusing only on getting to where I need to go.

If I can make it to the main house, they'll call Elliot. Then everything will be fine because they'll know. Gravel crunches beneath my shoes, so I focus on that sound rather than the pain in my body.

Almost there.

Bright lights illuminate me overhead, and I stop walking.

"Nova?" Tommy Hunt calls out as he steps into the beam of the lights, a rifle in his hands.

Tears fill my eyes, and I sink to my knees, my entire body finally giving in to the exhaustion. "It's me!" I call out. "I got here in time."

He rushes toward me then kneels down at my side. "Let's get you inside, okay?"

"He's coming for you," I tell him as he pulls me to my

feet then helps me toward the small utility vehicle. "He's coming for all of you."

"We'll handle that later. Let's get you back to the house, okay?" He helps me into the seat and buckles me in.

"How did you know I was there?"

"Security monitor on the front gate picked you up." He places the rifle back on the gun rack behind us then lifts his phone. "I'll call Lani."

"No. Please don't. The fewer of you that are here, the better. I'll be okay. It looks worse than it is."

He casts me a side glance as he drives. "It looks pretty bad."

"I'll be fine. I just need Elliot. Call Elliot. Keep Lani out of this, please. At least, for now."

"Okay." He comes to a stop in front of the house. Ruth rushes down the steps, and tears fill my eyes as I use what strength I have to rise to my feet and throw my arms around her.

"Oh, honey. Come on. Let's get you inside." She helps me out, and Tommy comes to my other side. Together, they help me up the stairs even though my body has all but given up on moving.

They guide me over toward the couch and help me down. She covers me with a blanket.

"I'm calling Elliot. Grab the first aid kit."

"What about Lani?" she asks.

"No," he says. "Nova said we need to keep her out of it for now."

She nods, lips flattened in a tight line, then rushes out of the room.

Tommy sits beside me and taps the screen of his phone. He puts it up to his ear, and I lean back, closing my eyes. *I made it. Thank You, God. I know You're the only reason I was strong enough.*

"Elliot. She's here," I hear Tommy say. "Nova is here."

CHAPTER 30
ELLIOT

Nova is here.

I sprint up the steps and burst into my parent's house, all of my brothers and Gibson on my heels. My first sight of Nova, sitting on the couch, covered in blood, brings a wave of red into my vision.

But then she looks at me, an expression of relief crossing her face, and all that anger drains away. She's alive. Here. With me. I rush over toward her and take a seat on the coffee table, directly in front of her. My mom hands me the first aid kit she'd been using to clean the injuries on Nova's face then squeezes my shoulder and leaves the living room.

I don't have to look back to know that everyone else went into the kitchen, leaving the two of us alone.

"I'm sorry," she chokes out. "I'm so sorry for what I said."

"Don't worry about that now." I dab the cleaning pad on her split brow, wiping crusted blood from it before using a butterfly strip to secure it. "How did you get away?"

"I made him angry," she replies with a half-smile. A cut on her lip has her wincing, though, and the smile falls. "He flung the chair I was tied to, and it broke. I was able to knock him out and get free."

"You made him angry so he'd break the chair?"

She nods. "I had to get free. He's coming for all of you, Elliot. He said he's going to kill you guys if I don't give him the evidence I apparently stole." Tears fill her eyes, spilling down her bruised cheeks.

I reach down and take her hands, trying not to lose my mind at the sight of red bands where zip ties were bound or the fact that there's still one around her right wrist. "He's not going to get to us," I tell her then reach into my pocket to withdraw my knife so I can cut it away.

She shakes her head. "Ivan is alive. There weren't any guards at the place I escaped from, but he'll have an army behind him."

"We've fended off worse," I tell her. "Right now, the only thing that matters is that you're here. You're alive." My own eyes fill, and I lean forward, resting my forehead against hers. "Thank God you're alive."

We sit like this for a few moments with just the sound of muted voices coming out of the kitchen.

Then, I pull away. "We're going to get you cleaned up, and then we'll figure everything out, okay?"

She nods. "I was so stupid. How could I not see?"

"None of us did," I tell her truthfully. "Not until Lani called."

Her brow furrows. "What?"

"You were on the phone with Lani when Brett showed up at the apartment. She heard the whole thing and called me."

"I was?" Her gaze goes distant as she thinks back over the course of the last forty-eight hours. I can see the moment it hits her. "I was. She was listening to the whole thing."

"Yes," he replies. "Brett didn't notice the phone was on. The call didn't end until she hung up to call me."

"And you came for me." It seems to surprise her that I did. Which makes absolutely zero sense.

"Why would you think I wouldn't?"

"After what I did. After what I said—"

"You were doing what you thought was right. I may not like it, but it would never have prevented me from coming for you, Nova. Nothing could have."

FRESHLY SHOWERED, Nova is no longer covered in blood. She also seems to have come down from the adrenaline rush, so her body is no longer shaking. But looking at her, all I can think about is tearing Brett apart. All I can *see* is the cut over her forehead, the bruises on the right side of her face, her split lip, and the red rings around her wrists.

I want to rip him to pieces for ever putting his hands on her.

She sits at the dining room table between my mother and Kennedy while Bradyn, Riley, Tucker, and our father take up all but one of the other chairs. I considered sitting, but with the fury pumping through my veins, sitting just isn't an option.

So I remain where I am, leaning back against the countertop. No one between me and that door.

"Tell us what happened," Bradyn says.

Tucker sits with his laptop, prepared to type up notes just as he is during every case we take.

"I was talking to Lani on the phone, telling her how ridiculous I felt being in that apartment. How there was no personality, nothing that even felt remotely like me, aside from the Bible with my name on it." A Bible she holds in her lap now since I brought it back with me. "She'd made a joke suggesting I look for a diary, so that's what I did. I was surveying the room when I had a memory of placing something beneath the nightstand. When I looked beneath it, I found a false bottom that popped off and a file tucked away."

"What was in the file? In as much detail as you can give me," Tucker says.

"Mostly notes. There was one that said, "Has he gone dirty?" Another that noted how his behavior had changed. And another about money popping up from nowhere. The last note that I read said that he'd met with Ivan." She closes her eyes, likely trying to recall more information. "September twenty-seventh, I think. 7:00 p.m." She sighs. "He came in before I could go through the rest of them. He asked me what I'd found, and I tried to play it off, but it was like he was a different person all of a sudden. The façade he'd been putting on was gone. Anyway, he attacked me, and I tried to get to the door. I felt him grip my hair—" She reaches up and touches the back of her head, and another burst of anger surges through me. "Then everything went black."

My mom reaches over and covers Nova's hand with hers. "You're safe now, honey," she says.

"I made a mistake." She looks at me now, her emerald gaze shimmering with tears. And I know, right now, she's speaking directly to me. "I shouldn't have gone. I should have trusted my gut instead of doing what I felt obligated to do."

"You're back now. And we're going to nail this guy," Riley tells her.

She looks away from me.

"I hate to do this, but I need to know what happened

afterward," Gibson says. He's been silent through most of this, taking his own notes as she talked.

"I understand." She smiles, but it's hollow. "I woke up tied to a chair. He told me that I'd stolen evidence and he needed me to tell him where it was. Said that, if I could, then he would plead for my life with Ivan so we could start all over again."

"He thought you were still going to move forward with the engagement? Even after the kidnapping and assault?" My dad shakes his head. "Unbelievable."

"He's also got some twisted impression that Ivan isn't going to kill him the second he gets his hands on the evidence."

"I should note that we spoke to your captain," Gibson says. "He hasn't spoken to Brett in weeks, and he wasn't the one you talked to."

"I figured as much." She takes a deep breath. "Ivan told me he always favored me and didn't want to hurt me but that he was determined to make me remember. Said that he found certain circumstances could make people open up."

"So Brett was working for Ivan."

"Not at first. According to Brett, I gave him back the engagement ring before I went undercover with my partner, Sam. He said he was worried Sam would get me killed, so he went rogue and initiated contact with Ivan outside of the PD. According to him, I was furious when I saw him there, but at that point, he was already in good favor with Ivan."

More anger. This time more subdued, but it's still there. They'd been separated, and Brett convinced her otherwise, trying to use the fact that she couldn't remember ending things to restart a relationship she didn't want to be in. No wonder she had no feelings for him. Her heart knew what her head couldn't remember.

"How did he get in good with Ivan?" Bradyn questions.

"I'm not sure. But he was the first person Ivan suspected of selling him out to a rival. Which, as it turns out, Brett did. And Rosalie was also working for that same rival. Whether she was contacted after I recruited her or not, I'm not sure." She closes her eyes a moment and shakes her head. "I was his head of security. He trusted me, but when he discovered Brett was the mole and went to kill him, Brett offered up Sam and me in exchange for his life."

I push off the counter and clench my hands into fists. "Coward."

"Yes," she says. "Exactly. He's the one who shot me. They thought they didn't need me. That Brett could find the evidence I'd stolen."

"Did they?" Tucker asks.

"No. They still don't know where it is. Ivan wants it bad though. And Brett believes finding it will land him a partnership with Ivan."

"It sounds like Brett owes Ivan a debt," Riley comments. "Let's just find and withhold the evidence, let that problem work itself out."

"Except that won't work," Bradyn says. "Ivan believes Nova has it. Unless we can find it and put him away, he'll keep coming after her."

"Do we have enough that we can get him for kidnapping?" I ask Gibson.

"We should have enough that I can get a warrant and search Ivan's Texas residence. But this isn't the first time he's dealt with the law. They've suspected his illegal dealings for years but haven't been able to pin anything on him. Chances are he has someone in his pocket that will alert him to the search."

"Then we don't give him a reason to believe one is coming," Dylan replies.

"Exactly," I add.

"And this is my cue," Gibson says as he heads for the door. "Just speaking in hypotheticals here, but if you were to go in without a warrant, what you find won't be admissible. You'll need that original evidence and Nova's testimony to put them both away."

"Noted."

"Let me know what you need from me. I'm going to do what I can to track Brett down—quietly." Gibson smiles kindly at Nova. "I'm glad you're okay."

"Thanks."

"Stick close to Lani until this blows over, okay?" Bradyn asks. "I doubt she'll go for another temporary relocation here, so if you don't mind—"

"I'll keep her safe," Gibson promises. "Call me if you find anything."

"We will," I tell him. With one final smile, he turns and leaves the room.

"Any idea where this evidence is?" Tucker asks.

Nova shakes her head. "Not a clue. I found that file under my nightstand, but there was nothing else. It's possible Brett missed it at my apartment; we could go back there and look."

"Tomorrow," I tell her. "You need rest."

"I'm not going to be able to rest until I know all of you are safe," she insists. "He said he's coming. That no one will see him coming until it's too late. He threatened your mother." She looks at my mom, who smiles tightly at her.

"I'm not as fragile as I look," she assures with a pat on Nova's hand.

"No one is getting to any of us," my father growls. "We'll make sure of it."

"We're safe," I assure her. "We've got security cameras around the residences, and one of us will be posted up here at all times monitoring them. Plus, the dogs will alert us if anyone gets close to the house. Nova and I will stay here in your guest rooms," I tell my parents. "Just in case."

"Elliot—" Nova starts.

"Sleep, Nova. Resting isn't weakness, it's storing up your strength. Get rest while you can. There's no telling when this is going to hit the fan." I leave the room, desperately needing some air.

A few seconds after I've stepped out onto the porch, my dad follows me out. "How are you doing, son?"

"She's alive."

"She is."

I let out a breath, feeling the fear of losing her lessen just slightly. "I'm struggling with what I want to do and what I know I should do."

"Then talk to me."

My dad has always been someone who understood the darkest parts of my brothers and me. The pieces that were shaded in by our time overseas. Which makes sharing with him easy. Maybe too easy.

"I don't want to wait for the police to find something. I want to hunt both Brett and Ivan down and put them in the ground so they can't hurt anyone ever again."

"That's understandable."

"It's murder. Regardless of whether or not I think they deserve it."

"I said it was understandable," he replies. "Not that it's the right thing to do."

"He could have killed her. You saw the bruises on her face. The cuts. They beat her, Dad." My throat constricts as my mind paints a horrific picture of what that could have looked like.

"But he didn't kill her. She's alive. God brought her back to us so you could do what's right."

"Which is where my dilemma is. I'm finding it hard to want to do the right thing. I could track him down. Him and Ivan. And they'd be out of this world forever. No justice system to make mistakes. I'm good at making problems disappear." It's the closest I've come to telling him what I did when I was in the service.

They'd been monsters—the men I'd dealt with. But they were human lives all the same.

"But at what cost?" he asks. "I know you've struggled with your faith since Renee, but you know what payment a darkness like that will require."

"I've pulled a trigger before."

"In life-or-death situations. When it was you or them. And we both know you're haunted by even those moments. How do you think it's going to feel when you're hunting them down and striking out of vengeance?"

"It doesn't matter. Because Nova will be safe."

He gently touches my left hand where it grips the porch railing. "Son. Nova's safety isn't all that matters to her."

I close my eyes, trying to breathe through the anger.

"She cares about you. And if you don't do this right, she's going to lose you."

"They don't play by the rules."

"No," he agrees. "But we're supposed to because vengeance isn't ours. It's God's. And the moment you take that from Him is the moment they've won. Regardless of what the outcome is."

"Then what do you suggest I do?" I turn toward him. "Just sit around and wait for them to strike? For them to come onto this ranch and take everything that matters to me?"

"You let Gibson get that warrant. You let the police go in, and you do what you do best." He grips my shoulders. "Find the truth. Even if he is tipped off that someone is coming, it won't matter once you have that evidence in hand."

CHAPTER 31

NOVA

Man, I look rough.

I lean in closer to the mirror, as though that might change the look of the bruises blooming on my cheeks. My right eye is black and bloodshot, my lip split at the corner.

I've definitely looked better. But have I looked worse? It would be nice if I could remember. Gripping both sides of the counter, I lean my head down and take a deep breath. I escaped, but that doesn't mean this fight is over.

And even though sleep is the last thing I want, I know Elliot is right. Running into a situation without being as prepared as possible is foolish. I can't risk my life that way, and I won't risk theirs.

Bootsteps in the hall have me straightening and opening the bathroom door. Elliot, duffel bag in hand, Echo at his side, opens the room right across from mine and heads inside.

Since he leaves it open, I cross the hall and stand in the doorway. Echo rushes over to greet me, so I lean down to pet him. "Hey, boy, it's good to see you too." He spins in a circle and rubs his body against me for more love that I will gladly give.

"You should be resting." Elliot sets his bag on the bed then turns to face me. His expression is shielded, those walls I first noticed put back in place. I know I put them there, and it makes me even angrier at myself.

How different things would look if I'd just taken him up on his offer to stay?

Would there be affection in his hazel gaze if I'd stayed?

"I was headed that way when I heard you come in."

He nods. "Riley is on monitor duty tonight. He'll keep eyes on everyone."

"I'm glad you're here," I tell him.

He nods then unzips the bag and withdraws a pair of shorts, which he sets on the bed. The cold distance is exactly how he acted before—well—everything. And it breaks my heart not to see the man who'd kissed me so passionately two days ago. I can't be surprised though—it's my fault. I put that anger there.

"I'm sorry, Elliot."

"I told you, you don't need to be."

"I do, though. I was trying to stay true to who I was being told I was, and I ignored who I'd become."

"As I said, you were doing what you thought was right."

"But I chose wrong. I listened to obligation versus how I really felt." How do I make him see that he's who I want? Who I've wanted all along?

"You still didn't choose me, Nova," he replies, turning to face me. He crosses both arms, and what's left of my heart breaks.

He's so closed off. What was I expecting? He offered me forever, and I threw it back in his face.

"I'm sorry," I say again because they're the only words I can put together right now.

"I am too," he replies. "But it is what it is. I need to get some sleep. We have a long day tomorrow." Grabbing his shorts and a small canvas bag I'm guessing are toiletries, he heads toward the door. I step out of the way, and he moves across the hall and into the bathroom. "I'm glad you're okay, Nova. Goodnight."

"Night."

The door closes with a soft click that might as well have been deafening.

"THERE'S NOTHING HERE," I say in frustration as I survey the mess in what was my apartment. Now everything is in disarray, with clothes in a pile on the floor, dishes on the countertops, and books pulled off the shelves, their pages checked for hidden messages.

So far, we've got nothing.

"You're good at hiding stuff," Riley offers, surveying the mess we've made. "I'll give you that."

Elliot is in the front closet, going over every nook and cranny in case I somehow managed to hide something in the wall.

We even checked the air vents. Nothing. Not a single shred of paper or a thumb drive. And since Elliot told me that Gibson got a team out to Ivan's place and they found nothing, I know we're running out of time.

Brett will come for me. And Ivan will back him.

Unless he puts a bullet in Brett himself.

"I don't get it. Why would I hide that folder on Brett here, but not anything else?"

"Maybe you were in a rush with the Brett folder," Elliot offers. "If he didn't make contact with Brett until after you were on assignment, it's likely you snuck away to hide that file." He sighs. "But I'm in agreement; there's nothing here."

"Do you think he came back and found it?"

"Nah," Riley brushes it off. "We would be able to tell because he wouldn't have bothered to put anything back."

"Who could tell with the mess I left behind?" I eye the blood staining the carpet in my bedroom.

"I can," Elliot replies.

"He has a freaky memory," Riley replies. "Always has."

"Good to know." I head back into the kitchen. I'm just turning when I see something move out of the corner of my eye, just outside the window. I rush over and peek through the glass, nearly jumping out of my own skin when I see a slender man duck back, eyes wide with fear.

He turns and rushes down the fire escape. I rip the window open. "Hey! Wait!"

"Nova!" Elliot calls behind me, but I'm already racing down after the man.

He hits the pavement and takes off down the alley with me right behind him. Still aching from the fight yesterday, I'm moving far slower than I would like, but the man running doesn't seem to do a whole lot of cardio, and by the time we've made it to the alley, he's wheezing.

He turns and takes a right, so I follow. The end of the alley is just ahead, and the man slows then turns to face me.

"Easy," I tell him. "I'm not going to hurt you."

"I kn—" His dark eyes widen further, and he rips a knife from his jacket as Elliot and Riley bound into the alley behind me.

"Easy!" I yell.

"Drop it now, or I'll drop you," Elliot growls, weapon

raised at the man. Riley is directly beside him, his own weapon trained.

"Wait!" I yell, stepping between them. I've got a feeling in my gut, a gnawing understanding that not everything is as it seems. I turn toward the stranger. The beanie low on his head and the tattered sweatshirt lead me to believe he's homeless.

He's gaunt, his skin pale. But he doesn't look angry or out of control. No, he looks scared. "Do you know me?" I ask.

"You told me to be careful," he whispers. "I tried to be careful. But when I saw them take you up, I knew I had to give you a distraction. So you could escape. I'm sorry. I messed up."

"You do know me?"

His gaze darts to me then back to Elliot and Riley.

"I was shot," I tell him. "I nearly died and lost my memories in the process."

"Nova, get back here," Elliot growls.

"She ain't going nowhere with you!" the stranger yells, holding up his knife. He takes a step forward, clearly wanting to protect me. But why?

My heart racing, I try to stay between the Hunts and this man. "Tell me what I told you."

He looks back at me. "You told me to be careful, and I was careful."

Hope. "You're not trying to hurt anyone, are you?"

"I'll hurt them if they hurt you." He bares his teeth. They're rotting, and he's missing a few on the bottom.

"They aren't going to hurt me." I turn around. "Put them away, please. Trust me."

Both Elliot and Riley look at me like I'm insane.

"Please," I say again.

Begrudgingly, they lower their weapons.

"I hope you know what you're doing," Riley mutters.

"I do." Shifting my attention back to the man, I ask, "What's your name?"

He lowers the knife just a bit. "You really don't remember me?" He looks almost hurt, and I feel a wave of guilt knowing I caused him distress.

"I'm sorry. I didn't even know who I was until recently."

"Milo," he replies. "We're friends."

I smile. "I believe you." I take a step closer.

"Nova."

"It's fine," I tell Elliot. "These are my friends too. Elliot and his brother, Riley. Elliot saved my life."

Milo looks past me to Elliot and narrows his gaze. "You did?"

"I did."

A heartbeat later, Milo is shoving the knife back into his pocket. "I'm sorry. I had to protect her. I thought you worked for that other guy."

"What other guy?" I ask.

"Not here," he says. "Eyes everywhere." He points to the top of the buildings then waves for me to follow him as he turns and heads toward a door on the back of the brick building.

"Nova," Elliot warns as I start to follow.

"He might have answers," I insist.

"Stay here," Elliot tells Riley. "Call for backup if you don't hear from me in ten minutes."

"You got it, be safe."

As Milo tugs on the handle, the door opens with a creak, and he heads inside first. I follow with Elliot right behind me. The door closes, plunging us into a dim backroom. A cot sits in one corner, a sleeping bag on top.

There's an electric cooktop and a kettle as well as a few milk crates with cans of food.

"Do you live here?" I ask him.

He nods. "You got it for me."

"I did?"

"Yeah." He surveys Elliot. "You're sure he's okay?"

"I'm sure."

"He looks like one of them soldier types."

I smile at Elliot. "He is a soldier type. But a good one." I turn back to Milo. "What were you going to tell me?"

He eyes Elliot one final time then heads over toward an old metal cabinet and reaches behind it. He tugs on something and removes a thumb drive with a piece of tape stuck to the back.

"What is that?"

"I kept it safe for you. Just like you asked me to. I made sure no one got it. I told you, you can trust me. I'll always be there for you." He hands it to me, and I stare down at it, praying it's the lifeline I think it is.

"Do you know what's on this?"

He shrugs. "I don't know. But you told me it was important I didn't give it to nobody but you unless time ran out."

I turn to Elliot. "This is it."

"What do you mean, when time ran out?" Elliot asks Milo.

"She told me that someone might be coming for her and that, if they did, she wouldn't be back to get the drive. She told me that, if I hadn't heard from her by her birthday, then I was to take it to the police station and give it to Lieutenant Crew. But only to him. Not the captain. You said explicitly, not the captain."

"I told you that?" If I didn't think I could trust the captain, then was he lying when he spoke to Gibson? Was he the man I talked to on the phone?

"Yes. You were adamant that I not trust him."

"You said you were going to protect her," Elliot says, moving closer. "Who were you protecting her from?"

"Those men. The ones that showed up right after you gave me that." He points to the drive. "They were really angry. I could hear them yelling, and I went to look, and they were making such a mess. I started to stop them, but you made me promise to keep that safe no matter what. I didn't want to risk letting you down, so I stayed away. They destroyed all your pretty things." He looks so sad for a moment; then his face lights up. "But wait! I saved something!" Milo rushes over to the corner and rummages through a bunch of stuff he has there. When he emerges, he's holding a black photo album. "I got this out of the trash for you. I couldn't get the rest of it. But I got this." Slowly, as though it's made of fragile glass, he offers me the album.

I take it from him and open it, my heart aching with grief as I study the images. An older woman with red hair like mine is smiling out of a photograph, her arm around me.

There's another with a younger me standing between that same woman and a man with dark hair. *My parents.*

I close the album and hug it close. "Thank you, Milo."

He beams at me, pride evident in his expression. "You're welcome."

"Can I ask you, when is my birthday?"

"May seventeenth," he says. "You didn't have nobody else to celebrate with you, so you'd have me over for cake. It was such good cake."

Emotion burns in my chest. A friend. I did have a friend. "I must have snuck the evidence out of my apartment right before Brett shot me." I turn toward Elliot. "I must have known they were coming for me."

"And you moved it to where Brett couldn't get it."

"Do you know him too?" I ask, turning back to Milo.

"Met him once. Not impressed. You promised not to tell him I was here." He points to a scar over his right eye. "He gave me this."

"I'm sorry." My heart falls.

"Don't be." Milo waves it off. "I'm just glad you're okay. I was worried about you. You know you're like my sister," he says. "We're family." He smiles, and I return it.

"Thank you for this," I tell him, holding up the thumb drive. "You just saved my life."

"I'll always protect you, Nova," he says with a wide smile.

"We got company!" Riley sprints into the room, weapon raised. "They must have been watching the apartment."

"We have to go!" Milo yells. "Come. You have to come." He grabs my hand and yanks me through another door. We emerge into a large empty room that looks like it was once a restaurant. Behind us, heavy boot steps and yelling have the adrenaline in my veins surging.

Elliot and Riley block the door, but we don't stop there. Milo keeps tugging, pulling me further and further through the building.

We emerge onto the street, and Elliot pushes past us, hitting the unlock button for his truck, which thankfully is parked right on the street.

A gun fires, and the bullet whizzes past us.

Milo stops running and pushes me forward. "You have to go!" he yells. "You can't have her!" he bellows, spinning to face the men with guns.

I turn and take his hand, trying to tug him with us. "Come on. You're coming too—"

A gunshot echoes along the street, and Milo stiffens.

"No!"

He turns slowly toward me, eyes wide as he stares back at me, fear and shock warring for control over his expression.

"No." Emotion burns in my throat. "No!"

He sinks to his knees. I try to pull him up as more gunshots are fired in our direction.

"I've got him." Elliot scoops him up and places him in the backseat then jumps into the driver's side.

Riley turns and fires—once, twice—before jumping into the truck. I get into the backseat and rip my sweatshirt off to apply pressure to Milo's chest. "We have to get him to a hospital," I insist.

"It's—it's okay." Milo smiles, eyes growing heavy. "You're okay. That's what matters."

"You matter too," I tell him, tears blurring my vision. "We're friends, remember? Family."

He smiles, though it's distant. "Family," he repeats. "I won't forget the day the pretty detective wanted to be my friend. You saved my life that day. I'm only glad I got to save yours too."

CHAPTER 32
ELLIOT

Nova hasn't said a word since we left the hospital. Unfortunately, Milo didn't make it. He was dead before we even arrived, but I know she'd hoped for a miracle.

I know I did.

The man threw himself in front of her, taking a bullet that would have surely robbed me of the woman sitting beside me. I owe him everything.

Tucker drove down and made a copy of the thumb drive. Then he and Riley headed back to the ranch. That way we could deal with the Lieutenant Milo claims Nova trusted enough to hand over the evidence that nearly got her killed.

Which is what we're doing now, sitting in an old diner on the same side of the booth, waiting for him to show up.

From the research I did, I know he's in his early forties.

Dark skin, bald, brown eyes. He was a Marine before leaving that life behind for one in public service. On the surface, he looks like a decent man. But after everything we've dealt with, I still worry.

"Are you all right?" I ask her then take a drink of my coffee.

"No. Not really," she admits. "I just keep hearing his voice in my head. Over and over again."

"It wasn't your fault."

"Wasn't it?" she asks. "I'm the reason he's dead."

"You gave him a purpose to live." When she doesn't respond, I lean over. "You trusted him with something so important people are killing for it. You took a man that no one would have looked twice at and made him a hero."

"He died," she replies.

"And I wish I could change that. But don't take away the heroics of what he did because you're feeling guilty. He made a choice to sacrifice himself for you. Honor that."

"Why did I let him stay in that alley?" she asks, still not looking at me. "If I trusted him enough to give him that drive, why didn't I give him somewhere warm to sleep? Warm food for his belly?"

Unsure what else to do, I reach over and cover her hand with mine. "Milo said you gave him that place to sleep, remember? You did that for him."

"It wasn't enough."

"You won't know anything until you get your memories

back," I tell her. "But I know *you*. You wouldn't have left him there if you weren't sure he was safe and cared for."

She starts to respond, but the bell over the front door dings, and Lieutenant Davin Crew strolls in, wearing jeans, a white T-shirt, and a black jacket. His gaze travels around the diner until it lands on Nova.

I watch him closely, noting how he visibly relaxes when he sees her.

"Nova."

"Lieutenant," she replies.

I note that he's a bit thrown off by her unfamiliar demeanor. "You still don't remember, do you?"

She shakes her head, and he slides into the booth across from us. "Sorry."

"Not your fault." He smiles. "I'm just glad you're alive." He shifts his attention to me and offers his hand. "I hear I have you to thank for that."

"Elliot Hunt," I tell him.

"Hunt? As in Hunt Brothers Search & Rescue?"

"One and the same." I'm a bit surprised he's heard of us since we tend to work mainly by word of mouth.

"You and your brothers are a legend around the precinct. We heard what your brother Bradyn did last year. Rescuing all those girls from that trafficking ring overseas."

Nova stares at me, her expression shocked. "Seriously?"

"It's what we do," I reply. We take no credit because it's God who guides our steps. Every single one of them. Even if I've struggled with my own faith, I've never doubted that.

"You're good men."

"So are you, from what we hear, Marine. Until you left the service for a job here in Dallas."

"My mother was sick," he replies. "She needed someone here."

"Family is something I understand." My respect for Crew grows. "I'm hoping you can offer us some help now."

"Anything." He turns to Nova. "What can I do?"

"Hi, honey, what can I get you?" the waitress asks as she crosses toward our table.

Crew flashes her a kind smile. "Just coffee, please. Ooh, you know what? I'll take a piece of pie too. Whatever you have."

"You got it." She writes something down then leaves the tableside.

"How long have we been working together?" Nova asks.

"This time or the time before?" When she doesn't answer, he chuckles. "Nova O'Conner, I have known you since you were a fresh-faced eighteen-year-old right out of Marine boot camp and ready to serve your country."

She looks honestly shocked. "I was in the service, too?"

"Here you go." The waitress sets down a mug of coffee and a piece of pie.

"Thank you," he replies.

"Anytime. Let me know if you need anything else." She leaves the table again, and I cast a glance at Nova, who's starting to look rather frustrated at the interruptions. I know she's desperate for answers. Even more so after what happened earlier today.

"So I served in the Marines with you?" She asks again.

He nods. "You're one of the strongest people I've ever met. After training, you got stationed in Oahu. I had already been there for a year." When she doesn't respond, he continues. "You were leaving a restaurant one night, and a couple Marines tried to get fresh with you." He grins. "I started to help, honorable gentleman that I am and all that, but before I got to you, two of them were on the ground, and the third was running away." He laughs. "I'd never seen anything like it. So I knew I had to meet you."

She looks at me then back to him. "So we were *friends*?" The inflection of her tone is the true question, and Crew catches on.

He arches a brow. "If you're asking if we were more, the answer is no. I was already engaged when we met, and you've always been a little sister to me. You and my wife have been close friends too. Sabrina is going to be happy to know you're okay."

"Really?" She's hopeful once more.

He nods. "Why do you look so surprised?"

"Brett told me I didn't have any friends."

If I hadn't fully trusted the man across from me yet, all of that would have changed the moment I saw the volatile fury on his face at the mention of Nova's former fiancé. "That man doesn't have a truthful bone in his body," Crew growls. "He never had anything but selfish intentions when it came to you. I never liked him. Begged you not to marry him."

"Why did I plan to?"

He shrugs. "After losing your mother, you felt alone. You worked a lot, and my guess is that you were tired of being lonely. Brett was charming at first—I'll give you that. But he was always a snake."

She nods. "He's the one who shot me."

Crew's expression morphs from anger to fury. "I'd suspected, but to hear he did—" He shakes his head. "I knew he was dirty."

"You did?"

He nods. "We had a fight after you got engaged. I told you it was a mistake, that there was something off about him. You told me that not everyone could have the kind of love Sabrina and I shared and that some of us had to settle. I, of course, told you that you were wrong, but things weren't the same between us after that. Even at work, you avoided me." He shakes his head in frustration, clearly hating that he's recalling such a memory. "Anyway, a few weeks before you left for your latest undercover op, you came to me and told me that you were ending the engagement. That something felt off and you wanted to reconnect when you got back."

"I didn't say what felt off?"

He shakes his head. "But a few months ago, you showed up out of the blue and told me that Brett had taken it upon himself to show up on mission. You said you didn't trust his motives and thought he'd been working with Ivan long before the mission was even authorized. That him showing up had nothing to do with you and everything to do with him trying to get close enough to keep an eye on you. You asked me to look into it."

"Did you?"

"Oh, I did. Took what he did to the captain and insisted he pull the plug and get you all out, but he refused."

"We don't think he can be trusted," Nova says.

"You'd be right there. I can't prove it, but some of the decisions he's making lately don't make any sense."

"Like what?" I question.

"Aside from not pulling the plug even though Brett went rogue? There were quite a few things. Telling us to drop certain cases. Denying surveillance requests despite insurmountable evidence. Then there was the other thing with your op," he says then takes a bite of pie.

"What about it?"

Crew washes down the pie with a swig of coffee.

"Whenever an officer heads undercover for any length of time, we take precautions to ensure that the true identity is hidden. But this time, they *erased* both you and Sam."

"That's not typical? Brett told us they'd done that, but I just assumed it was because of the type of mission," she replies.

"It's not typical for them to go that deep. They erased your life. A specialized team removed every image of you they could find from the internet so no facial ID could be used. They removed your records, both from the service and work at the precinct. Your fingerprints were taken out of the system. It was like you never even existed."

"They did a thorough job," I tell him. "The only thing we managed to dig up was a surveillance video of her outside a shop."

"They were intent in what they did. When I asked about it, the captain said you were going deep undercover and they wanted to be sure because it was suspected Ivan had contacts as high up as the FBI. It's why they sent you and not one of their own agents. Or so they said."

"You don't believe any of that," I say, not even bothering with a question. His answer is clear in his expression.

"Not a word of it. But before I could really dig, they'd already sent word you'd accepted, and you didn't want to back out because you believed you could do good work."

"I wish I could remember any of this." Nova groans in frustration. "It's all missing. My entire life is gone."

"It'll come back." I have to fight the urge to put my arm around her and pull her closer, if only to offer the slightest comfort.

"Tell me what led you to me." Crew takes a bite of his pie.

"We were at my apartment, looking for the evidence Brett claims I have. We didn't find anything, but there was a man outside my window. At first, I thought he was spying on us."

"Milo," Crew says with a smile.

"You knew him too?"

"Of course. You had him over for Thanksgiving every single year. Sabrina and I were there too, and we met him then. Nice guy. Rough life. But you've been trying to get him clean and sober ever since. You'd worked out an agreement with the guy who owned that building adjacent to yours, and you'd been trying to help him get his own place. Is he doing okay?"

Nova looks down at her hands.

"He's dead," I tell Crew, sensing that she doesn't want to speak the words. "Took a bullet meant for Nova."

Crew looks genuinely upset. He shakes his head. "I'm sorry to hear that. He was a good man, Nova. You saw the best in him and gave him every chance."

"So people keep telling me." She raises her gaze back to Crew. "He told us that you could be trusted. That I told him, if I didn't come back, to go to you."

"Go to me with what?"

"This." Nova reaches into her pocket and withdraws the thumb drive then sets it on the table between all of us.

"Is that—" Crew starts.

"Surveillance photos. Transaction receipts. Locations, dates, and cargo manifests. All of it linking directly back to Ivan. My brother Tucker was able to access it."

Crew's eyes go wide. "You got it."

"I got it."

"Nova, this is big." He reaches forward and pushes the drive back to her. "But I can't take it."

"Why not?"

"The captain is dirty, I'm certain of it. And if you give that to me, you run the risk of losing it. They're watching me. Every move I make. I had to slip two tails just to get here without incident."

"They're tailing you? Why?"

He shifts his gaze to me. "Ever since I went to the captain with my fears about Brett, they have. And now internal affairs is sniffing around the precinct. It's a mess."

"Are they interested in the captain?"

He nods. "But not just him. After Sam's body was found, we thought it was only a matter of time before yours washed up too. When that happened, I went to a friend of mine at the bureau and told him my concerns. He took it to his superior, and the next thing I know, IA is requesting access to files and taking up office in our conference room."

Frustration tugs at me. If he can't help us, who can? "Can your contact help us?" I ask him.

"No. I wouldn't trust it. I thought we were friends and he would look into things quietly, but now I'm thinking he's just looking for a career climb."

"Then what do we do? How do we make sure this gets into the right hands?" Nova asked. "Sam and Milo died for this. It has to mean something."

"It will," Crew assures her. "Let me do some digging. I'll see what I can find out." He turns to me. "Do you have anyone you can trust? Anyone with reaches high enough to make sure that evidence doesn't end up buried?"

I run through the list of contacts I've made over the years. Agencies both here and abroad, as well as contacts I still have in the military. "Possibly. I'll make some phone calls."

"Excellent." Crew turns back to Nova. "You have to keep that evidence safe, Nova. Without it, Ivan walks. But be careful who you trust. He has deep pockets, and his reach is wider than we ever considered before."

"You stay safe too," she tells him. "Hopefully, when all of this is over, I can get to know you and Sabrina again."

He flashes a smile. "We'd like that."

CHAPTER 33

NOVA

I believe I've spent a lot of time in churches. Even if I can't remember the place, day, or time, or what I was wearing. What the verse was or how the altar looked.

It's a feeling. A knowing understanding that I've been in God's house many times before. And chasing that feeling is exactly why I'm here now.

Elliot is beside me, sitting completely silent, his shoulders squared. He looks more comfortable than the last Sunday we were here, but there's still a tension to the way he sits. Nerves clearly present.

Pastor Ford steps out of a door off to the side of the altar, his gaze sweeping the sanctuary. When he sees us, his eyes widen, but he smiles warmly.

"Elliot Hunt. It's good to see you, son," he greets.

"Pastor Ford," he greets.

The pastor turns to me. "And Nova. It's good to put an actual name to your face." He offers his hand, so I shake it. "Word travels fast in this town. I believe we knew your real name mere minutes after you found out." After releasing my hand, he takes a seat in the pew in front of us then turns. "How are you both doing?"

"Feeling a bit lost," I admit.

"This is the perfect place to be when you're lost," he says, casting a quick glance at Elliot, who remains staring straight ahead.

I long to reach over and take his hand in mind, hopefully offering some assurance that he's not the only one feeling the weight of being within these four walls. But aside from the kindness he's shown me since Milo died, he's made it clear that's not what he wants, so I keep my hands in my lap.

"I'm struggling with the fact that I've lost so much. I can't remember anything about my life, not my family, friends, the place I grew up. Whether or not we had a dog." I shake my head. "Someone who cared about me died today, and I couldn't even offer the assurance that I would remember him because I don't know who we were to each other."

"You think just because you can't remember who you were that you won't remember who he was?"

I shrug. "If memories are so easily lost, who knows?"

Pastor Ford smiles softly. "God's plan is a mystery to

everyone but Him. What we have, though, is His Word. His promises. You are in the middle of a storm, Nova, but it doesn't have to take you under."

I snort. "It definitely feels like it might."

"And at times, it will feel that way. But just a little faith can move a mountain. Yours can get you through what you're dealing with now. He can calm the storm."

"Why take my memories, though? If I'm meant to stop —" I trail off, not wanting to say too much. "If I'm meant to do good, then why erase everything and everyone I've ever known?"

Pastor Redding lets out a sigh. "I wish I had an answer for you, Nova. What's happened to you is a horrible tragedy. But that doesn't mean something beautiful won't come out of it." He smiles at me and glances at Elliot again. "Oftentimes, God takes what is broken and creates a masterpiece like only He can."

Elliot's on monitor duty tonight, so I make an extra cup of coffee and carry it into his dad's office where he's been watching the cameras since Tucker headed to his house.

Both Ruth and Tommy retired to their rooms an hour ago, and I've been up in my room, unable to sleep. So I decided to make good use of my time and use the laptop

Tucker loaned me to research ways of helping me remember my past.

My hope is that, if I can just remember, then there will be someone else we can go to for help. Someone who will be able to take that thumb drive, make the arrests, and then I can go on with my life.

I step into the office and pause in the doorway, my heart leaping within my chest.

Elliot is bare-chested, his eyes closed, as he does decline sit-ups on a bench in the corner of his father's office. Every muscle in his body is tense, his skin gleaming with sweat. The bullet wound beside his heart is still red and raised but closed.

My mouth dries.

The ink from his left sleeve spans over his chest, nearly hiding an older puckered scar. There are four more scars along his chest and abdomen, and I recall him telling me he'd been shot multiple times before.

I swallow hard. *Oh my.* He's gorgeous. Stunning. And I can't seem to tear my gaze away from the pure power he displays with every movement.

Before he catches me gawking, I clear my throat. He opens his eyes and finishes his current sit-up. Then, he gets up and retrieves the shirt he left on the back of the chair. "What are you doing up?"

"I couldn't sleep, so I thought you could use some

coffee." I carry it over to his desk and set it down beside an open Bible.

"Thanks."

"Sure."

Elliot checks the cameras then retrieves a bottle of water from a mini fridge in the opposite corner.

"Any word on the search to find us help?"

"I've notified some guys I know in Maine. They're looking, too, but since we have to be careful who to trust on this one, they're doing some extra digging."

"That's good."

"Thanks for the coffee," he says again. He's dismissing me, asking me to leave without actually asking. I nearly listen, but I really don't want to be alone. Especially if it means I can't be here with him.

"Thanks for taking me to the church today."

"You already thanked me for that." He crosses his arms and leans back against the desk. I can't help but drink him in. The pure masculine strength that is Elliot Hunt. While he is quite wonderful to look at though, there's more to him than what's on the surface. The haunting darkness in his eyes has captivated me from the moment we first met.

"I know, but I wanted to say it again." I move around the room, studying photographs on the walls of his father and all of them out on the ranch. There are pictures of all five of the Hunt brothers in uniform with Lani standing in the center in her scrubs. They all look so happy. I turn toward him. "Can I ask you something?"

"Sure."

"How did it feel being in church today?"

"Excuse me?"

"How did it feel?"

"The same as when I was there with you on Sunday."

"Which was?"

He eyes me, clearly trying to understand why I'm asking him. "A bit nervous," he finally says. "But a step in the right direction."

I nod in agreement. "It felt like home for me. Like even though I can't recall the names of my family, I'd found my way back home." I look over at the Bible. "You're reading?"

"I lost myself for a while," he says. "As you know. But I'm working on getting back there."

"Is Renee the only reason you stopped going?"

He eyes me, expression unreadable. "We're just diving into all the hard conversations, aren't we?"

"I want to know more."

"About what?"

"About you. About why you pulled away from the church. About"—I swallow hard— "Renee."

"Why do you want to know about her?"

"She mattered to you."

"That doesn't answer my question."

"Doesn't it?" I ask. I know I hurt him, but these walls, they're killing me. "I want to know you better."

"Why?"

"Are you seriously going to make me spell it out?"

"Yes," he replies, pushing to his feet. "Because I offered myself to you. I opened myself up, and you threw it back in my face when you left with him. So yes, Nova, I want you to tell me why. I want you to be honest with the both of us."

I close my eyes, tears stinging the corners. My heart is so heavy it might as well have been pumped full of lead. "I told you, I made a mistake. I'm sorry." When I open my eyes again, he's running a hand through his hair.

"I don't need your apologies."

"No? Because you don't seem to understand how absolutely sorry I am for what I did. How, even as I was making that choice, I *knew* it was the wrong one." I take a few steps closer.

Elliot's nostrils flare, and he crosses his arms.

"Even if Brett had turned out to be everything I'd thought he was at first, if what he'd told me was the truth, he was still a choice someone else made. I'm not her anymore. It just took me too long to realize it."

"And what, now that your fiancé turned out to be a murderer, you're interested? I'm not a second choice, Nova. I deserve better."

"You were never my second choice, Elliot. I may not

remember anything, but I do *know* that." I take a step closer then remain where I am. If he wants what's between us, then he can take the next step.

And if not? Well, I'll deal with that if I have to.

"From the moment I woke up on that horse and saw you holding me, I've been drawn to you."

"Then why did you walk away? Was it really just obligation?"

"It was that and hope that, if I returned to my old life for even a little while, I'd remember who I was. I didn't feel whole. I still don't. But I'm beginning to think that doesn't matter. Not in the way I thought it did."

He uncrosses his arms, and his expression turns tortured. "Nova—"

"Please, Elliot." Risking my pride, I step forward. "Please don't close me out again." I reach up and place my hand on his chest. "Please, Elliot," I repeat, this time my voice barely above a whisper.

He slips a hand around the back of my neck and pulls me closer. Heat twists in my stomach, a burning desire that only he stirs. "I won't let you go again, Nova. If we take this step forward and you try to leave, I'll track you down."

I look up into his eyes and smile. "The same goes for you."

Elliot slams his mouth onto mine, and the broken parts of me come back into place. Even if I can't remember who I am, all I need is right here. God brought me to Elliot Hunt for a reason, of that I'm sure. He saved me and brought me home.

My cell rings, killing the moment between us. I pull back and take it out of my pocket. I read Crew's name as it flashes across the screen. "Hey, this isn't a good time. Can I call you back?"

"I can't guarantee he'll answer."

The blood turns to ice in my veins, all the desire I'd felt moments ago gone like a puff of smoke on a windy afternoon. I level my gaze on Elliot then place the phone on speaker. "Brett. Where is Crew?"

"Still breathing," he replies. "For now."

"What do you want?" I know better than to tell him to leave my friend alone, that his fight is with me, because Brett won't operate that way. He'd thrive in knowing how rattled he's made me.

"You know exactly what I want, Nova. And until you get it to me, I'll be hanging onto your buddy. We have some catching up to do, anyway."

"If you hurt him—"

"I've already hurt him," he replies. "And if you don't do exactly what I say, I'll finish him off then head over to deal with the rest of his family."

I hear a muffled plea, and I can't help but imagine Crew, bound and gagged, struggling to get free so he can protect his family.

Elliot grabs his phone and fires off a quick text.

"Then tell me what to do. But if he doesn't make it out of this, you should know—neither will you."

"Big threats for someone who doesn't even remember her own middle name."

How did I *ever* even consider marrying this man? "Tell me what you want."

"Bring me the drive in one hour. I'll be waiting in the creek at the park. And come alone. Don't even think about bringing the cowboys. They'd be in well over their head, anyway. You'd be marching them straight to the gates of hell. Goodbye, darling. I'll be seeing you soon."

The call ends, but my focus is elsewhere.

Darling. The word sparks an assault on my mind.

Plunging me headfirst into a memory.

PAIN IS a reminder that I'm still breathing as I sprint through the trees. It's not my first choice, running barefoot through a Texas forest, but he left me no option after bringing me out here.

The Lord is my Shepherd; I have all that I need. *I start repeating Psalm 23. My mother told me to write it on my heart for moments just like this.*

Tears sting my eyes.

He lets me rest in green meadows; he leads me beside peaceful streams.

Every move is agony, but I keep going. Keep moving.

He guides me along right paths, bringing honor to His name.

I have to keep fighting until there's no more breath in my chest. I won't go down without a fight. Too much has been lost already, and if something happens to me, the truth will also be buried six feet beneath the cold, hard ground.

Ahead, I can see the bright illumination of headlights on the highway. Hope fills me with renewed strength. If I can get up to the roadside, I can get into a car before he reaches me. Then I'll be able to survive. Then I can get help.

I push harder. Faster. I've got this.

Until—I slide to a stop at the edge of a river.

Water roars, blocking me from the highway. Thanks to the heavy rains we've had over the past couple of days, there's no hope of me getting across without being swept away. Still, maybe—

"I told you I'd find you. I will always find you."

Even when I walk through the darkest valley, I will not be afraid, for You are close beside me.

Dread coils in my belly as I turn to face my attacker. His smile is sinister, his eyes dark. How I ever trusted him, I'll never know. Unfortunately, it's a mistake that will likely come at the cost of my life. "What, you don't think you can take me on without that?" I ask, eyeing his weapon, trying to keep my tone level.

Your rod and Your staff protect and comfort me.

He raises the gun and levels it on me. "I have nothing to prove to you, darling. I gave you a chance. You failed. Now I have no choice. You gave me no choice. Why couldn't you just take the deal? Why couldn't you play ball?"

"You know me well enough to know I never would have gone along with it. You sold your soul, and that's something I'll never do."

You prepare a feast for me in the presence of my enemies. You honor me by anointing my head with oil.

"Always dramatic. Things could've worked out. I'm sorry, but you've truly not given me any choice."

My cup overflows with blessings. Surely Your goodness and unfailing love will pursue me all the days of my life…

A single tear slips down my cheek. If this is the end, at least, I stayed true to myself. At least, I didn't—a gunshot echoes through the trees, and the bullet tears through the flesh of my abdomen. I fall backward, hitting the ground with a heavy thud.

I can barely breathe, every muscle in my body contracting with the pain.

It hurts so bad.

So bad.

I'm going to die here. Amongst towering trees and the scent of wet dirt.

Get to the creek. *The words echo through my mind, and I glance behind me. The creek is a few feet away. It'll take a miracle to get there before Brett kills me.*

Still, I scoot back a bit.

Brett moves closer and stares down at me. "We could have had it all, you know. All you had to do was bend just one of those ridiculous rules of yours."

"You mean the rules that kept me from becoming a dirty cop like you?" I continue moving slowly, trying to keep my moves calculated so he doesn't sense my desperation for escape. I'm not sure how, but I know that, if I can just reach it, I'll be free. Maybe, just maybe, God will save me so I can save them.

"Don't you see it? Look where playing by the rules got you!" he roars, pointing at me with the gun. "Bleeding on the ground."

"If you think for a second that Ivan is going to save you, you're an even bigger fool than I thought."

"Ivan needs me. He needs someone on the inside."

"Ivan is sadistic. He likes to play with his food before he devours it." I should know. I've worked alongside him for over a year. Playing the game, waiting for my escape.

Brett's expression twists. "I'm sorry it has to be this way. I'm already in too deep, Nova. There's no going back for me."

"Yes, there is," I insist. "You can help me take him down." I keep scooting every few seconds. I need to keep

him talking long enough to reach the water. "We can do it together." The lie is vile on my tongue. I'll never forgive him for what happened to Sam.

The image of my partner, kneeling in front of me, tears in his eyes as he stared down the barrel of a gun, will haunt me forever.

"It's too late," Brett insists. "I'm sorry, Nova, but this is it."

Gathering what little strength I have, I sweep my leg out and knock him off his feet then plunge into the river. Cold envelops me as the current carries me away. Brett roars my name then fires his weapon in my direction.

But I'm already out of range. My last thought is the final line of Psalm 23.

And I will live in the house of the Lord forever.

CHAPTER 34

ELLIOT

"I remember," Nova says, eyes wide as she stares back at me.

"What do you remember?"

"All of it. I—" She stops speaking a moment, and I hold my breath as she stares toward the wall across from me. "I think all of it. I remember Brett attacking me in the woods. I crawled into the creek, Elliot. He didn't push me. When he shot me, I fell onto the ground, a few feet from the creek. But I heard this voice—" She pauses. "Telling me to get to the creek, and I just knew it was my salvation." She raises her gaze, staring straight at me. "God saved me."

"We already knew that," I tell her.

"I know, but… He really saved me." She smiles, a blinding smile that radiates. But then it falls. "We have to get to Crew." She starts for the door, but I grip her arm and pull her back.

"Wait, Nova."

"For what? You heard Brett. He's going after Sabrina and the kids!"

"Kids?"

"Yeah, they have two," she replies then stops and looks up at me. I can see the war on her face, the joy that her memories are returning mixed with fear for her friend and his family. There will be time to go through all of it, but right now, we're up against a clock.

I check my phone as it dings, signaling an incoming message. "Dylan is heading to their place now. Tucker got him the address. He'll get them out."

"He's just one person," she insists. "Ivan could have an army waiting to strike."

"You clearly don't know Dylan. If there was an army facing me and I only had one man at my side, it would be him." I retrieve the thumb drive from my desk and shove it into my pocket. My phone dings again, so I check the messages coming through the group chat I share with my brothers. "Bradyn and Riley are loading up right now. They'll head to the park first."

"He said to come alone."

"And he won't know we're there," I reply. "You're not doing this alone."

She considers then takes a deep breath. "I remember everything, Elliot. Every late night when I was undercover. Every shower where I cried frustrated and lonely tears because I was in so deep. Even Sam— Oh, Sam." She closes her eyes. "He'd tried to help me, but he was struggling too."

"Being in deep like that must have been incredibly difficult," I reply. "But you're out of it now, and you're not alone."

"I know that. We have to handle this delicately though. Elliot, I don't want to lose anyone else. First Sam then Milo —I can't lose Crew."

"You won't." I only pray it's the truth. That we're not already too late. "Let's gear up. Then we'll head out."

"Okay." She turns and heads for the stairs, taking them two at a time, and as soon as she's gone, I lower my head.

"God, I know You are with me. Even though I've struggled with my faith, battling against my own doubts and insecurities. I ask that You protect us tonight. That you bring Crew home to his family and help us stop Brett and Ivan from hurting anyone else. In the name of Your Son, Jesus Christ, I pray. Amen."

***

"IF YOU CAN HEAR ME, brush the hair behind your right ear," I tell Nova through the earpiece. I watch her through the scope on my rifle as she does just that then heads deeper into the trees.

Tucker is to my left, camouflaged in some brush.

Bradyn is somewhere in the distance, scanning the surroundings while I watch Nova. Riley is in one of the tall pine trees, hidden well above the ground but prepared to drop down if need be.

All of us working as a single unit, just as we have so many times before.

Dylan messaged us right as we arrived to let us know he got Sabrina and the kids out. There was activity—three armed men sent to capture the family—but Dylan handled them, and he's headed back to the ranch with the family, where they'll be safe.

Here's hoping we'll be reuniting them with Crew too.

"Where are you, Brett?" Nova calls out. "I came, just like you asked." The shrill tone of her phone cuts through the earpiece. "What is it?" she asks after raising it to her ear.

"You didn't follow my instructions," Brett replies after Nova's put the phone on speaker.

"What are you talking about? I came just like you asked me to."

"But you didn't come alone," he snarls. Even with the static of her phone being on speaker and coming through the earpiece, I can hear the irritation in his voice. Irritation that undoubtedly leads to instability. Unease snakes up my spine as I realize, with horrible clarity, that this is about to go sideways.

"There's no one with me."

"Lies," Brett replies. "I tell you what, because of our history, I'll give you one final chance to claim your friend. There's a car pulling into the park right now. Get in the trunk."

"First you asked me to come here; now you want me to get into a trunk? Do you think I'm an idiot?"

"I think you'll do whatever it takes to save your friend."

Don't bite, Nova, I urge silently. *Please don't bite.*

"How do I even know he's still alive?" she asks. The moment the question leaves her lips, I know she's going to do whatever Brett requests. And even though I want to sprint from these trees and run to her, I remain where I am because a man's life is at stake.

"Talk to her," Brett orders. When nothing happens, there's a loud crack.

"I'm going to enjoy removing that hand," Crew growls through the line.

"There. Now you know. Get in the trunk, Nova. Time's ticking. And don't forget to leave your weapon on the ground. You won't need it. See you soon." The call ends.

Nova doesn't hesitate before she starts sprinting through the trees.

"Nova, you can't get into that car!" I push up from my position and shoulder my rifle then rush after her. "He's going to kill you!"

"He's going to kill Crew if I don't. I won't lose anyone else." She's breathless as she runs faster, and I honestly can't tell if she's trying to get to the car in time or outrun me so I can't stop her. Truthfully, I'm betting on the latter.

"Please, Nova. We can find him!" I yell as I sprint.

"If it were anyone else, you'd let them go," she says. "You know you would. It's the right play."

She's right. But I don't tell her that.

I keep running as fast as I can when weighed down by the armor attached to my chest. Someone moves in the trees beside me, and Riley comes into view. He's running, too, his gaze trained straight ahead. "You're not anyone else," I tell her.

"I'm a cop," she argues. "And I have to do this."

I leap over a chain hung to close off the trail.

"I'll see you soon, Elliot. I know you'll find me. You told me you would if I ran. I'm counting on it."

Her earpiece goes dead seconds before I hear a trunk slam shut.

"Nova!" I bellow and burst out from the trees as a dark sedan spits gravel and races out from the parking lot. I race after her on foot, not wanting to waste time getting into my truck when I could be getting the license plate.

But there isn't one.

And she's gone.

Riley's truck slides to a stop beside me. I jump in, and we take off after the car. He presses the pedal as hard as he can, and the engine growls, but the car is long gone.

"Where are they?" I ask, frustration and fear at war within me. "God, where did they go?"

"They must have pulled off onto a backroad," he replies. "Let's double back for the others, and we'll see if Tucker can track her."

I know it's our best bet, but with Nova out there somewhere, doing the smart thing is not a choice I can make. Not when I want to tear apart this town until I find them.

"THE EARPIECE IS TURNED OFF," Tucker says. "I can't track it, but I can set up an alert so, when it comes back online, we'll be notified. Until then, I'm searching all traffic and ATM cameras in town and those on the outskirts."

"Gibson put out an APB on the car," Bradyn adds. "Everyone is looking for her."

It should make me feel better, but since it's been four hours and we've got nothing, the pit in my stomach only grows.

"They may have had her ditch the earpiece," Dylan says. "If so—"

"No. There wouldn't have been time for them to make her turn it off." We found her cell phone on the ground alongside her weapon, but the earpiece was nowhere to be found. "The line went dead before she ever got in that trunk. We have to believe she hid it on her somehow."

"If she did, they could have found it." I whirl on Dylan, hands clenched into fists. My younger brother holds his hands up in surrender. "Not trying to be a downer; just trying to consider all possibilities."

"She's smart," I growl then push out of the office, my earpiece still in place. I'll sleep with it if I have to. She has to make communication. Somehow. Someway. *God, please don't let anything happen to her.*

The image of Renee covered in blood assaults my mind. But instead of her face, it's Nova's green eyes staring back at me, dulled by death.

I grip the porch railing so hard my knuckles turn white. The door opens behind me. I don't have to look back to know my dad has followed me out. "I can't lose her too," I tell him.

"You won't," he replies, coming to stand beside me. "Nova is strong. She'll make it out."

"Renee was strong too," I remind him.

"She was," he agrees. "But not in the way Nova is. Nova is trained, Elliot. She's a Marine. A police officer. Which means she's also resourceful. Have faith, son," he says, clasping a hand on my shoulder.

"I've struggled with my faith for a long time."

"Then now is a great time to lean on it, wouldn't you say?"

I look over at him. "I don't know if I deserve His help. I'm praying. I'm trying. But I turned my back on Him three years ago. When I should have been leaning on Him the most."

He smiles softly at me, the lines at the corners of his eyes crinkling. "'We can rejoice, too, when we run into problems and trials, for we know that they help us develop endurance. And endurance develops strength of character, and character strengthens our confident hope of salvation. And this hope will not lead to disappointment.'"

"Romans," I reply. It's a verse that's tattooed on my chest. Right above my heart. I'd had it done right after I got back from my first tour. A fitting verse given I'd had every bit of innocence stripped from me and returned a man tainted by war. Death.

"Romans chapter five," he says. "And it's truer each and every day." He releases my shoulder and faces the ranch. "I wish I could take your pain, son. I wish that it were possible for you and your brothers and Lani to have never suffered, but that's not what God intended. Not in this life, anyway. What comes next? Now *that* is going to be perfection." He smiles at me. "I'm sorry for what happened with Renee, for what's happening with Nova now, but you have to find your will to push on despite the outcomes. You have to lean on God even when it's hard—especially when it's hard."

"You've always been so steady, Dad. I'm not that strong. I don't know how to hang on to my faith when the world is burning around me."

He snorts. "Son, you are stronger than I've ever been. All of you are. It's been my greatest blessing to watch you all grow into wonderful adults. As a parent, you never know just how much you're doing, or how much damage you'll cause even as you're doing your best. I'm glad to see that my best resulted in such fantastic adults."

My chest tightens, and a bit of the weight I'm carrying lifts. "We got lucky with you and Mom," I tell him truthfully.

He smiles again. "We got lucky with all of you."

I look out over the ranch, wishing I could picture Nova walking up the drive. Right now, though, all I can see is her lifeless body lying on the ground. My dad covers my hand with his then bows his head.

"Lord, we come to You today asking that You watch over Your precious daughter, Nova. Please, God, keep her wrapped in Your holy light and send Your angels to protect her in this fight. Please guide us to her, Lord, so that we may bring her and Crew home. In the name of Your Son, Jesus Christ, we pray. Amen."

Another weight lifts, and the pit in my stomach shrinks slightly.

"Amen," I repeat.

"Keep the faith, son. God always has a plan. Even if we can't see it."

CHAPTER 35

NOVA

The car comes to a stop, and I jolt, rolling slightly in the trunk. There was nothing in here but carpet, so if it comes to a fight, all I have is myself. Not terrible odds, but not great given they're all going to be armed.

The earpiece I'd pulled out before I'd stepped from the trees is tucked safely in my bra, hidden even if I get patted down. I can only hope we're not out of range when it comes time to use it.

I have mere minutes to get to Crew because as soon, as Brett has the drive that's in my pocket, I'm no good to him. And neither is my friend.

Lord, keep me steady, I pray. *Help me stay strong so Crew and I can get out of this. Please, Lord, free us from this trial. Amen.*

The trunk pops open, and a light momentarily blinds me

as two sets of hands reach in and rip me from the trunk. I blink rapidly, trying to clear the white spots from my vision as I'm dragged up a sidewalk and onto a porch where a man I'd hoped never to see again waits.

Neal Austin, Ivan's second-in-command, crosses his arms as he glares back at me. His hair is shaved to the scalp, just as it was the last time I'd seen him, though there's a jagged scar over his right eye from the coffeepot I broke over his face when he'd tried to force me into his bedroom.

Memories continue to assault me, but I can't even enjoy the fact that I remember. Not yet, anyway.

"Nova," he greets with a sadistic smile. "How great to see you again."

"I wish I could say the same, Neal."

He chuckles. "Search her."

Swift hands travel over my body, checking for any concealed weapons. "She's clean," a man growls.

"Good. Bring her in." He steps out of the way so the two men can drag me into the house. Once we're in the light, I study them both. They're new, likely brought in after Brett was supposed to kill me and failed.

I'd seriously hoped this place would be just like Ivan's old compound—uninhabited—but it seems I'm not that lucky.

No problem.

I'll pivot.

"What are your names?" I ask the men, trying to keep my tone level as they practically drag me down the hall. "Not chatty, then?" I add when they both refuse to answer. The one to my right, an angry-looking man in his early twenties, releases my arm to pull open a door to the right.

The man to the left, who looks to be about the same age as the other one, his expression less twisted, tightens his grip. His blue eyes dart to my face nervously. *He doesn't want to be here. Interesting.* This could work.

"What's your name?" I ask as he guides me through the door.

"You don't ask the questions," Brett says. He stands from behind a mahogany desk. "Let her go and leave us," he orders. The men do as he says, and the door closes behind them. Brett comes around the desk and crosses his arms. He looks different than before, more stable—his expression less wild.

"Where is Crew?" I demand.

"Where is the evidence?"

I reach into my pocket and take it out.

He holds out his hand. I note the bruises on his knuckles. *Crew.* What shape is my friend going to be in when I finally find him?

"Not until I see Crew."

"You do realize I can take it from you, right?"

"You can try," I retort.

"Do you really want to taunt me? Don't you remember what happened in your apartment?"

"Before I knew who I was, sure. But I remember all of it now, Brett," I growl. "I remember every single detail. Which means I also recall just how easy it's always been for me to beat you. Brawn doesn't beat skill after all."

His expression darkens, and he taps the pistol holstered at his shoulder. "I won't miss this time."

"What, you're not going to try and charm me anymore?"

"It won't work, so why waste my breath? We both know you've already decided on the cowboy."

"Didn't stop you before," I reply, trying my best to keep my head level. I'd counted—as twisted as it is—on his attachment to me. If he considers himself in love with me, then maybe he won't be so eager to put a bullet in me. Then again, it's not like that worked the first time around.

But this cool demeanor is worrisome.

"I'm far less patient this time," he replies. "Now." He holds out his hand. "Give me the evidence, or I'll kill you and take it."

"What's going to keep you from doing just that the second I hand it to you?"

"Nothing. But if you give it willingly, I'll at least let you speak to Crew before Ivan decides what he's going to do with the both of you."

Knowing I don't have much choice, I hold out my hand.

If I don't give it to him, then he's going to do just as he threatened. I won't even have a chance to find Crew before they start tossing dirt over my body.

Brett plucks the drive from my hand and shoves it into his pocket then painfully grips my arm and rips the door open. "For your sake, I hope that's what we're looking for," he growls as he leads me down a hall and pulls open a door on the right.

My heart plummets when I see a bruised and bloodied Crew strapped to a chair. The floor beneath him is covered in blood-splattered plastic, and when he raises his head to look at me, I see that Brett's bruised fists were in fact caused by my friend's damaged face.

"You shouldn't have given him the satisfaction of showing up," Crew snarls, his gaze murderous as he glares at Brett.

"You know me better than that," I reply. "You have the drive," I tell Brett. "Let Crew go."

Brett doesn't answer as he leads me over toward a bed then withdraws a set of cuffs and handcuffs me to the old iron bed frame. "I'll go check the drive. If it has what I'm looking for, then I'll tell Ivan that you're requesting Crew go free. Though I can't say that's what I'll be pulling for." He glares at my friend. "And unless Ivan thinks he can make good use of Crew alive, I wouldn't count on it."

"Five minutes," Crew says. "Let me free for five minutes, and let's fight fairly."

"Not a chance. I have nothing to prove." Brett turns back to me then reaches up and cups my cheek. I fight the urge to withdraw from his touch. "I really am sorry it came to this, Nova. I really am."

"No," I reply. "It's me who's sorry. Sorry that I *ever* trusted you." Even though the relationship has been over for quite some time, knowing just how twisted the man I'd once believed myself in love with hurts. It hurts bad.

But not as bad as his face will as soon as I get a fist free.

Brett withdraws his hand and steps out of the room, closing the door behind him. A lock clicks, so I start checking the room for cameras. "Are we being watched?" I ask Crew.

"Not that I'm aware of," he replies.

"Okay. It's a risk I'll have to take. Close your eyes." I lean forward over the bed as best I can then pull my hands as close as I can. After tugging the front of my shirt down, I'm able to shake the earpiece loose. It falls to the bed, so I grab it with my lips then drop it into my hands. "You're good," I tell Crew.

He opens his eyes and studies me curiously. "What is that?"

"Help," I tell him with a smile as I press the button and slip it back into my ear. "Hello?" I say. "Can anyone hear me?"

"Nova?" Elliot's voice is heaven in my ear.

"Yes. It's me."

"Thank God."

"I don't know how much time I have. But Crew and I are chained in a bedroom in some old house. I was in the trunk maybe an hour before we stopped moving. Do you know where we are?" I ask Crew. He shakes his head.

"No worries," Elliot says. "Now that the earpiece is active, Tucker can track it. Can you hide it somewhere again but leave it on? Just in case they find it."

"Yeah. I can do that." I swallow hard, tears burning in my eyes as reality sets in. "I don't know if I'm going to survive this," I tell him. "And if I don't—"

"You will," Elliot interrupts. "Tucker has a fix on you. We're coming, Nova. And I'll be right here the entire time."

"Okay." Even as I know I should do as he suggested and remove it from my ear, I can't bring myself to do it. Because even though he's miles away from me, having his voice right there makes me feel less alone.

"Are you still there, Nova?"

"Yes. I don't want to say goodbye yet."

"Me neither." I can tell he's moving, likely getting packed up and in his truck to come for me. "How bad is Crew?" he asks.

"How badly hurt are you?" I ask Crew.

"Not as bad as I look," he replies. "I've been worse off."

"He says he's been worse," I repeat into the earpiece.

"Okay," Elliot says. "How far out are we?" he asks one of his brothers—likely Tucker. I can't hear the response, but a second later, Elliot says, "We're forty-seven minutes from you."

I want to cry in relief. Less than an hour. He's less than an hour away. "Don't alert local police," I warn him, remembering just how deep I'd discovered Ivan's pockets to be. "Ivan will have ears everywhere."

"We're not dealing with local police," Elliot replies. "The five of us are coming for you," he says. "Bradyn also called in a favor, so we've got backup coming from Dallas."

"How far out are they?" I ask, lowering my voice as soon as I hear heavy bootsteps outside the door.

"They're a bit closer," he says. "But I have more motivation. Either way, someone will get to you. Just stay alive. Please, Nova."

"I'll do my best. I—" I trail off when the door opens and Brett steps in.

"Is this the only copy?" he demands.

"Yes." It's a lie, and one I hope doesn't show on my face.

"Are you lying to me?" He grips the front of Crew's shirt then slams his fist into my friend's face.

"Hey, stop!" I yell. "I told you it was the only copy!"

Brett withdraws a knife and holds it to Crew's throat.

"Do it, you coward," Crew growls.

"Tell me the truth, Nova, or I start cutting."

"It's the only copy," I insist. "I gave it to Milo to keep and didn't have time to do anything other than confirm what's on it."

Brett stares at me then releases Crew and sheathes his knife. "Fine."

"Stay calm, Nova," Elliot whispers into my ear. "We're coming to you."

"Let him go. You have what you want," I say again. It won't work, I'm sure of it, but I have to try.

"Ivan's not back yet," Brett replies. "As I said, he gets to decide whether or not to give in to your request. If it were up to me, he'd be dead already." He glares back at Crew. "You'll have a decision to make if he does."

"I won't be a dirty cop," Crew spits out.

"There's nothing a man won't do if given the right motivation." Brett leans forward. "And it just so happens I know of three pressure points that would make you fall to your knees and kiss my ring."

Crew's eyes widen. "If you touch them, I'll rip you apart. I swear, Brett. There will be nothing left of you when I'm finished."

"From where I'm standing, you have no grounds to make threats." He pulls back and turns to me. "As for you, I wouldn't count on such mercy. You've already betrayed

Ivan once, and he's made it clear to me there won't be a second time."

Which is why he's distancing himself from me. Because he knows what I feared—I was dead the moment I got in that trunk. *Focus, Nova. Crew can make it out of this even if you can't.* "When is Ivan going to be back?" I ask.

"Any minute now," Brett replies. "So I'd start coming to terms with yourself. Get right with God and all that."

"I'm already right with God," I tell him. "But am I allowed to make a phone call?"

"No."

"Not even just one?"

"Why?" he asks, taking a step closer. "So you can say goodbye to your cowboy? Don't worry, I'll make sure he knows what happened to you. Maybe I'll drop your body back in that creek. Let it wash up on his ranch again. This time though, there will be no saving you."

I swallow hard as Elliot growls in my ear.

God, please. If I can't be saved, let them be safe. Let Crew be safe.

"I'm not afraid to die," I tell him honestly. "I know where I'm going when I do."

"So certain." Brett clicks his tongue. "Then tell me why your God isn't saving you right now? Why would He let you die?"

"I don't know. But I do know there's a reason for everything, and if my life ends here and now, something good will come from it. Maybe not right away, but eventually." I smile at him. "Who knows, maybe Elliot dealing with you will be the good that comes from it."

"He won't be able to touch me," Brett replies. "Not without losing everything he cares about."

"I don't think he wants to count on that," Elliot snarls in my earpiece.

I grin at Brett, a carnal smile I hope shows him just how unafraid I am. "He's going to come for you. And you won't be able to do anything about it."

Brett charges forward and grips me by the throat. Pain chokes me as he squeezes.

"Let her go!" Crew roars.

"Maybe I'll keep you alive long enough for me to deal with your cowboy. Then we'll see who's the last one standing."

"He will be," I manage, choking on the words. "There's no wondering for me."

"Stop taunting him, Nova," Elliot says, keeping his voice low so it's barely a whisper in my ear. "It's not worth it."

But it *will* be worth it. Because my fingers grip the keys barely sticking out of his pocket. I cling to them, keeping my gaze firmly locked on Brett.

After a few heartbeats, Brett releases me and steps back. The keys slip from his pocket, so I hide them in my hands. Someone knocks on the door. "What is it?" he calls out.

"Ivan is here," a man calls through the door. "He's requesting you in his office."

"I'll be right there." Brett turns away from me then pauses by the door. "I wouldn't count on breathing much longer," he says to me then leaves the room.

I suck in a deep breath, my throat burning.

"Why would you do that?" Crew demands.

"Because of this," I choke out then show him my hands.

Crew smiles. "You're brilliant, O'Conner."

"I try."

"What is it?" Elliot asks.

"I have the keys to my cuffs," I tell him as I work to remove them from my wrists then rush over to free Crew. I untie the ropes binding his arms behind his back then work on one of his legs while he frees the other. "Get here fast, Elliot, and we'll hold them off as long as we can."

CHAPTER 36
ELLIOT

"Be careful," I tell her, having to fight to keep my tone level as my fear hits an all-time high. She and Crew are two against who knows how many, and they're unarmed. Even if he wasn't injured, those are terrible odds.

"She still good?" Riley asks from behind the wheel.

"For now. She got the keys from Brett and released Crew."

"That's great," Tucker replies from the backseat. "We're only twenty-eight minutes out now."

Twenty-eight minutes may not be a long time, but it's a lifetime when the woman I love is trapped in a house full of armed enemies. "How far out is Loyotta's team?" I ask Bradyn.

"He just checked in. Their ETA is 11:17," he replies.

I check the clock on the dashboard. Thirty-one minutes

out. Which means we've made up some of the headway they had on us, and we'll have less than five minutes to get into the house and secure Nova and Crew before the sirens arrive and it turns into a hostage situation.

That's not a lot of time, and we're all operating on little to no sleep—I'm in the latter category. Since the call came in so late last night, most of my brothers had only just gotten to bed themselves. I know that there have been times over the years, during and after we were out of the service, that we've operated on days of no sleep, but it's never a recipe for success. More of a "let's hope the adrenaline carries us through."

Echo whimpers at my feet, so I absently pet his head.

"Take this," I hear Nova say through the phone. "The door is locked, but when he comes in, you swing the chair, and I'll go for his weapon."

Every word she says is another moment of panic because it's a reminder that she's alone. One split second, and her life could be over.

A single gunshot and the light forever out of her eyes.

God, please.

"Faster," I urge Riley.

"Dude, if we get pulled over with all the heat we're packing, it'll raise more questions than we have answers for at the moment. I'm going as fast as I can."

I know he's right. The last time we got stopped, it took Gibson, Loyotta, and four hours to get us back on the road again. We don't have that kind of time. But every minute is torture.

Absolute torture.

***

THE HOUSE NOVA is being held in is nothing impressive. At least, not compared to the compound Ivan abandoned. Likely, it's a staging place for him to gather the evidence from Nova then disappear.

She's been silent in the earpiece, though silence is a good thing when she's in a locked room. It means I have more time to get to her. And maybe us breaching the house is what will distract them from going for her at all.

Or it could have the opposite effect.

Either way, I'm not waiting around to find out.

"Elliot will take the back with Echo, Riley, and Romeo," Bradyn says. "We'll go in the front with Bravo, Tucker, Tango, Dylan, and Delta. Our job is to draw atten-tion so Elliot and Riley can get to Nova and Crew. Sound good?"

We all offer him nods. Taking a deep breath, I hold my weapon at the ready and wait for Riley and his dog, Romeo, to fall in line behind me. Normally, we'd all go in on the same side, but with such little time and no clue which side of the house Nova is being held on, we're having to take the risk of splitting up.

"We're coming in, Nova."

"Okay. Elliot—" She trails off.

"I'll be seeing you soon," I promise her.

"I'm going to hold you to that, cowboy."

I smile then start toward the house, doing my best to keep out of sight by sneaking through the tall oak trees bordering the property. There's no one out patrolling, but that doesn't mean he doesn't have people posted inside, watching.

"Someone's at the door," Nova says.

My heart begins to race.

"Ready?" she asks Crew. I can't hear his response, but I do get muffled movement.

"Tell me how many," I tell her. "As soon as you can."

She clears her throat in response. I hear a door crack and muffled yelling.

And then—a single gunshot.

"Nova!" I whisper loudly then pick up the pace.

"Keep your head," Bradyn warns through the earpiece. We're all linked though, so I know he heard that shot too.

"Nova, talk to me!"

Nothing.

"Nova!"

I make my way around the side of the house and toward the back door. After peeking in the window, I wait for Bradyn's signal even though I want nothing more than to kick the door in now.

But there are five of us on this team, and any wrong movement could lead to the plan falling apart and someone else getting shot. The lives of my brothers are on the line too, and I won't risk them further by going off half-cocked.

Nova, please talk to me.

"Breaching in three, two, one—" Bradyn says. "Go!" I wait a single heartbeat so all attention will be at the front—then nod at Riley before slamming my boot into the door. It splinters and we rush in, dogs between our legs.

"Clear," Riley says.

"Clear this way too."

A gunshot.

Then another.

"Get her!" Bradyn yells. "We're drawing fire. Ten hostiles that we can count."

"Likely more upstairs," I say.

Riley nods and falls into step beside me. We head for a set of stairs off the kitchen. We're not two steps up when a bullet whizzes past my ear. "Contact!" I call out then come out with my rifle.

One shot.

Enemy down.

I keep moving up, stepping over the body as I make my way higher.

"Two down!" Dylan calls out.

"Another!" Tucker adds.

"We're heading up the stairs. Man down in the stair-well," Riley adds.

Nova, come on.

We reach the top and push out into a hallway. It's empty. As quickly as possible, we make our way down the hall, checking door by door.

I stop at the last door on the right and nod at Riley.

He repeats the gesture, letting me know he's ready. Gripping the handle, I shove it open.

My heart stops beating.

Or, at least, it feels that way.

Because on the other side, Brett has a gun to Nova's head. Blood soaks the left leg of her jeans, and she's not putting any weight on it. Her face is scraped up, her lip bloody. Crew is on the ground, and Ivan is standing over him, a gun in his hand. Ivan's bleeding too, crimson staining the front of his white cloth shirt.

"Drop it, or I'll put you down," I tell Brett.

"Same for you," Riley warns Ivan.

"Not before I can pull this trigger," Brett says then gently squeezes. "I've already shot her twice now; it really wouldn't be too hard to do it again. Practice does make perfect, after all. Third time's the charm."

"I will kill you," I tell him.

Echo growls from his stance between my legs. The dog is ready to attack, and if I weren't so worried Brett would shoot her or my dog, I'd send him after the coward now.

"You won't kill me if it means risking her," Brett sneers.

Nova remains silent, but her piercing gaze is on me, and in it, I see permission to take the impossible shot. Just as I'd trusted her to save us back in those woods, she's placing the same faith in me.

Her gaze flickers from me to Crew then back to me.

She smiles.

Then slams her elbow into Brett's gut.

"Echo, *fahs!*" Echo lunges for Brett, who's bent at the waist. Nova falls to the side.

"Romeo, *fahs!*" Riley orders. His dog goes for Ivan, latching onto his arm.

I sprint forward, grabbing ahold of Brett as he goes to raise his gun against my dog. I hit him with the full force of my body, taking him to the ground. The gun clatters off to the side. We roll, and I pin him then slam my fist into his face.

Bone crunches, and blood spurts from his nose. He roars in pain, and it takes everything in me not to hit him again. Again. Again. Until there's nothing left.

But vengeance is not mine.

Stopping this violence is my job. And he's no longer a threat.

So I leash the feral rage shooting through my veins and, instead, flip him over and zip-tie both hands behind his back.

By the time I straighten, Riley's done the same to Ivan.

Nova is on the ground by Crew, looking him over. She turns to me, and the world comes to a stop. Tears fill her eyes, and she pushes to her feet. Limping, she makes her way toward me, but I eat up the distance in two long strides. She wraps her arms around me, and I hold her, clinging to my lifeline.

Because that's what she is.

Nova is everything to me.

"Are you okay?" I pull back and kneel so I can check her leg. She keeps herself steady by placing both hands on my shoulders.

She nods. "The bullet grazed me." I grip the bullet hole in her jeans and tear just enough to get a good look. It's not deep, but it'll likely need a few stitches.

Gripping the bottom half of my black long-sleeve tactical shirt, I tear it and wrap the fabric tightly around the wound. She hisses through clenched teeth.

"Where are we at, Bravo?" Riley asks through the coms, using Bradyn's code name.

"All good down here. Loyotta arrived, and they're wrapping things up. Where are you?"

"Top floor. Last room on the left."

"All good?"

"Nova and Crew are both alive. Ivan and Brett are secure. Send some of Loyotta's boys up to grab them."

"You got it. Ambulance is on the way. Should be here any minute."

"Great. Nova's been shot, and it looks like Crew has too."

"So have I!" Ivan screams.

"You'll live," Riley tells him. "Maybe. Either way, buddy, I hate to break it to you, but you're not top priority." He bends down and helps pull Crew to his feet. "Can you walk?"

"I'll manage. My family—"

"They're fine. My brother got to them just in time."

"Thank God."

I don't even ask Nova if she can walk. Because her answer doesn't matter. I scoop her up into my arms, and to my relief, she doesn't argue. With one arm draped around my neck, she rests her head against my chest and lets me carry her out of the room.

We're just stepping into the hall when two of Loyotta's men come into the room. They offer us nods as they head in to retrieve Brett and Ivan.

"You know, life would be boring if you stopped saving my life," Nova comments.

I start laughing, her words catching me off guard. "I wouldn't mind a little boring once and a while."

"Fair enough," she replies with a smile then rests her head against my chest again. "Thanks for getting here so fast."

"Thanks for fighting."

We reach the bottom of the steps, and Bradyn holds open the front door for us. We're just stepping outside as the second ambulance arrives. Paramedics rush out and pull open the back.

They take Nova from me while Riley guides Crew over toward the other waiting paramedics.

Everything begins to move at an impossibly slow speed as the adrenaline surging through my system slows.

She's alive.

She's secure.

I turn back toward the house as Ivan and Brett are walked out. Brett's expression is murderous while Ivan is clearly terrified. *Cowards.*

"You boys are going to get me more raises than I know what to do with," Frank Loyotta comments as he comes to stand beside me. "I'll own the company before the end of it. They'll just hand over the keys," he jokes. While he's not officially a member of the police, his program has rescued more trafficked people than any other government organization.

Because of that, he has permission to operate on an as-needed basis. So when things go wrong and we need backup without alerting the authorities, he's who we call. Vice versa, too. We've worked quite a few missions alongside his people.

"You deserve it," I tell him, offering my hand.

"And I appreciate that." He returns my handshake. "You know, I told Bradyn, you boys ever want to come work for me, I'd love to have you."

I smile at him. "As much as I appreciate that, we're happy where we are."

"Yeah, that's what he said too." He grins. "Good seeing you, Elliot."

"You, too. Thanks for the assist."

"Thank you. The FBI's been after Ivan for a while now. I'm happy to be the one to turn him in. Turns out he's knee-deep in trafficking himself. Drugs and weapons mainly, though according to that intel Tucker emailed over, he was getting ready to expand into people. You boys brought him down before he could do that."

Thank you, God. Pride swells in my chest as I look over at Nova. "Nova O'Conner did all the work on that," I tell him. "She risked her life for this."

"Then maybe she's who I should offer a job." He winks. "I'll see you around, boys."

"See you around," I reply.

I take a deep breath then watch, amused, as he heads over toward Nova. Undoubtedly to do just what he said and offer her a job.

"He try to get you to come work for him?" Riley asks, coming to stand at my side.

"He did."

Riley chuckles. "The man sends Tucker weekly emails.

If I didn't appreciate his help, I'd be offended that he's trying to break up a brotherly bond."

"He's harmless," I say then head toward the ambulance.

"You going to the hospital with Nova?"

"Yeah. Can you take Echo back to the house?"

"Sure thing. We'll see you there, brother." Riley shakes my hand then pulls me in for a hug. As soon as he's released me, I offer a wave to Bradyn, Tucker, and Dylan, who are off talking to some of the local police Loyotta alerted after things were wrapped up.

They return the gesture, so I head over toward the ambulance.

"You let me know," Loyotta says then offers Nova a wave and me a smile.

"Room for me?" I ask.

"Always." She smiles, so I climb up into the ambulance, sitting off to the side as the paramedic climbs in and sits opposite.

"Let's head out," he says to the driver.

I reach over and take Nova's hand. "So what did Loyotta offer you?"

"A job," she replies with an exhausted smile. "Says he's been trying to get the Hunt brothers for quite some time now and you all keep turning him down."

"Why break up a good thing?"

"So true." She chuckles and turns her head to look at me. "Hey."

"Hey." I lean forward and run my free hand over her forehead. "What did you tell him?"

"That I already have a job, I think. And that things are messy right now, so accepting something new isn't on the table."

I try not to let her words sting, especially since she's talking about a job and not me, but they burrow deep within my heart anyway. I hadn't given a whole lot of thought to what comes next, but it's true.

Nova does have a life that has nothing to do with me.

A career.

An apartment.

Just as I have my own life that I can't leave.

What if, even after all of this, even after all of the promises we've shared, we still don't get a happy ending?

CHAPTER 37
NOVA

"You're sure about this, Nova?" Crew asks, studying the piece of paper in his hands. It's been six months since we were rescued from that house, so all of his bruising has faded, his injuries healed. While my physical injuries have also healed, the damage Brett's betrayal caused still haunts me.

When I combine that with the darkness I had to endure while undercover in the first place, I know that I'll never be the same again.

"You're really sure?" he asks again as he sits behind his desk in the Dallas Police Department while I remain standing in front of it.

"I am."

He smiles, but it's hesitant. "I want you happy, but I'd be lying if I said I wasn't sad to see you go."

"This isn't where I belong. Not anymore." I turn to look

out into the bullpen, my gaze landing on the desk coupling I once shared with Brett.

"You're one of our best detectives," he says. Since the captain was arrested after Brett sang like a canary, desperate to cut a deal for himself, Crew was promoted.

With me put into his spot as lieutenant.

Turns out the captain was taking payments from Ivan too, offering to look the other way as he attempted to become the largest trafficker in the country. Which is why they went after the shipping company. Using high-profile clients to hide guns, drugs, and people was one way to get things in and out of the country without a whole lot of attention.

I'd brought Rosalie in to help us, but Brett convinced her the payout from Ivan's rival was far too great an opportunity to pass up.

Together, they traded information for cash, and when things got too hot for Brett, he sold her out. Just like the coward he is.

"And I appreciate every opportunity you've given me, sir. But this is just not where I want to be."

The promise I made to Elliot all those months ago, standing in his dad's office, still lingers. And while we've talked occasionally over the last six months, I know he's been giving me my space. Space that I no longer want or need.

.   .   .

"And where do you want to be?" Crew asks. "A small town with a certain cowboy?" He arches his brows, and I feel my cheeks heat even as my stomach churns.

"Maybe. I won't know until I try." I can only hope the space he's given me didn't give him a reason to change his mind.

It's been a whirlwind of wrapping up loose ends, packing my apartment, and praying my way through life-changing decisions that make me ill just thinking about them. I haven't even told Elliot that I'm handing in my resignation because I wanted the decision to be one hundred percent mine.

And it is.

I've known from the moment we met that my life is nothing without Elliot Hunt in it.

Even before I remembered who I was, I knew that.

Crew stands and comes around the side of his desk to place both hands on my shoulders. "Well then, as your captain, I'm sad to see you go. But as your friend, I couldn't be happier for you. Hunt is a good man. You picked well. This time." He winks.

Smiling, I lean into his hug. "Thank you, Crew."

"Anytime, O'Conner. Come back. Visit."

"You too." I pull away. "Who knows, maybe Elliot will have changed his mind and want nothing to do with me. I could be back sleeping on your couch tonight."

He laughs and releases me. "We both know he'd have to be an idiot. And Elliot Hunt doesn't strike me as a fool."

Heart full, I retrieve the duffel at my feet. Everything else I wanted to bring with me is in boxes in the back of my Telluride. An entire life of belongings in the back of a single SUV. But after donating all of my furniture, there wasn't much left since Brett destroyed and trashed most of my things when he'd tossed my apartment.

I'm truly starting over.

And it's honestly more terrifying than getting into that trunk six months ago was.

HERE LIES MILO ANDERSON. BELOVED FRIEND. 1987-2025. GREATER LOVE HAS NO ONE THAN THIS: TO LAY DOWN ONE'S LIFE FOR ONE'S FRIENDS.

After placing a bouquet of flowers on his grave, I run my hand over the cool marble. "I miss you, my friend," I say. He'd had such a hard life. So many cards stacked against him. But in the end, he'd made a choice that saved my life.

He'd come through in a way most wouldn't have.

A true hero, that's who Milo was. Tears burn in the back of my throat. "I wouldn't be here if it weren't for you, Milo."

I can recall the first moment I met him. He'd stolen a loaf of bread from a grocery store I was shopping at. The moment I took him to the ground and heard his sobs, I had this overwhelming feeling that he needed me.

So, I'd taken him back in, bought him groceries, and had him over for dinner. Shortly after that, I'd worked out the deal with Mr. Kerry so he could stay in the back room of the old store as it was being renovated.

He was my neighbor. My friend. My family.

"I'm so sorry," I say, a tear rolling down my cheeks.

The Hunts came out for the burial. All eight of them, as did Gibson Lawson, Crew, and his family. Everyone paying their respects to a man who sacrificed everything despite having next to nothing.

"I'm going to go out to the ranch. Tell me, how am I more nervous now than when I'm staring down the barrel of a gun?" I laugh as though he's standing beside me. "I may not be here to visit as much as I have been for the past few months, but I hope you know it's not because I've forgotten you. I'll never forget you, Milo. Not as long as I live. I'll see you on the other side, my friend. Keep a seat open in Heaven for me."

THE DRIVE OUT to the ranch feels like the longest two hours of my life.

I nearly stopped to call Elliot a dozen times, just to make sure he's okay with me coming out. But the last thing I want is to give him a chance to think I have any doubt in my mind at all that this is where I want to be.

I did, however, call Lani, who was more than happy to offer me her guest room until I could find a place. She'd wanted me to drop my stuff off first, but if things don't go well with Elliot, I really don't want to have to go to his sister's place to grab everything all over again.

Not that I don't think things will go well.

Do I?

Oh, God, please let this go well.

Parking in front of his parents' house, I climb out and run my hands over the front of the pale green summer dress I chose to wear today. It's one of the only dresses I had in my closet.

I even styled my hair, not that I think it matters how I look, but it gave me something to do that helped distract me.

Butterflies dance in my stomach as Ruth opens the front door. She smiles and waves. "He's in the auto barn," she says, pointing toward a structure just past the main barn.

"Thanks."

She nods then heads back inside.

I turn toward the auto barn. *Here we go.*

On legs that feel heavy as steel, I make my way into the barn. Tucker's standing beside an old truck, and when he sees me, he arches a brow and grins. He crosses over and offers me a quick hug then leaves the barn silently.

Elliot is beneath the truck, his legs sticking out. "Can you hand me that crescent wrench again?" he asks, holding his hand out.

His voice wraps around me, and my stomach twists, nerves taking control.

"Crescent wrench?" he asks again. "Come on, Tuck, I don't want to be under this thing all night."

I cross over and retrieve the wrench then squat down and offer it to him. As my fingers brush his palm, warmth radiates through me. His hand closes around the wrench, so I stand and take a step back.

Elliot doesn't pull the wrench underneath the truck, but he doesn't move, either. Several heartbeats pass before he's pushing out from under the truck. His hazel gaze locks on me, and all of the fear of rejection I'd felt melts away.

Because I see the same love I feel reflected in his eyes.

"Nova." He stands and tosses the wrench to the side.

"I'm sorry that I took so long," I say, starting the speech I've memorized over the past week. "I needed to figure out how to step away from that life, how to close that door the right way." Nerves twist in my stomach, and I toy with the front of the dress again. *Why did I wear it in the first place? I've never been a fan of it. Why did I pick this one?* "But I meant what I said in your dad's office. From the moment we met, you're all I've wanted. That old life was never going to feel like home again. Because it's not." Tears fill my eyes, and I raise my gaze to his. "You're my home, Elliot Hunt."

He rushes forward and grips the back of my hair before crashing his mouth down onto mine. The moment our lips meet, the nerves I've carried inside of me for the last six months vanish. His kiss obliterates the darkness still lingering around me. None of it matters.

Nothing but Elliot.

But us.

His other hand cups my cheek as he deepens the kiss. I lose myself in it. In him. In this moment.

He pulls away and rests his forehead against mine, our ragged breathing loud enough to drown out all other noises. "I wasn't sure how much longer I could wait before I went after you," he says.

"You were going to come after me?"

"I told you I would," he replies. "But I wanted to give you time. That way, we could figure out where I fit in your life."

"You *are* my life," I tell him.

"And you're mine." He kisses me again then steps back. His eyes widen, and he chokes on a laugh. "I am so sorry."

"For what?" I look down at the front of my dress and laugh. Grease smears the front of the pale green. "So worth it," I reply, grinning up at him.

"It's on your face too."

Laughing harder than I have in months, I step forward and run my hand over the front of his shirt then wipe the grease onto his cheek. "Now it's on yours too. Look at us, matching already."

He wraps both arms around my waist and spins me in a slow circle then kisses me quickly before setting me back down. "I love you, Nova."

Warmth spreads through me, heating me from the tips of my toes to the top of my head. "I love you too, Elliot. And there's no adventure I wouldn't take with you."

He smiles down at me then brushes some hair behind my ear. "Same. But let's hope our lives are rather calm for a while."

CHAPTER 38
ELLIOT

S ix months later

"You're sure?" I whisper, taking the binoculars from Nova's hands.

"Positive. Four armed, three unarmed."

Only because I need their placement and not confirmation, I check through the scope, tracking the movements of the men guarding the woman we're here to save. "Unarmed might be civilians."

"Or they might be unfriendlies," Nova says as she checks her weapon one final time before our final assault.

"Delta, Tango, are you ready to move on the east side?"

"Ready," Tucker replies through the coms.

"Locked and loaded," Dylan adds.

"November and I will go west," I tell him, nodding at Nova.

"Understood. Let's go get our target."

I raise my weapon and look down at Echo, still sitting between my legs. "Ready, boy? Let's do this."

"He's always ready," Nova comments with a smile. Her thick red hair is braided down her back, and she's dressed in all black just as I am. Tactical boots and bulletproof vest as well. A black hat is pulled down over her eyes.

She's been working with us for the past six months, helping out as needed, and today is her first boots-on-the-ground mission. Pride swells in my chest. God gave me a wonderful woman.

"Move out," Tucker orders. Since it's his op, he's running the shots, his plan going seamlessly—so far.

But we know how fast things can change.

Nova and I move through the brush with me in the lead and Echo at my side. Our weapons aimed and ready, we do our best to keep our steps silent. We're deep in the marsh-lands of Louisiana, so I keep watch for predators while treading carefully so I don't step onto unsure terrain.

So far, the ground is dry. I'm only hoping it's this way all the way to the house.

The teenage girl we're after is a runaway. A foster kid burdened by the weight of the world. She'd left one nightmare only to end up trapped in hell when she was abducted by a drug dealer and used as a mule. But today we'll bring her back to the light—if all goes well.

"Two hundred yards out," Dylan whispers.

"Same," Nova replies.

We hit the side door, and I look to her. She offers me a nod. "Breaching in three—two—" I trail off and slam my boot into the door. It splinters open.

Gunfire rings out, and we both seek cover. Echo remains at my feet, silently watching, both ears perked as he prepares to strike. I withdraw a stun grenade from my waistband and throw it in. It goes off with a piercing bang, so Nova and I push inside.

Moving quickly, we put down two armed gunmen with their rifles aimed at us then manage to locate the room where the teenage girl is being held.

"Hey, honey," Nova says softly as she rushes over toward the teenager. "Are you Susie?"

"Yes. Wh-who are you?"

"I'm November, and this is Echo. We're here to bring you home," she says as she cuts the zip ties on the girl's wrists.

"I don't have a home."

"Then we're going to take you to safety," Nova says. She helps the girl to her feet. "Are you injured?"

"Just my head. I tried to run, and one of them hit me."

"You're a fighter, that's good." Nova smiles again. "Stay behind me, okay? We're going to get you out."

"All clear, we have the package," I tell Tucker and Dylan through the earpiece. Seconds later, the gunfire ceases.

"We've secured all the unfriendlies," Tucker says.

"And secured the unarmed civilians," Dylan adds. "Team is two minutes out," he adds in reference to Loyotta and his men, who were called in for the final assist.

"We're bringing her out now," I tell them. "Stay behind November, okay, Susie? If you hear any gunfire, drop to the ground."

"Okay."

"Ready?" I ask Nova.

"Ready."

"Let's do this." Just in case any more guards are lurking, I keep my weapon up as I make my way out of the house and toward the rendezvous point. This place will be swarming with Loyotta's men in minutes, and we don't want Susie out in the open when it is—just in case there are any more conflicts.

We make it to the small clearing that serves as our rendezvous point at the same time Loyotta's men storm the compound.

Dylan and Tucker, along with Delta and Tango, step into the clearing. Dylan's shoulder is bandaged, but he moves as though he can't even feel it.

"You hit?"

"I'll be fine," he replies, brushing it off. It's just like Dylan. The boy who used to save spiders from being squashed has now suffered so much that a gunshot wound barely fazes him.

"How you doing, kid?" Tucker asks her.

"Better," she replies. "For now."

"We'll make sure you're safe," Nova tells her.

Susie smiles, but it doesn't reach her eyes. There's a darkness there, her innocence lost years ago when she'd first been placed into a broken system. "Thanks. What happens now?"

"Now we wait. In a few minutes, we'll all be on a truck and headed back to civilization where I plan to eat the largest cheeseburger known to man," Tucker replies.

Susie's smile widens. "A cheeseburger sounds nice."

"Then we'll make sure you get one too," I tell her.

TWELVE HOURS and a plane ride later, Nova, Echo, and I are stepping into our house. Echo heads straight for his water bowl while Nova and I stash our weapons in the safe and hang our gear up in the hall closet.

Then, she crosses over, and I wrap my arms around her, pressing a kiss to the top of her head. "Some honeymoon, huh?" We'd gotten married only a week ago, right beside the creek where I'd found her what feels like life-times ago.

She laughs. "Some honeymoon. It all turned out okay though, didn't it?"

"I think so. I'm a bit worried about Susie though," I tell her truthfully. "I hope they find her a good family. Someone who won't make her want to run."

"I hope so too," she replies. "I really do. Help me?" She turns and lifts her braid, so I undo the chain of her necklace and wait as she slides her wedding ring off before securing the chain back around her neck.

She slips the ring onto her finger, and I do the same with mine after I remove it from the chain around my neck where it has rested, right beside an iron cross Nova gave me on our wedding night.

"Right back where it belongs," she says, stretching up on her toes to kiss me.

She starts to pull away, but I deepen the kiss, savoring the way she fits me just right. "I love you, Nova Hunt."

My wife.

My love.

My life.

"I love you, too," she replies with a wide smile that sets my heart ablaze, just as she's done every day since the very moment I met her and will continue to do until the day I meet the God who brought her to me.

The same One who never left me, even when I'd abandoned all hope myself.

Keep reading for a sneak peek at Riley's book, Romeo! Coming soon!

CHAPTER 39
ROMEO CHAPTER 1- JULES

I cover my mouth with a shaking bloodstained hand and do my best to stifle my breathing. Through the sliver between the accordion closet doors in my grandfather's study, I can see the masked thief working through the safe where my grandfather kept nearly everything of value.

How he even knew the code, I'm not sure. It's something my grandfather kept close to his chest. Not even I know what it is.

Grandfather. His crimson blood soaks the floor at my feet, saturating the carpet as it moves beneath the closet doors. I have to keep myself from looking at the body lying just in front of the doors. It's the *only* reason I haven't been seen.

The only reason there aren't two bodies on the floor.

He's protecting me even in death.

Tears burn in my eyes as grief sears the inside of my throat.

All of this for jewelry. For money.

Gems that are considered more important than the blood of the greatest man I ever knew. A man who *never* gave up on me. Even when I gave up on myself.

"Stay in and stay down, girl," he'd told me before shoving me into this closet. *"Don't make a sound. No matter what you see or hear."*

"We need to call the police!"

"And you will. But nothing in this room is more important to me than you are, Jules. Never forget that."

His smile will haunt me for the rest of my days. The thief didn't even give him a chance to hand anything over. They'd pulled out a gun and fired. Two shots.

Bang. Bang.

That was the end of my grandfather.

The thief drops something to the ground, and the jarring noise has me jerking within my hideaway. I accidentally bump into an umbrella leaning against the side.

It clatters to the ground, and the sound is deafening.

Oh no.

The thief straightens slowly, his face covered in a black mask as he turns toward the closet. On footsteps so quiet they might as well be silent, he crosses over and peers inside. I try to hide, to tuck myself into a corner, but there's nowhere else to go.

Even with his eyes shielded, I know the moment his gaze meets mine.

He steps away from view, and my grandfather is drug out of the way.

Panic shaking every inch of my body, I know that if I don't fight, I won't survive. Even if I do fight, I may not survive.

But my grandfather raised me to meet death with fists.

So, I grab the very umbrella that gave me away and wait. The doors open, and I explode out of them with a scream, driving the umbrella into the gut of my grandfather's killer. He grunts and stumbles back, so I dodge to the right and try to make it to the door.

I haven't even taken a single step before I'm ripped backward and slammed into a hard body. An arm bands around my throat, and breathing becomes a nearly impossible struggle.

"They'll think you did it," he growls into my ear. "I know you. I know you're trouble. And I'll make it look like you did it," he says, hatred lacing his tone. "Deranged former alcoholic murders beloved actor. I can see the headlines now. You just handed me a get-out-of-jail-free card."

"Who are you?"

"Someone owed something," he snarls.

My gaze lands on my grandfather. He will *not* have died for nothing. I slam the heel of my shoe down into the top of my attacker's foot.

He mutters an obscene remark that I can't even focus on as I turn to make a mad dash to the closest exit—a window my grandfather left open after I'd come in and insisted he air out his office tonight.

The killer tackles me to the floor, and my head hits the corner of a table on my way down. Pain radiates through the side of my head as warmth trickles down. I'm nearly blinded as blood slides down over my eye, but I turn and slam my foot into his face.

He releases me again, and I waste no time as I rush toward the window and climb out onto the ledge. After wiping my hand over my eye, I slide further onto the ledge and take careful half-steps to put myself out of reach of the window. I just need to buy enough time to find a safe place to fall—

The attacker is leaning out the window, the gun he used on my grandfather in his hand.

Without much choice, I leap from the balcony.

A bullet whizzes past me.

I hit the top of my grandfather's car with a heavy thud, then roll off.

"I will find you!" the stranger bellows. "You can't hide from me!"

Adrenaline in my system is my only saving grace as I sprint toward the estate's sprawling gardens even as every inch of my body aches from the impact.

The security building at the gated entrance. I just need to make it—another bullet whizzes past me.

Tears burning in my eyes, I have to keep wiping them —and the blood—away from my face so I can see. I know these grounds better than anyone. Most of my childhood was spent playing hide-and-seek with my grandfather.

Which means—I veer to the right into a group of trees.

Breathing frantically, I find the space that has been my victory spot since I was seven years old. And if my grandfather couldn't find me, then maybe—just maybe—it will be my salvation.

Doing what I can to avoid leaving a blood trail, I drop to my knees and slide into a large tunnel that leads up into the trunk of an old tree. Then, just as I did when I was a kid, I reach through and pull a bunch of old leaves toward the hole so it doesn't look disturbed.

And then, with the horrific image of my dead grandfather on the floor and the echo of heavy boot steps just outside, I stay quiet.

Quiet as the dead.

Otherwise, I'll be joining them.

CHAPTER 40

ROMEO CHAPTER 2-
RILEY

"Oh, Romeo, Romeo, where are you, Romeo?" I grin as I jump around the trunk of a large tree. "There you a—" But my service dog is not there. "Hmm. Getting better at hide-and-seek, are we?" I ask, tone amused.

How else am I supposed to spend a Tuesday morning than playing hide-and-seek with my best pal?

A low bark signals that I'm not even close, so I turn and run through the trees. After jumping over a fallen branch, I leap down the embankment toward a low spot in the creek.

Romeo barks happily, his fluffy tail wagging back and forth in absolute delight. "Hah! You shouldn't have given yourself away!"

He lunges forward, and I let myself fall back to give him the victory. Both paws planted on my chest, he stares down at me happily, his long tongue hanging out of his mouth.

"You're the best boy, Romeo. Don't let anyone tell you otherwise." The German shepherd has been with me for the last five years. Each of my four brothers have their dogs, as well. While our dogs are from two separate litters, they do share the same dad, who gave them all the same long fur and sharp ears.

The shrill sound of my ringtone cuts through the silence, and Romeo steps back and sits, going into what I like to call "alert mode." After checking the screen and seeing my oldest brother Bradyn's name on it, I answer. "What can I do for you, big brother?"

"Are you at home?"

"Nah. Romeo and I are out for some partner bonding time." I rub his head as I get to my feet. "We're headed back though."

"Great. Swing by here afterward, please. I have an assignment for you. The client is en route. Should be here in forty-five minutes."

A spark of joy surges through me. I *love* the job. Everything about it. Hunting bad guys, returning good people to their homes—helping deliver monsters to justice. "On our way." After shoving the phone into my pocket, I look down at Romeo. "You ready to do some running, boy?"

He barks in response.

I grin. "Race you home!"

I sprint over a small hill and down through more trees as I race Romeo back to the house I had built on my family's ranch. Our dad gifted each of his six kids an acre for our own home, though we share everything in between.

It's been our home for generations and will remain our home for generations to come. The only one of my siblings who hasn't built a home here yet is my sister, Lani. She's the youngest of us and runs a medical clinic in town, so she still lives in her apartment on the other side of our small town of Pine Creek.

With Romeo on my heels, I crest the small ridge that overlooks my home. Nestled in a small valley and surrounded by still-growing fruit trees I planted a few seasons ago, my two-story farmhouse is a beacon.

The wraparound porch is something I'd dreamed of having all those years I'd been deployed, a place to wind down with a glass of sweet tea or a steaming cup of coffee in the morning.

It's home.

My home.

I smile as Romeo continues down the ridge, not stopping until he reaches the bright red front door. "Fine, bud!" I call out as I climb the porch steps. "You win."

He barks in response and spins in a circle before taking a seat and waiting for me to unlock the door. It's something I know I don't technically have to do, but I do it anyway because years of working missing persons cases have made me hyper-aware to just how easily someone can breach your private space if precautions aren't taken.

Sometimes even if they are.

Romeo immediately heads for his water bowl, while I retrieve a bottle of water from the fridge, then make my way down the hall and into my bedroom. The place is sparsely decorated, but it's mine. And I've come to realize that I really don't need that much stuff.

A bed. Blankets. A dresser. And my books.

As I always do, I take a minute to grin up at the bookshelves covering two walls in my bedroom. Floor-to-ceiling, the titles housed there range from thrilling spy novels to nonfiction, history, and everything in between.

I've even been known to read my fair share of Christian romance, though my brothers will never let me live it down. These aren't even all of them. I have an entire wall of books out in my living room, and ten plastic tubs still waiting to be shelved in my office.

Books are my happy place. My escape from the world when things get too heavy.

After stripping out of the T-shirt I'd been wearing, I head for the bathroom and crank on the shower. Water sprays out of the nozzle, turning hot in seconds thanks to the tankless water heater I installed when I built the place.

Best. Decision. Ever.

I take a moment to look in the mirror and study the bullet holes marring my chest. Angry red scars that serve as a roadmap to the hell I've survived. For some, scars are a painful reminder. For me, they're fuel to the fire in my soul. I walked away from every single attempt made on my life. And as a former Special Forces Operative responsible for taking on monsters masquerading as men, in missions no one will ever hear of, there have been quite a few.

The silver cross around my neck is the very reason why I walked away, and I'll never let myself forget it. God was in the fire with me, right beside me as the flames got so hot I could barely stand it.

And He brought me through. Which is exactly why I will keep fighting for the innocent until He calls me home. It's more than a job. It's a calling.

One I will answer until there's no more breath in my lungs.

The Hunt Brothers Search & Rescue office is inside a renovated barn on our property. Up until a few months ago, we were using Bradyn's home office, but now that he and his wife Kennedy are in the process of trying to start a family, the decision was made to do something more permanent.

Since Dylan and Tucker are out repairing fences,

Bradyn, Elliot, and his wife Nova, are all sitting at the table with our newest client, Odie Landers. I remain standing against the wall, arms folded, Romeo at my feet. This gives me a vantage point when studying Odie's body language.

He's relatively collected for a man who just lost his grandfather and quite possibly his sister too, but that could also mean that he's used to a stressful environment. Given the family's celebrity status, I'm betting on the latter.

"What's the status on the authorities looking for your sister?" Nova questions. As a former detective herself, she's always making notes and surveying every case with the scrutiny of an officer seeking clues.

"Things have been kept under the table," he replies. "They're looking for her, but only locally. And given the media storm it would bring raining down upon my family, they're keeping the story as close to their chest as they can."

"You don't believe she's hiding near your grandfather's estate?" Bradyn questions.

"No. If she had, we would have already found her." He takes a deep breath. "Do you have a sister, Mr. Hunt?" he asks Bradyn.

"I do," he replies.

"Then you must know what I'm feeling right now. Or at least part of it. I know Jules is troubled, she always has been, but to kill? I can't imagine what would have driven her to that. I just want answers. I want to know she's safe."

"You believe she killed your grandfather and took off with $14 million in jewels?" I ask.

He turns toward me. "They're gone, and so is she," he says. "Her blood was found at the crime scene, but her body wasn't recovered."

"Still, there must be something else that drove you to believe she's the murderer. Even with all of that considered, there are at least half a dozen other explanations." Bradyn crosses his arms. "As I said, I have a sister too. And my first thought would've been that she was abducted by the killer. Not that she was the killer."

Odie's gaze momentarily drops to the folder sitting in front of him—something he brought in but has yet to open. His reaction is one I've seen before. There's something in there he wants to keep hidden. Something that will likely answer a lot of questions but bring bad light to either his family or his sister.

Question is: will he be honest with us?

"Look, I don't want this to be public knowledge. Our grandfather was incredibly famous, one of the greatest actors of his time. I don't want to stain the legacy he left behind."

"Nothing you say to us will be shared outside of our team and anyone necessary to this case," Bradyn assures him. "But if you don't give us everything, we can't help you."

He takes a deep breath. "Jules has been in and out of

trouble for most of her life. She's an alcoholic who's spent more time in rehab than not."

"Being an alcoholic is a far cry from being a killer," I say.

"Maybe. But Jules has problems. And if she were innocent, why would she run?"

"She was scared. Abducted. Unsure who to trust. I can think of quite a few reasons," I retort.

"You said that your mother married her father?" Nova questions before Odie can respond to me.

He nods. "After our parents died, our grandfather took us in."

"Grandfather on your side or hers?" I ask.

"Hers. He's her—our—dad's dad." Odie closes his eyes. "Was our dad's dad. I must remember that. It's still just so fresh." He takes a deep breath, then opens his eyes. "We were young when our parents got married. Jules was only seven and I was ten. But losing her mother took a toll on her, and she never recovered. Then when our parents died—" He fidgets with the file in his hands. "My grandfather had a lot of money, but he'd always considered us his greatest possessions. And now he's gone and so is she." A tear slips down from his eye, and he wipes it away. "You asked why I jumped to my conclusion." He slides the folder to Bradyn, so I push off the wall and lean over Bradyn's shoulder as he opens it.

Images of bloody handprints on the side of brick. Blood smeared on the dented roof of a car.

"It's her blood," Odie says. "No one could have abducted her, then climbed down the side of a two-story house. And they wouldn't have needed to, as she and my grandfather were the only ones home and the security alert was never even triggered. No one was coming."

"She could have been grabbed from the grounds," Bradyn offers.

"It's possible, but unlikely. Jules knew those grounds better than anyone. No one would've been able to find her unless she wanted to be found. Even injured. She was an expert hide-and-seek player when she was little."

My thoughts drift back to the hide-and-seek game I was just playing with Romeo. A strange coincidence for sure.

"You have a lot of faith in your sister's hiding abilities under duress." Bradyn closes the file. His tone is flat, emotionless. Out of all of us, he's the best at reading people. Which makes me wonder just what he's seeing when he looks at Odie Landers.

"As I said, Jules is troubled. She ran away when she was sixteen and didn't come home again until she was eighteen. No number of private investigators we hired could find her."

"That's a long time to not know where your sister is."

He nods, clearly distressed at having to relive the past.

"That's not all, either." He reaches into his pocket and withdraws a bracelet with embedded diamonds the size of blueberries. "It was our grandmother's. Someone pawned it at a gold shop in Oregon. Security footage shows that it was Jules." He sticks it back into his pocket. "She's a good person, Mr. Hunt. She's just— Losing both of her parents traumatized her, and it's not something she got over. If she isn't responsible, then she's out there scared and hurt. And if she is the one who killed him—" He trails off, emotions playing out over his face. "Then she's in trouble and needs help. Either way, I just want her home in time to lay our grandfather to rest."

Bradyn glances back at me. Since we work on a rotation, I'm up next. Meaning this is my case to accept—or decline. I look down at the photograph Odie provided us with of his sister.

It's a family photo, with him and her on either side of an elderly gentleman sitting on a bench. Odie is smiling widely, his hand on the man's shoulder, while Jules looks a bit less enthusiastic. She's gorgeous, there's no doubt about that. And she's smiling, her red lips curved just slightly. Her blonde hair is cut to just above her shoulders and styled in waves so it curves around her face. But there's darkness in her green gaze. Pain shielded beneath armor. It's something I recognize easily enough. The question is, what put it there? Was it truly losing her parents? Or something else?

Perhaps something during those two years she was missing from home?

"I'll take the case," I say.

Odie looks about ready to hug me. I'm grateful he doesn't. While physical contact doesn't typically bug me, when it comes from complete strangers, I'd rather pass.

"You'll keep it confidential?" His gaze darts from me to Bradyn, then back to me. "As I said before, our family is very well-known. The last thing we need is a scandal with Jules's name attached to it. Especially when we don't know the truth just yet."

"I assure you, Mr. Landers," I start, popping a piece of gum into my mouth. "The only thing I'm better at than keeping secrets is tracking those who don't want to be found. I'll track your sister, and I'll do it without anyone knowing why."

"Thank you so much." He gathers his file and stands, then leaves the office without so much as a backward glance. As soon as the door is closed and we're alone, I turn to Bradyn.

"What's your radar saying, big brother?"

"That he knows more than he's telling us." Bradyn crosses his arms. "Just watch your back, Riley. And if something seems off, trust your gut."

"I always do."

nother day. Another name. Another place.

I pull the baseball cap lower on my face, hoping to shield the still-healing injury on my forehead, as I watch the screen on the other side of the restaurant I'm sitting in.

I keep waiting to see my grandfather's face up there. Waiting to see if anyone is out looking for the killer—or me. But it's been radio silence for the last week. Fear has kept me from going home and reaching out. Fear that the killer will find me and Odie will get caught in the crosshairs.

And worse, fear that the killer did just what he said he was going to and find a way to make it look like I murdered the man who raised me. A man who I loved more than life itself. I can only hope Odie saw through it, but with my past—

I shake my head.

"You are not defined by your past. Moses was a murderer. Noah was a drunk. Yet God still used them. Jesus died so you could have a chance to live. So, what will you make of that life, girl? What will you make of your second chance?" My grandfather's words echo in my mind, a reminder that I am *not* a dunk anymore. I am *not* broken. And I will find a way to bring the killer to justice and reunite with my brother.

We may fight more than we get along. We always have. But he's still my brother. Blood or not.

Despite the tension between us, I felt like we were right on the verge of turning a corner and growing close. Maybe even closer than we'd ever been.

Until grandfather's killer knocked us down and scattered us again. This time, permanently. My throat constricts with emotion I've tried to ignore for the last week. Tears won't get me anywhere.

"Hi, is this seat taken?" A deep baritone fills my ears as a man points to the chair beside me.

"It is," I tell him without looking up. *Don't let them see your face.* As famous as my grandfather was, both Odie and I have been seen at various red-carpet premieres. While it's been years for me, the last thing I need is to risk anyone recognizing me.

"Oh, my mistake." He keeps moving along, but not before I get a glimpse of him as he turns away.

Tall. Broad shoulders. Likely muscled beneath that leather jacket.

In another life. Before any desire I had to get close to anyone was ripped away from me.

I take a sip of the coffee in front of me, then toss some bills on the table before I stand and turn to leave. The restaurant is crowded, though it could be like this every single night, and I wouldn't know. Aside from hotels, I *never* visit the same place twice.

Another rule for not being noticed. Something I've become quite adept at over the years.

After stepping out into the warm summer air, I make my way across the street toward the hotel I'm staying at.

It's far from the Ritz, but the bed is comfortable and the room is clean. It'll be my home for one more night, then I'll be moving on from here too. Likely to another city since the pawn shops here are claiming they know nothing about any jewels fenced.

Aside from the ones I sold, of course. Jewels I grabbed from the floor of my grandfather's study after returning to check to see if he'd somehow survived. I'd known he hadn't, but I'd been praying for a miracle.

It broke my heart to sell such prized possessions, but to survive, I need untraceable money. So here we are. My grandfather's life was worth far more than anything I could sell. Which means getting vengeance for his death is also priceless.

After unlocking the door, I step inside and immediately flip on the lights. The place is clean, everything exactly where I left it. I toss the keycard on the table and remove my hat, letting my blonde hair fall loose to my shoulders.

I run both hands through it and let out a deep breath before retrieving the notebook I've been using to jot everything down over the past week. "Back to square one—"

A large masked figure lunges from the bathroom.

I barely have enough time to react before he's on me, slamming my body against the door.

"Hey there, trouble. I told you I'd find you," he snarls against my ear.

I bring my knee up and slam it into his groin. He groans and stumbles back, giving me just enough time to get to the door. I grip the knob. If I can get out to the hall, I can call for help.

He won't get away this time.

I get the door partially open before he grabs me and throws me back into the room. The man towers over me, hands balled into fists. "You're going to suffer for what you've put me through."

Adrenaline coursing through my veins, I shove my panic down and focus only on the task at hand—getting free so I can call for help.

He lunges for me, and I dive to the side, then scramble to my feet as I sprint out into the hall. I've made it two steps before I'm hitting a hard body at full force.

"Let me go!" I scream as hands grip my shoulders, steadying me on my feet.

A dog barks.

"*Ruhig*, Romeo," a deep voice orders. *I know that voice.* "Easy, I'm not going to hurt you." He releases me and steps back. The man from the restaurant is standing in front of me. *Coincidence?* "What happened?" he asks.

"I was attacked," I tell him. "In my—"

He shoves past me. "*Such*, Romeo," he orders what I now see is a large, fluffy German shepherd.

The dog races into my room as the man draws a gun and follows him in.

All while I remain in the hall, staring after him, trying to come down from the panic clawing at my throat. I should run. Should leave now, but as the adrenaline wanes, all I can do is lean back against the wall of the hallway.

"It's empty," he says as he comes out.

"It can't be, he was just there." I force myself to walk on shaking legs, only to find myself staring at a messy— but empty—motel room. The window is flung wide open, curtains spread apart. "No! Come on!" Panic turning to frustration, I cross the room and peer outside. The street isn't busy, but someone had to have seen him.

"Were you hoping he was hanging out in here waiting for a round two?"

I turn toward the stranger, who's popping a piece of gum into his mouth and leaning back against my door. His dog sits at his side, ears perked straight ahead. Unease snakes through my belly as I recall where I know that voice from.

"You were at the restaurant earlier."

"I was. I'd been hoping to have a bite to eat while we talked, but you shut that down pretty quick, and I wasn't looking to make a scene." He grins at me. I imagine it's meant to be charming and disarm me, but all it does is set off alarm bells in my head.

Charming men cannot be trusted.

It's a lesson I learned time and time again.

"Who are you?" I back away from him, getting closer to the window. If I have to, I'll leave what's left of the jewelry and my pocketbook and find a way to start over again.

"I was hired to find you."

"By who?"

"Your brother."

The mention of Odie has me pausing my retreat. "I don't believe you."

"Believe me or don't. It really doesn't matter."

He's blocking the easiest exit for me, but I take a step back toward the window. Wouldn't be the first time in the last week I've had to escape through a window.

"If you jump out that window, I'll just find you again. It is what I do, after all. And that's if you can get out before Romeo here catches you."

I look at his dog. I've always been fond of animals. Cats, dogs, horses, goats—all of them. I'd even briefly considered going to veterinary school before my dad died. But now I eye the canine warily.

Could he catch me before I'm out the window? My money—what little I have—is on yes.

"What do you want from me?"

"A confession would be nice. But I'll settle for you just coming quietly."

"A confession?" I choke out. "For what?"

"Murder. Thievery. Espionage. Whatever it is you're into."

"I'm sorry, *what?* Murder? Espionage? Are you kidding me?"

"I notice you didn't balk at thievery."

"Let me get this straight." I cross my arms. "You show up as I'm being assaulted, and your first go-to is that *I'm* a murderer, a thief, and a spy?"

"I just threw the espionage bit in there for color," he replies.

Arrogant jerk. It's quite literally the only two words I can formulate as the adrenaline continues to wane in my system. "I don't have time to deal with all the ways you're wrong. I have a real killer to catch."

"That's who was supposedly in here?" he asks, looking around for dramatic effect.

"He *was* in here." Anger wars with the fear rooted in

my chest. "And if you were truly hired by my brother, then you should know that the man who was killed was my grandfather. I would never have hurt him. Never. Not for anything."

"Which is exactly what a murderer would say."

The accusation infuriates me. I clench both hands into fists and take a step forward. The dog lets loose a warning growl. "I would *never* have hurt my grandfather. And you must be the worst type of arrogant jerk to take a tragedy and turn it around that way."

He studies me in a way that makes me feel an awful lot like an ant beneath a magnifying glass. And I *really* don't like it. "Your brother should be able to clear it up then." He withdraws a cell phone from his pocket.

"No. You can't call him."

"And why is that? If you're not a murderer, then you have a worried brother out there looking for you. One phone call, and I can put his mind at ease."

"He can't know that you found me. I can't risk leading the killer back to him. He could get caught in the crossfire."

"Or he could turn you over to the police."

"Which is exactly what the real killer wants," I say, putting both hands onto my hips. "I don't even know why I'm talking to you." I drop my hands and ball them into fists again. "Let me leave."

"You're more than welcome to try your luck with the window," he says. "But you're better off staying here until we get this squared away. If you are telling the truth, then there's someone trying to kill you too. Do you really want to risk them catching up to you again?"

"I thought you didn't believe me."

"I never said I do, and I never said I don't. I'm merely making observations."

"Why would I make up someone attacking me?"

"Because you saw me coming. Maybe you made me as a threat at the restaurant."

"Yes, because every arrogant man in leather thinks every woman notices them."

"That's the third time you've called me arrogant, Miss Landers," he says as he takes a step closer. "You don't even know my name, yet you feel like you know me well enough to insult me."

"Fine, then. What's your name?" If he's a hire of my brother's, then I will have likely heard the name said around a time or two. Odie and my grandfather always used the same PIs. Even if I don't know their faces, I made it a point to know names. Made avoiding them a lot easier.

He flashes another handsome smile that churns my insides even as it sets my heart racing. "Riley Hunt," he replies. "And as I said, I've been hired to take you home."

ABOUT THE AUTHOR

A *USA Today* bestselling author of over sixty novels, Jessica recently felt her faith pulling her in a new direction. Now, her focus is inspirational romantic suspense with characters who fight to find their faith in even the darkest of moments, because, as she has learned, it's then we should lean on God the most.

She lives in Texas with her husband and homeschools her three kids. She is an Army veteran and has written multiple bestsellers since debuting in 2016. Find out more on her website, www.jessicaashleybooks.com or by joining her Facebook group, Coastal Hope Book Corner.

ALSO BY JESSICA ASHLEY

<u>Coastal Hope Series</u>

Pages of Promise: Lance Knight

Searching for Peace: Elijah Pierce

Second Chance Serenity: Michael Anderson

Tactical Revival: Jaxson Payne

Perilous Healing: Silas Williamson

<u>The Hunt Brothers Search & Rescue</u>

Bravo: Bradyn Hunt

Echo: Elliot Hunt

Romeo: Riley Hunt

Tango: Tucker Hunt

Delta: Dylan Hunt

9 781964 579146